Sasha the Witch

Sasha the Witch

Iris Vradenberg

Library of Congress Control Number: 2024907701

ISBN 979-8-9901184-0-9 (paperback)

ISBN 979-8-9901184-1-6 (ebook)

For my parents

Chapter One

In a bedroom in a suburban house, a witch stood in front of her open closet, drink in hand. It was a late August morning, the blinds shut to the warm sun.

"I don't want to go," the witch, Sasha Hoffman, said, flipping through dresses. Sasha wore an old silk robe, the sleeves frayed, the collar torn at the nape of the neck.

Courtney Johnson, her best friend and the only other witch in their town, sat on the edge of Sasha's bed. She wore the gray A-line dress she'd picked out when the luncheon invite arrived several weeks before.

"What about that one?" Courtney asked, pointing to the middle of the closet at one of the many black dresses.

"Sleeveless? Nah." Sasha took a gulp of her drink. The event was hosted by the Westchester Board of Witches, and she knew what it would be like. Stuffy. Boring. Full of all the annoying older witches.

"How many times have I sat here while you decide between two or three slightly different black dresses?" Courtney teased.

Sasha tossed her hair over her shoulder. "Fewer times than I've done it myself."

Courtney laughed. Needing some movement, she walked to Sasha's dresser and picked up the items there. A wooden jewelry box, a glass holder with the end of a candle that had burned out years before stuck in it, and a glittery pink plastic heart that she gave Sasha as a joke gift when they first became friends in high school. Courtney turned back around and watched Sasha pour more vodka into her drink.

"Do you want some?" Sasha asked.

Courtney waved her off. "I'm hungover from last night, but thanks," Courtney said. "I can't believe you're not." She had woken up with a headache, and then immediately threw up her omelet after breakfast.

"Hair of the dog," Sasha said, holding her drink up to toast.

"As I get older, I'm starting to think that's not effective."

Sasha pulled out a black dress with a low back. "I think this is the one."

Courtney nodded her approval.

"You're not annoyed to be spending your actual birthday at a board event?" Sasha asked.

"I like the events," Courtney countered quickly. "They're fun. You get to catch up with everyone and the food is good."

Sasha stepped into the dress and pulled her long dark hair into a bun. She turned in front of the full-length mirror in the corner, hung high to accommodate her height. They were ready.

Courtney drove, as she always did. Sasha didn't have a license. Pulling out of the driveway, Courtney waved at a woman walking her dog. For a town of under five thousand, two witches was normal. For some people, they'd be happy to have fewer. Sasha and Courtney would have liked to have more.

New York was one of the fourteen states where witchcraft wasn't banned. As long as the witches stayed on the right side of the law, no one could do anything to force them out of town—or send them to one of the Exile states. But the right side of the law, as upheld by the Witches' Guard, had a way of seeming shaky. The law stated, *Spells and potions are allowed as deemed appropriate by the Witches' Guard.*

Every town and city had a Witches' Guard. Theirs was in a building right next to the police station. "Theirs" because in a way, the witches and the Witches' Guard were linked, as there was no Witches' Guard without witches.

Sasha watched as their neighbor waved back at Courtney, her green bracelet visible. The bracelets were from the guard. Everyone wore them except for witches. They were made of thick plastic and worn tightly so they couldn't be taken off by anyone except the guard. If a witch performed magic on someone their bracelets sent a signal to the guard headquarters, triggering an alarm loud enough to be heard from miles away. This had all been set up with magic—always a bitter thought for Sasha.

Neighbors knew each other in their town, labeling houses by the family name that lived there, sometimes for multiple generations. Sasha had forgotten many of her neighbors' names, hadn't bothered to learn the names of new ones, but everyone knew her house as the Hoffman house. "The witches live there," her neighbors would say to people new to town. Plural even though her mother hadn't lived in the house for almost a decade.

Their small town was carved out of a tamed wilderness. In the older part of town, where Sasha lived, trees hung over the curving main roads. When the wind blew too hard, the neighborhoods lost power for an hour. Stone walls lined property, becoming squat and unkempt along wooded areas. Small lakes and ponds dotted the landscapes, sometimes jutting up against the road, appearing suddenly around a sharp turn. The wilderness looked as if it'd let the town be built but would be happy to take it back.

Over time, new houses had grown larger and larger, money collecting into the town. It busied the sleepy main street with new stores and a new town square, but let the trees stay.

They were out of their town quickly, traveling south. The Westchester Board of Witches had been in a brick building in

North White Plains since its inception in the 1950s. This luncheon was held to mark the end of the summer. Ella Chow, one of the thirteen witches on the board and a professional party planner, had been head of events since before Sasha came into her powers.

Ella stood inside the front door. The foyer, well-lit with natural light, had a high ceiling with an elaborate crystal chandelier.

Ella wore bright red lipstick and a crisp white button-up shirt with a subtle ruffle detail at the sleeves and collar, tucked into a black suede pencil skirt. The outfit differed little from her usual appearance, as witches were largely creatures of habit and uniform. Ella was a country club witch—Sasha's mother's term for witches that dressed to blend in with their Westchester neighbors. Ella's hair—black with a thick streak of gray—was pulled back into a chignon.

Ella greeted Courtney with a hug. "It's been too long," she said, pulling away and squeezing Courtney's arms.

"I know. I was thinking the same thing," Courtney said with a genuine enthusiasm for the older witch that made Sasha want to roll her eyes.

"And Sasha, how are you?" Ella said, holding out a hand, which Sasha shook.

"I'm fine, Ella, thank you."

"Of course," Ella said and shifted her attention to another group of witches arriving behind them.

Sasha turned to Courtney as they made their way to the next room. "I could've said, 'I just found out I have cancer, so kinda bad, thanks,' and she would've said, 'Of course.' She's always so stiff with me."

Courtney swatted her arm gently. "Don't joke about cancer."

The main room was already full of witches making their way around circular tables to greet each other, hugging and laughing. The place was crawling with country club witches, Sasha noted.

They spotted their friends Pooja Barik and Faye Torre, two

young witches that made up half a coven in Bronxville. Courtney was friendly with a lot of other witches and kept on stopping to hug and chat as they made their way across the room. Sasha crossed her arms, gave brief nods, stared at her feet, checked to see that Faye and Pooja hadn't moved, and watched the bewitched carts zipping around with meals and drinks.

Finally, they reached their friends. "Happy birthday," they sing-songed to Courtney, who struck a mock pose. Sasha gave them both big hugs.

Settling down at the table, Sasha picked up the pen and parchment in front of her. Pooja said, "You write your full name on that, which activates a cart to bring your meal. Isn't it cute? Gail helped come up with it."

"That is clever," Courtney said.

Their cart arrived with two plates with croissant sandwiches, a cup of coffee for Courtney and two mimosas. The glass was cool in Sasha's hand. "How about a toast?"

Faye and Pooja raised their glasses. "To fall," Pooja said.

Sasha tapped her flute against theirs and took her first sip. Pulpy orange juice. She ran her tongue over her front teeth. Just like Ella to ruin a good drink, she thought.

Courtney looked down into her flute, "Honestly, I can't stomach this this morning. Anyone want mine?"

"I'll take it off your hands, thank you very much," Sasha said, and they all laughed.

"Last night was so fun. That's the right way to turn twenty-five," Faye said.

"It was almost too fun," Courtney said, rubbing her temple. "But I really appreciate you guys coming out and celebrating with us."

"Of course. We all still have a couple years before we're"—Faye gestured at the other witches in the room—"only going out for luncheons."

"This is nice, though," Courtney said. "Well put together."

"Teacher's pet over here," Sasha teased.

Pooja waved a hand at both of them. "Courtney, we love you. We'll celebrate you any day of the year."

Courtney raised the coffee cup as if to toast again. "And I feel every single one of the twenty-five years I've been alive."

Sasha finished her drink and moved it aside for the next one. The conversation ambled on. Faye wanted to go on a trip for her twenty-fifth birthday next year but couldn't decide where yet. They all wanted to know the theme for the board Halloween party (the only board event Sasha enjoyed) so they could begin planning their outfits.

Pooja showed off a new ring she'd been saving up for, a glittering light blue stone on a gold band. Pooja worked as a copywriter, and even wrote items for the board's quarterly newsletter, which Sasha usually threw out unless Pooja mentioned she'd written something in one. Some witches made a living using their magic, like Courtney did, creating potions. Others worked non-magical jobs like Pooja or Faye, who worked as a personal shopper and stylist. But magic had a way of creeping in. For an extra fee, under the table, Pooja could spell the copy to make people immediately want what they read about. And Faye was known for her transformation spells. If her client bought a blue dress and wanted it turned silver for an event, she could do that. Gained or lost weight? She could change an item's size. Her customers went crazy for her services, but Sasha wondered how many turned their nose up at magic publicly.

Sasha did not have a job. She had family money. Her grandfather ran a successful department store in Westchester through the 1980s before selling it to a larger national company. When he'd passed away, the money was left to his wife and his one child, Sasha's mother. When her grandmother passed away several years later, she left everything to Sasha's mother, and when Sasha's mother was exiled, the money was given, per law, to her next of kin —her daughter.

Sasha finished the second mimosa and tapped her nail against the empty flute, admiring the ring with Courtney. Leaning back from Pooja, she saw Ella making rounds. Their eyes met. Ella pursed her lips and moved her attention to someone new. "I don't think Ella likes us being here," Sasha said.

"Wait, why?" Faye asked.

"I don't know. I always feel this, like, laser beam of judgment when she looks at me. Maybe because we haven't been a coven in years. We're an embarrassment."

It had been four years since they'd had a coven in their town, and they did not know how long before a third witch would come into their powers and make them a coven again. Four years since Catherine Darley, their last coven leader, died.

The people who did seek out a witch went to Courtney. If things had gone differently, the people of the town would have probably been more inclined to go to Sasha for help, the daughter of a witch, and a white woman in their mostly white town. Not that many would have admitted to themselves that Sasha being white and Courtney being black was an important distinction. But even before Sasha did what she did, the town began to notice her mother, Deborah, was acting differently. Then she was gone, exiled. And the town left her daughter alone. Some days, if Courtney was busy, Sasha went the whole day without speaking to anyone. She didn't even notice.

"Does she really mind that much? There's nothing you two can do. The next witch hasn't come into their powers yet," Pooja said. Witches came into their powers before they were eighteen, with some showing powers as early as thirteen.

"That's probably not how Ella feels," Courtney cut in. "And if it really is bothering Ella, well, we don't like it either."

"You know, Gail's aunt is a witch up near Syracuse, and she told us she was the only witch in her town for like thirty-five years starting in the sixties. Then, *bam*, two witches come into their power in a row," Faye said. Sasha spotted Gail Bayers, their coven leader, across the room with a group of other witches. Faye and Pooja always gushed about Gail, but Sasha couldn't help noticing that, in a black tweed dress and matching jacket with two strands of pearls, she fit the country club look. But then, Sasha thought, so did Courtney.

"It's totally unpredictable," Pooja added. "And when you live in a smaller town like you do there's less of a chance at there being new witches to come into their powers."

"I don't know why I even said anything. I don't really care what any of them think," Sasha said.

"Nobody wants to be thought of as the odd ones out," Courtney said.

"We're witches. We're always the odd ones out," Sasha said.

"Yes, but the point of this community is so that we don't have to be," Courtney countered.

"Here's to that," Pooja said, raising her glass.

The speeches started, Ella and other members of the board making toasts to each other, certain coven leaders, everyone present. They recounted all the wonderful things the board had done over the summer and how excited they were to tackle the fall and their goals for the end of the year. Several non-board coven leaders were scheduled to speak, presenting projects their covens had been working on. Courtney took out a notebook and pen. She made notes as they spoke.

Sasha saw two young witches—even younger witches than she and her friends and witches she didn't know—look at Courtney and exchange a glance with each other. One giggled. As the first coven leader wrapped up and Courtney started re-reading her scribbles, the giggling witch whispered to the other, "Will there be a test?"

Courtney looked up slightly but returned her eyes determinedly to flip the page of her notebook.

Sasha pushed her chair back towards the two witches. "Hey," she said, "did you have something to say to us?"

The giggling one blushed. "Uh, no."

"Good."

Sasha started moving her chair back. The witch that hadn't spoken rolled her eyes at the other. Sasha opened her mouth to speak again, but Courtney put a hand on her shoulder. "It's okay," she whispered.

Sasha settled in with a glare shot behind her.

The third coven leader launched into a presentation on different organizational methods for writing your grimoire, a speech which turned out to be twenty-eight minutes long. A numbing feeling crept steadily over Sasha's entire body, and after the next coven leader stood to start a speech, Sasha whispered to Courtney that she was going to get some air. Courtney nodded while listening raptly, her pen poised.

She walked through the hallway towards the kitchen. No one was in the large room. A dozen carts stood still, waiting. Several bottles of champagne lined the sink, all empty. The window above the sink was open. From outside, Ella's voice rang out—"I agree" —and Sasha ducked down by the cabinets. Apparently, she found the speeches as boring as Sasha did. Another witch's laugh floated into the kitchen.

She was considering making a silent return to the main room, when she heard her name. "...Sasha Hoffman, with someone like that..." The rest of the sentence was lost.

The "someone like that" beat against her chest. This untangling her name from herself, that she was just "someone" and worse, a someone "like that." Sasha being "like that"—it sounded as if these witches had talked about it before, the way it was easily shorthanded. She moved closer to the open window.

"It's too bad there haven't been any new witches in their town yet. Mentoring someone could be the distraction she needs," the other witch said. It wasn't a voice Sasha recognized, so she didn't know why this witch felt she knew what Sasha needed.

"Maybe. A new witch will come into powers there, eventually.

I have faith in that." Ella paused. Sasha leaned forward. "It drives me crazy." She drew out the last word.

"I don't think it's too late for her. She could still live up to the talent Catherine thought she had."

"I'm glad Catherine didn't have to see her like this."

Sasha didn't want to hear anymore. Like this. Like that. She readied to stand and retreat when the French doors opened.

Sasha hadn't heard their voices moving or maybe they'd been closer than she realized. She slid into the corner of the cabinets, suppressing a gasp. They clicked across the tiles in their sensible heels and out of the kitchen.

A deep breath in. Thoughts hissed through her with fire. How dare they. Ella said Sasha drove her crazy. Stop thinking about me, then, Sasha thought. And anyway, why were they thinking about her? It's like they were all saying at the table—Sasha and Courtney couldn't do anything about their not being a coven. Of course, Ella liked Courtney. Maybe Ella blamed Sasha. They'd lost covenhood when Catherine died four years ago, but four years before that, Sasha's mother had been exiled. If she hadn't been, they'd still be a coven. And Sasha could admit that that blame could be laid on her shoulders.

But bringing up Catherine. Ella and Catherine had never been close, never more than friendly. And this other witch—whoever she was—what did she know. Talking as if she had been some confidant of Catherine's. Where were these women when Catherine was sick? They didn't care. They were bored old women, prying into others' lives and digging up the dead. They knew nothing.

Sasha pushed herself up and walked towards the dining room. In the hallway, empty carts zipped past her. She stood at the dining room's entrance. Witches in their finery, crisp shirts and draped shawls, witches she didn't know, laughing, listening, interjecting. Layers of them together. As close as she stood to them, no one noticed her. There was a barrier widening between her and these witches. They were a painting come to life. While she, the viewer, was frozen in time. Sasha turned away and walked back into the kitchen. She started looking for champagne.

An hour later, Sasha sat on the kitchen floor, tucked into the corner of the cabinets. She snapped her fingers, sending thin shoots of flame into the air. Hearing someone come in, she rushed to hide the bottle she'd opened, letting the flame linger in the air.

"Sasha?"

She scrambled up, leaning on the countertop. "Courtney?"

"What are you doing in here?"

"I—" What was she doing in there? Drinking, being alone. "Sort of felt I wanted to be alone. There were so many people out there."

Courtney nodded. "Well, I was thinking of leaving. Are you ready?"

"Yes, extremely."

They returned to the dining room to say goodbye to Faye and Pooja. When Courtney went to say goodbye to Ella and the other board members, Sasha walked to the foyer. She stood leaning against the wall with arms crossed until Courtney joined her.

In the car, Courtney said, "Some of the board members said to give you their regards."

"Is that what they said? God, those witches are old."

Courtney laughed. "Stop, I thought it was nice of them."

Because they're not talking about you, Sasha thought.

Sasha opened her mouth to tell Courtney what she'd overheard in the kitchen. The words—that Catherine didn't have to see her some way, and that that was a good thing—curled sour in her mind. She couldn't repeat them.

She said nothing.

CHAPTER TWO

Courtney had scheduled a call with her parents for 3:00 p.m. on her birthday, and she'd given herself plenty of time to get ready. Her birthday weekend was planned out carefully, the same as any other weekend. Friday she'd gone to her salon for a blowout. Saturday she did errands in the morning, and then she and Sasha got ready for the night before meeting Pooja and Faye at the restaurant. Sunday morning was the board luncheon and now she had an hour before her parents called.

She filled up her tea kettle, an orange one from her childhood. It was one of many household items her parents left for her when they'd moved to North Carolina, where her father was from. Courtney was their youngest child, and with her graduation and her mom's retirement from teaching, they moved south to North Carolina, weary of the cold. It was a banned state.

Courtney knew what people in banned states said about witches—what people in New York said, too—saw politicians on TV saying, "What sort of influence on young people can witches exert?", or "Why do *they* have powers? And what are they going to do with them? Who will they corrupt or seduce?" The last part became a slogan for a time: "To corrupt and seduce."

She could visit her parents, with permission from the guard in their town. The rules for witches going to banned states differed from state to state. For North Carolina, she would have to visit the state guard headquarters and have a bracelet put on her for the duration of her stay. If she performed magic, the bracelet would shock her and notify the guard. Stories of how guards acted in banned states spread online—large fines, being locked up and harassed for a week, being sent to exile for even minor infringements—and Courtney wasn't interested in finding out about them firsthand. Witches who lived in banned states wore bracelets, created by witches working in the government, just like the non-witches' bracelets.

The kettle whistled. In Courtney's mind, the tea kettle was as bold and bright as it had been when she was a child, but occasionally she saw it with the eyes of visitors—mostly women from town that came to commission potions from her. Whatever the townspeople needed help with, Courtney would look for the solution. When Sasha said she was too good to them, Courtney reminded her that Catherine had told them over and over that is what witches did—they helped people.

In those first moments visitors entered her kitchen, she was struck with an urge to move the kettle out of sight and make some apology for it, but quickly her pride and love for it flared stronger than the initial impulse, and she never did move it. Sasha liked to pat the side of the kettle before Courtney fired up the stove and say, "Hey, ol' girl."

She poured the water into one of her favorite mugs—one of an orange set of four that her parents bought to match the tea kettle. With a bag of green tea steeping, Courtney opened her laptop. She had several emails to respond to—returning clients and prospective ones. Then she went to Witches Talk, a forum site she frequented. It was only available to witches, protected by spells and run by witches in tech, and she had waited almost a month to be admitted after applying for membership.

There were groups and subgroups, and she'd read through them all in order to find relevant advice she was looking for but some of her favorite groups were for black witches, New York witches, young witches, black witches of New York, witches working on potions, and for witches not yet in a coven. The last was one she frequented the least. It gave her solace to read witches talking about similar feelings of impatience, anxiety, and shame, but clicking on the group name also stirred up all those emotions.

She went to post in the black witches of New York group, which she considered a home base. She typed, edited, reread, edited, then reread again, and finally posted: *Good afternoon, everyone! Today I'm celebrating my twenty-fifth birthday. Well, I started celebrating last night with my friends and had a great time but am admittedly a little hungover! I'm over hangovers, and I'm thinking about drinking less this year. I'm still enjoying my day, though. I always feel reflective on my birthday. Twenty-five in particular is such a big milestone in US culture (A quarter century! I can rent a car now! Not that I travel much to be honest, but at least I know I can). I've been reading lately to see if twenty-five is an age of significance in witch culture but haven't found anything yet. Does anyone else know of anything?*

She read over posts in her other groups (she skipped the non-coven one—staying nice, homey) until her phone rang. It was her parents, calling over video, prompt as always.

They were squeezed together on their couch to both fit on the phone screen, her mother holding her phone out in front of them. Courtney saw her own uninhibited grin on the small square in the corner, holding one hand to the still warm orange mug, while her parents softly jostled one another to lean towards the phone when talking. They moved with the practiced choreography of people who have known, loved, and lived with one another for over three decades.

"Hey, Court," her dad, Norman, called, looking at her over his glasses. "Happy birthday, baby girl."

"Happy birthday," her mom, Dorothy, chimed.

"You're as beautiful and as wonderful as this day twenty-five years ago when you came into this world. You know you'll always be our baby. You are a miracle to us and forever our pride, along with your brother, of course, who said he'll give you a call today too. Pester him if he forgets. I know he's busy, but you're his sister and birthdays are important. Anyway, we think about you all the time, and we miss you a lot."

Every birthday, he made a speech about her virtues, and she always looked forward to it.

It was her mom's turn. "Happy birthday, Courtney. We love you so much. I love you so much. It's so good to see your face and that bright smile. And we're sorry we couldn't make it up to celebrate with you this year. You know we were going to drive up, but then Dad's back acted up again and we're so sorry. We really are."

"It's okay. I get it. And thank you for the birthday wishes. I got your presents in the mail too—"

"Oh, good, good."

"How's your back today, Dad?"

He sighed. "It's okay. It'll be okay."

"He's being stubborn," Dorothy interjected. "The doctor is struggling to follow doctor's orders."

"Well, I just—"

"Think you know best," Dorothy finished. Courtney laughed.

"Never mind all that. Court, you're the star today. How's everything going?"

"Everything's going well. There was a Westchester Board of Witches luncheon earlier that Sasha and I went to. There were a lot of really interesting presentations. Plus, I saw some witches from around the county I hadn't seen in a while."

Her parents nodded along. "Right, your witch group," Dorothy said.

"Well, it's not my... It's actually sort of large, with over one hundred witches. And they do a lot..." She trailed off as their smiles set in politeness.

Dorothy said, "Of course. You know us, with witches, it's still unfamiliar. But you're having fun with it?"

Fun was a hobby, Courtney thought, not an inextricable aspect of yourself. "Yes," she answered. And then she added something that she had been thinking about, a seed germinating in her mind so delicately that she hadn't told Sasha, or Ella, or anyone yet. "One day, I want to be on the board." She paused, to take a needed deep breath, and continued, "You have to be a coven leader to be on the board, and we don't have a coven yet. But I think we could have one soon. I'd love to be the leader. I think I'd be the right pick."

Leadership positions, being on boards... These were concepts her parents could relate to, and they began nodding with serious consideration. "Remember, it's not that you think; it's that you are. You are a natural leader. We've always seen that," Dorothy said.

"And there's never been a black witch on the Westchester Board, so that would be a big deal," Courtney added.

Both of her parents hemmed. "Do you even want to be involved then? With a group that isn't bringing black folk into leadership positions?" Norman asked.

"You make it sounds as if it's a club I've joined. These witches —they are my people. It's not about wanting to be involved. You are together. I wouldn't be the first black witch to be a coven leader, and if I can get on the board, I can make changes, and show how a black witch can be a leader for the whole community."

"Okay, I just hope they appreciate you as their people too. Would they speak up for you the way you're speaking up for them?" he countered.

"Yes," she said, with true certainty. "The next time you come up to New York, I'll introduce you to Ella Chow. She's on the board and she's a real mentor to me, a great leader, and a great witch."

"Okay, you sound confident, and we believe in you," her mom said. "They better deserve you, because you're someone special, and if it's enough for you, being a witch—"

"It is enough," Courtney said.

After their call ended, Courtney returned to check her forums. There were half a dozen birthday wishes posted, including one witch that wrote, *Oh, I remember being young and drunk all night long. In some ways I miss those days, and other ways I don't at all.*

Another responded, *Yeah, I've got twenty years on you and two drinks gives me a headache the next day. Enjoy it while you still can! But seriously, happy birthday. Twenty-five is a good one. I don't know about the year being big for witches specifically, but it is one of those time periods of clarity and shifts.*

CHAPTER THREE

Every morning after the luncheon, Sasha woke up thinking about covens.

She was happy with herself and Courtney. They were a great duo. But they were not a coven. It was the natural order for witches, being a coven, being a tight-knit group among the communities—both the one they lived in and the larger witch community. She tossed the idea of it around all week, as the phrase "I'm glad Catherine didn't have to see her like this" kept pushing through her consciousness. She didn't know what that meant, which made it hard to dismiss. When it wouldn't stop popping into her head, she got drunk.

One day at the beginning of the next week, she sat in Courtney's living room, on the couch with an untouched coffee in an orange mug in front of her. Courtney sipped from her own mug and sat in a chair with her feet up on the ottoman. They sat in the silence of two people who had known each other for years. Courtney was thinking of potions, she'd been toying with the idea of a new one she wanted to try. Sasha was thinking of covens.

Sasha broke the silence. "I think we'd make a good coven."

"Of course, we were a good coven with Catherine. And your mother," she added quickly.

"I mean with someone younger. We'd be good as, like, the elders."

Courtney smiled broadly. She raised her orange mug slightly. "I agree."

"I wish the new witch would hurry up," Sasha said with a sigh.

"Yeah," Courtney said softly. Everyone knew that waiting was part of the process for new witches. On Courtney's forum, witches liked to write, *A watched cauldron will not boil!*

Sasha grabbed the pen and light green pad of paper on the coffee table in between them. There were several items listed already. She started writing underneath them. "Do you want to head out soon?" she asked.

This was their routine. One day a week they had an errand day where they would go together for tasks around town. Usually, the bulk of the errands were Courtney's, but Sasha would add one or two of her own—going to the bank because she liked to have cash on hand, stopping at the liquor store, bringing a box from online shopping to return at the post office.

"Yeah, I have a potion to drop off at the high school."

Sasha paused, her eyes flitting to the top of the list where she saw *high school* printed. "Ugh," she groaned.

Sasha hadn't been back to their high school since they'd graduated. In her last few months as a student, she stopped attending most classes, hiding out behind the stacks in the library with her phone, mindlessly reading and watching whatever caught her attention. Some days she completely skipped school, several times to get drunk in her living room. The teachers and administration never said anything about her absences. She walked across the stage at graduation to a smattering of polite applause and snatched her diploma out of the principal's hand.

"It'll be super quick. We're going to drop off Denise's order and then we'll be on our way."

· · ·

Courtney drove them down the hill, the curving lane through the thin woods that surrounded the high school. Below, the building was gray and one level, with trapezoid-shaped windows and bushes along the walls. It was a small building, fitting a student body of less than a thousand.

"It's not like I enjoyed school ever, but why did we have to spend four years in such an unglamorous building?" Sasha asked. "This is a building that has no self-respect."

"At least we don't have to come by it often," Courtney said.

At the bottom of the hill, other than the school, there was a dry cleaner and a burger joint, neither Sasha frequented, and several houses of people she didn't know.

"Denise asked you to come by with her order?"

"Yeah, usually she comes to pick it up, but it's been busy with the start of the school year, so I offered to bring it by. This is the sort of thing that makes me like Denise, honestly. Even if I did drop-offs, you know a lot of my customers wouldn't want me coming around, letting people know that they're using potions. Denise doesn't care."

Sasha nodded. "I can appreciate that."

"And she's not in the seventy-five percent who wants another cream to get rid of wrinkles." Courtney gestured to the backseat, where the glass jar filled with a lilac cream sat in her bag. "This is for her arthritis."

They parked in the visitor lot and walked to the front door. Sasha balled her fists. She focused on putting one foot in front of another. Her past whispered through the halls. At least the students gave them a wide berth.

Courtney led them to the front office. Sasha saw Denise Petrini, who had been the principal's secretary since before they started high school, through the large glass window. When they pushed open the door, she looked up from her computer screen and smiled. "Courtney and Sasha, how are you two?"

Sasha could give Denise credit that in her last months of high school, while the principal and vice principal scowled whenever they saw her, Denise still greeted her with a smile.

"We're great, thanks," Courtney answered.

"Thank you so much for coming by. There's school and the stuff with my mother—it's been a lot these last few weeks."

Courtney brought out the cream, and launched into some new ingredients she'd added and why.

Sasha drifted to a board covered in flyers for sports tryouts, theater auditions, and tutor services. All those tests, she vaguely remembered them. And *Get your school gear before Homecoming!* Who cares? Even when she'd been in high school, when her friends were excited and nervous about various events and plans, the lives they were piecing together seemed small and irrelevant to Sasha. She leaned against the wall to wait.

Courtney and Denise continued talking, Denise describing her mother's most recent visit to the doctor. Courtney nodded along, raising her eyebrow when appropriate, agreeing at other times. Denise sorted through her purse to get her check book and Courtney said, "You know, after the surgery, I have a potion for easing pain. I made it for my father after his knee surgery and he said it really helped."

Sasha remembered Courtney had to argue with her father for weeks to get him to accept the potion. He kept saying, "The doctors don't need magic's help, they know what they're doing." She finally convinced him when she found an interview with a retired baseball player he liked, where he said he'd used a similar potion to recover from hip surgery. "I'm not afraid to admit that it helped me," the athlete said. "You know what, admit isn't even the right word. Why should something that helped me be shameful?"

Denise put her hand to her heart. "Courtney Johnson, you are a blessing. That would mean the world to me, thank you."

Courtney hurried past the compliment, but Sasha saw as she tried to hide her smile, that it warmed her. So Sasha could appreciate that about Denise also.

Both took out their day planners so Courtney could schedule making the new potion.

Sasha looked out the large window into the hallway. It was emptier now, with students in classes. One student walked past, shoving a textbook and a large binder into her open backpack. She gripped a pen between her teeth, and as she struggled with the bag, her sweatshirt, which was tucked in the nook of her arm, started to slip. This was exactly the image to represent their high school, Sasha thought. Balance everything at once however you can. Sasha had been glad to leave it behind. A small life. Worrying about tests and essays. But Sasha didn't know this girl. And Sasha? Sure, she could do magic, but she rarely did. And when she did, little things and little things only.

The student grabbed for her sweatshirt, and as she did, the pen fell. Sasha chuckled and thought, No hand left to grab that, when the pen froze in its tumble.

It was only for a second, and the student snatched it out of the air.

Sasha burst into the hallway. The student flinched and immediately the binder and textbook crashed to the ground.

"Did you just do that?" Sasha asked.

Courtney and Denise ran out also, alerted by the crash.

The student's eyes widened. Because she had been caught?

"You just did that," Sasha repeated.

Before the kid could respond, Denise was fussing her. Helping her get everything together, while chatting away about class schedules and soccer tryouts. And while the student answered, she kept looking back at Sasha, the pen gripped in her hand.

.   .   .

"What was that about?" Courtney asked as they walked out of the building.

"I saw that girl do magic," Sasha said.

Courtney grabbed her arm. "Are you sure?"

Sasha nodded fervently. "She dropped her pen, and then froze it in the air. Probably not on purpose. You know how it is when you first come into your powers. You have a strong emotion and the magic shoots out. I guess her strong emotion is school supplies."

"Or," Courtney mused, "avoiding embarrassment at school. But you're sure? You weren't standing close to her."

"Do you not want her to be a witch?"

Courtney shook her head. "I don't want to get my hopes up."

They were back in the visitor parking lot. As she moved away from the interaction, she wondered if she had exaggerated it, her mind seeing what it wanted.

Courtney stopped walking, pulling Sasha short. Howie March leaned against the passenger side door of Courtney's car. Waiting for them. Howie had been in charge of the Witches' Guard in their town for twenty-three years and had been part of the guard for nearly as long before, since he'd been a young man. The guard wore all black uniforms similar to the police, but Howie always wore plain clothes. And his wire-framed glasses. Sasha dreamed of breaking those stupid glasses.

He pushed off the car as the witches approached. Sasha avoided his eye contact. Courtney walked with a quick pace and her shoulders back. "Good afternoon, Officer," she said.

"Please, Courtney. You know I prefer Howie."

Courtney smiled and nodded. "Good afternoon, Howie. I hope you're well."

"I am. And Sasha, how are you?"

"I'm fine," she muttered.

"That's great. It's great to see you two girls, really. But unfortunately, we have a problem."

"A problem?" Courtney said, still smiling.

"This visit to the high school. It's a problem."

"Sasha and I were bringing an order to a customer of mine who works at the school. She asked me to."

"That may all be true, but there's no way for me to know if that was your real intention. I can't let these visits become a regular occurrence." Howie took a small leather-bound pad and a pen out of his jacket pocket. He flipped the pad open and started writing.

"We weren't planning any return trips," Sasha snapped.

"I don't want parents to have to worry. I don't want anyone to get hurt."

"No one got hurt. We didn't even speak to any of the students."

"Sasha..." Courtney warned.

Howie ripped off the paper and handed it to Sasha with a smile. She snatched it from him. She got into the car and slammed the door. Courtney moved with more deliberation, but Sasha saw she was shaking. She heard Howie's muffled voice through the door say, "You two have a great day, Courtney."

Once she was driving away, Courtney said quietly, "I hate him."

Sasha watched him in the rearview mirror. He stood in the same spot, hands in his pocket. They started the climb up the driveway away from the school. He became smaller and smaller in the mirror. Sasha stabbed at his figure in the reflection.

"I fucking hate him," she screamed.

Courtney cracked up, leaning against the wheel.

Sasha said, "He's the only one who should be worried about getting hurt." She balled the ticket up in her fist.

Courtney stopped laughing. "Don't say that in front of him."

"I won't," Sasha said, still watching him. She could tell he watched them, a motionless speck.

"What does the ticket say?"

She spread it out and read it. "Two hundred dollar fine for trying to manipulate young minds."

Courtney groaned. "Well, Denise just paid me one fifty."

"Forget that, we're not paying this."

"Sasha, we have to."

"No, this is not a real ticket. This is, 'Hey kids watch me put the mean witches in their place.'" Sasha tore the ticket in half, then in quarters. She lowered the window and let the pieces fly away. Courtney gasped, but started laughing again.

"It's one of his stupid power trips. It's for the show of it. And he'll have some new petty idea tomorrow," Sasha said. She tilted her head towards the open window, the fresh air rushing in. "And if he doesn't drop it, I'll pay it, okay? Don't worry about it."

Chapter Four

When Sasha was younger, she was best friends with a girl named Juliet Roth. They met in the third grade. On the first day of school, Juliet wore a big white bow in her hair. Halfway through the day, Juliet took the bow off and clipped it in Sasha's hair. "We can share it," she said. When Sasha dragged her mother across the school parking lot to meet Juliet's mother, Mrs. Roth put down her cell phone to attend to her daughter tugging on her other hand. She looked up at Sasha and her mother striding towards her. Deborah put her hand out. "I know who you are," Mrs. Roth said.

Deborah kept her hand out and Mrs. Roth shook it. Sasha and Juliet remained friends up until high school and Sasha called Juliet's mother Mrs. Roth the entire time, even the last time she saw her, when Mrs. Roth spit in Sasha's face.

When Sasha started showing powers the summer before their senior year, Juliet was the first person she told after Catherine and Deborah. And Juliet was as excited as Sasha was, enthralled by every new spell Catherine taught Sasha.

At the same time, Courtney started to show powers too, but hadn't told anyone yet. For years, Courtney was just the nerd rushing to copy down every word the teacher said. She was someone Sasha sat next to because of alphabetical order and didn't take note of otherwise.

Sasha was over at the Roth home for a sleepover. They always stayed at Juliet's house. When Juliet's parents went to sleep, the two crept downstairs in the dark, giggling and pushing each other. They each took a tall glass from the kitchen, then Juliet led the way to the liquor cabinet. She poured half a glass of rum, careful to keep the bottle from hitting the top of the glass. "I want vodka," Sasha whispered.

Juliet shook her head. "We took too much last weekend. I heard my dad asking my mom about it."

"I told you. You should've filled it with some water."

Juliet shook her head again and forced the bottle of rum against Sasha's chest. "This is what we're having tonight."

Sasha took her share, and they tiptoed upstairs, shielding the glasses against the sides of their bodies in case Mr. or Mrs. Roth came down the hallway. It would've been easier and quieter for only one girl to make the retrieval, but they were never separate and wouldn't miss out on the clandestine adventure.

In Juliet's room, they sat on the floor on the side of the bed farther from the door, the lights out.

Sasha took a big gulp and made a face. "I hate rum."

"Shut up, you'll drink it anyway," Juliet said. She took a sip and smacked her lips. "I happen to think it's tasty."

"That's because you have bad taste."

"You bitch," Juliet laughed, and then slapped a hand over her mouth. She glanced at the door. "You have bad taste."

"No, you really do. Like Mark?"

"Mark is cute." Juliet smacked Sasha's knee and they both giggled. Juliet stopped laughing. "I don't get why he isn't into me."

"He's a dumb jock. You're sophisticated. You're too good for him."

"He's not dumb. Honestly, if you'd talk to him, you'd see that. And if I'm too good for him, why isn't he chasing after me?"

Sasha didn't have an answer for that. "I saw Alex Torrance staring at you during lunch again this week."

"Yeah, he's okay, I guess." Juliet took a big sip of rum and sighed. "I think Mark likes that junior Paige Kaplan."

"Well, she might not be into him."

"Do you think you could make him like me back?"

Sasha's stomach dropped. "I don't know that sort of magic," she said.

Juliet leaned forward, stared at Sasha, as if waiting her out. Even in the faint light that came in through the window, Juliet's stare burned into her.

"Fine," Juliet said finally. "What about Paige? You could curse her with a ton of acne. Or make her sick, just a little sick, like give her mono. It'll keep her out of school for a while."

"I don't know that magic either. I've only learned like three spells. And besides, I can't do magic on people without their permission." She nodded to Juliet's green bracelet. Sasha still wore her own bracelet also, as Catherine wanted to wait to register her with the guard. She wasn't even supposed to have told anyone about being a witch, but Catherine had allowed an exception for Juliet. "You know that."

Juliet leaned back.

"Maybe he has a thing for blonds? We could dye your hair."

Juliet rolled her eyes with a smile. "Sasha if I were to go blond, I'd go to salon, not do it out of a box."

"That's what I meant. You'd pull it off too."

In the next few weeks, Juliet would nudge Sasha whenever they saw Paige Kaplan in the hallways. Sasha tried to change the subject, but that stopped working. Juliet pulled her into the bathroom one day. Fussing with her hair in the mirror, she said, "What about you take away all her family's money? They'd have to leave town. And it's not like you'd be doing a spell on them directly. And—"

"Stop."

Deborah had fallen down the stairs in their house earlier in the week. A save-the-date had arrived from Sasha's father David and his fiancée, and Deborah was drinking more and more. Sasha heard the thump and ran to help her. "I'm fine, I'm fine," Deborah said, pushing away her daughter.

Each night since, Sasha lay awake in bed, listening until her mother stopped pacing in her bedroom down the hall, and only then could she fall asleep. Whenever Catherine came over, she and Deborah fought. Sasha didn't want to hear any more about Paige Kaplan.

Juliet raised her eyebrow in the mirror. The silence stilled the space between them. Juliet turned slowly to face Sasha.

"I saw Alex staring at you again today," Sasha said. "I know he used to be a dork, but maybe he's not anymore. He really grew up over the summer, looks wise."

Juliet rolled her eyes. "What do you know about anything, Sasha?" She brushed past her to the door.

Juliet didn't bring it up again for weeks. Sasha thought it was done. When she went into her mother's room to see her, Deborah lay smoking cigarettes in bed, her blinds closed, and Sasha went to pick up the empty wine bottles on the floor.

"Leave them," Deborah snapped. She had started smoking cigarettes again, something she said she'd only stopped because David hadn't liked it when they were first dating.

Sasha was sleeping less. Each day felt endless, but they added up without her noticing and suddenly it was winter. Sasha was jittery from the lack of sleep.

There was a voicemail from her father. Deborah saw the

missed call over her shoulder. "Play it," she said and when Sasha tried to change the subject, Deborah grabbed her phone out of her hand.

Catherine had started coming by the school to check on Sasha, buttoning up Sasha's coat absentmindedly on a chilly day, but had stopped visiting their house.

Deborah put the phone to her ear to listen. When the message was finished, she said with a fake sweetness, "You haven't responded to his texts about holiday plans. You should respond. It's rude to keep him waiting." She threw Sasha's phone at her, and it smacked against her collar bone.

"Ow," Sasha said.

"Grow up," Deborah snapped.

Sasha walked upstairs to her room, rubbing the sore spot. She turned some music on and then turned it up to cover the sound of her mother walking downstairs.

Sasha would sleep well that night. Her mother could take care of herself.

The first snow fell before midnight. Slow, lazy snowflakes. There was a thin cover on the ground. Sasha watched the snow through her window, which looked out over the backyard. Her mother stepped outside.

Deborah wasn't wearing a jacket and held a glass of wine clutched in her hand. She held out her other hand, catching snowflakes. She watched her palm. Sasha watched her.

Sasha had never seen her mother be sentimental about anything except her father and magic. Was she even excited about the snow? Sasha couldn't see her face. Deborah walked forward and slipped.

Sasha gasped and started for her door. But for a second, she stopped. Let her stay there, she thought. She was shocked at herself and ran out of her room and down the steps. She pushed the thought down. She would never tell anyone that she paused. Deborah was groaning. She'd fallen onto the wine glass, and her hand was slashed open red. Shards of glass stuck out of her palm. Deborah's eyes were unfocused. Sasha pulled her mother onto her lap.

"Fuck, fuck," Sasha said.

"David?" Deborah slurred. She reached up to Sasha's face. "David?"

Sasha fumbled for her phone in her pocket. "No, Mom, it's me."

"Oh."

Sasha looked at her screen. It didn't feel right to call Catherine or Juliet. She thought of Courtney. Courtney Johnson, the nerd who'd approached her in school in October and confessed to Sasha that she thought she was a witch. Sasha brought her to Catherine's home and Catherine said to them, "You're sisters now."

Courtney showed up thirty-six minutes later. Sasha had dragged Deborah back inside and wrapped her hand in a towel. "What took you so long?"

"I had to walk. I don't have my own car yet. And besides, it would've woken my parents up if I started the car and opened the garage door and then—"

Sasha held up a hand. "I get the point." Sasha and Courtney sat on the floor on either side of Deborah. Sasha unwrapped the towel. Deborah squinted at Courtney. "Who are you?"

"It's Courtney, Mrs. Hoffman. We've met a few times?"

"Mrs. Hoffman," Deborah laughed. "Yeah, I bet that's what she'll call herself."

Sasha held her mother's hand up with both her hands. The blood had mostly stopped. "You left the glass in?" Courtney said.

"Aren't you supposed to?"

"I think that's if you're stabbed with, like, a knife?"

"Okay, let's take them out then."

They both looked at Deborah's hand. "She's your mom. Why don't you—"

"Fine," Sasha snapped. She plucked out one of the smaller shards.

They worked quietly. There were seven pieces total. Sasha traced a finger above the cuts, Deborah softly moaning. "We should heal this," Sasha said.

"Um, I don't know that sort of magic. Do you?"

"Don't just sit there and say 'um,' okay? It's pissing me off. I feel like you've said 'um' fifteen times since you've got here."

Courtney looked at Sasha in shock. Then she stood up. "Why didn't you call Juliet? These cuts probably just need to be cleaned."

Courtney started walking towards the front door. Sasha struggled to stand. "I didn't call Juliet. I called you. You can't leave."

"Actually, I can."

Sasha carefully laid Deborah on the floor and followed her. "Please. Please don't leave."

Courtney looked back at her. Blood on her hands and her pajamas. Her face swollen, likely from crying. "Okay. But stop being so rude."

Sasha took a deep breath. She started crying. Courtney wasn't sure what to do, to go to her or not. She settled with hugging her arms around herself and not looking at Sasha's face. Sasha stopped quickly. She sniffled and wiped at her nose. "You're right," she mumbled.

They went back to Deborah. "Do you have bacitracin? Hydrogen peroxide?"

Sasha stood up. "I'll go check."

She came back with everything they needed to treat the cuts. Courtney held Deborah's hand aloft, like an offering. Deborah cringed at the hydrogen peroxide, then Sasha dabbed on bacitracin. She covered each cut with a bandage. Deborah moaned and mumbled throughout it. "Let's take her to her room," Sasha said.

They pushed her into a sitting position. "Okay, Mom, let's go to bed."

"Hmm," Deborah said. "Where's David?"

"Not here." They pulled Deborah up, supporting her between them. They shuffled to her bedroom, half dragging her. Sasha opened the door and saw it through Courtney's eyes. The dirty clothes piled on the floor. The empty wine bottles clustered on the bedside table. A ripe smell of body odor and abandoned food. The smoke settled in the air. "It's not usually like this," Sasha muttered.

"Yeah, of course," Courtney said in a falsely bright voice that jangled off every surface.

Sasha bit back a snapped retort. Courtney was here. She'd showed up, and she'd stayed.

They laid Deborah on the bed. Courtney was pulled onto the bed and leapt up. This time Sasha couldn't stop herself from saying, "It's not that bad."

"No, it's not, I'm sorry, I'm..." She trailed off, looking at her feet.

"It's fine," Sasha whispered. She pulled the duvet over Deborah, who already had her eyes closed.

The two younger witches left the room. Back in the living room, Sasha said, "Thank you. For coming over and helping."

"Of course. Is your dad out of town?"

Sasha looked at Courtney with a jolt. *She really knows nothing about me*, she thought. But then, Sasha considered, she didn't know much about Courtney either. "No. They're divorced."

"Oh. I'm sorry. That must be difficult."

Sasha laughed. It was almost a bark. She felt like her smile would burst through her cheeks. "Yeah." Had Juliet ever told her she was sorry about her parents breaking up? Sasha called her right after her parents had told her, ran up the stairs, and slammed the door.

"He lives in New Jersey now."

"At least it's easy for you to visit," Courtney said.

"I guess."

"I meant, Jersey isn't a banned state, so you wouldn't need permission from the guard."

"Oh. That." Sasha hadn't been to visit her father since he'd moved.

Courtney looked around, lowered her voice, as if they could be overheard by the guard. "They've always freaked me out."

Sasha thought of when Catherine finally took her to register as a witch at the guard. Howie March, the head of the guard, had smiled and circled his hand around her wrist while the other guard member went to get the tool to take off her bracelet. "I hate them," Sasha said.

Courtney wrapped her arm around herself again. "Yeah. Anyway, I should get going," she said.

"Yeah, totally. Thank you, again."

At the door, Courtney said, "I hope your mom will be okay."

Sasha couldn't string together a response—her thoughts on her mom and what "okay" might look like for Deborah could fill up the whole room, knock her over, claw out of her throat and leave her empty. Instead, she nodded and waved goodbye.

Courtney registered as a witch two weeks later. Someone must have seen her leaving the guard headquarters with Catherine, Deborah, and Sasha, because even before she came into school without her bracelet on, people knew. As she walked down the hallways in the morning, students turned and stared. Darren Murphy, one of the popular crowd and someone she'd never spoken with before, announced loudly when she walked past that he was looking at protective amulets online because he wasn't interested in a witch sinking her claws into him.

Josh Keller, who she was friendly with and was widely considered the frontrunner for valedictorian, approached her later in the day in the empty hallway and quietly offered to help her with the *Macbeth* essay for their English class in exchange for her help with "some stuff."

He looked at his feet while he said this, red creeping up his neck. She had finished the *Macbeth* essay the weekend before, she let him know, and would never find out what the "stuff" he wanted help with was. The acne that had stubbornly perched on his cheeks since eighth grade? The jeans that were now too short on him after his recent growth spurt, that he kept wearing while many of their peers showed up in new clothes every other week? Some idea he harbored of a love spell for someone he was too shy to ask out? Maybe he wanted a witch to sink her claws into him.

When they talked about *Macbeth* in English class, every student and even Ms. Andrews looked at her each time the witches were mentioned. The topic of discussion that day was how the witches' prophecies moved the story forward. Courtney did not participate.

She had lunch next and looked forward to sitting with her friends and having a chance to breathe. But when she got to the lunchroom, her friends weren't at their usual table. She searched the room, trying to see if they'd relocated.

At a table nearby, Sasha sat with Juliet and their other friends. Sasha had checked in with Courtney between morning classes—as instructed by Catherine—to see how she was handling the stares and whispers. When Sasha registered, it didn't warrant many second looks. With her mother a witch, most students had considered her a witch already. Skyler Bannerman saw Courtney out of the corner of her eye and leaned forward to the rest of the table. "I overheard her friends say they were going to eat in the band room today. It didn't sound like they were going to let her know." She smirked.

They watched Courtney sit down at the table, still looking around, as if maybe her friends were running late. Juliet giggled. "Who knew that group had that pettiness in them?"

"She always needs to be the person with the right answer. She's so annoying."

Juliet and the others all laughed harder. Sasha stood up. "Shut up, Skyler," she said. Skyler snarled her upper lip. Juliet arched an eyebrow. "You've never given Courtney more than two seconds' thought. Now you're obsessed with her. You must be jealous." She collected her lunch and walked over towards Courtney's table.

"Sasha, where are you going?" Juliet called out, an edge to her voice.

Sasha sat down across from Courtney with a huff. Courtney looked up at her mid-chew, her eyes wide.

"I cannot stand the morons we go to school with," Sasha said. Courtney smiled.

Courtney shared some of the things people had been saying to her and around her throughout the day. She said it under her breath, with people craning their necks to look at them, taking a route to walk past them.

Sasha said, "They're pathetic."

At the end of lunch, they walked together towards their next periods. Before they split in opposite directions, Sasha said, "Listen, your friends..."

"Let me guess. They ate somewhere else and didn't tell me."

Sasha nodded. "At least it shows you who your friends really are."

Courtney sighed, "So, no one."

Sasha looked at the ground; she didn't know what to say. Courtney started down the hall. Sasha called out, "Maybe you could come over some time, not just during coven stuff. To hang out."

Courtney smiled. "Yeah, I'd like that."

Sasha and Juliet had a free period after lunch. Sasha went to the bathroom in the languages wing, where they always went first to touch up their makeup and redo their hair. Juliet, already there when Sasha pushed open the door, looked at her in the mirror, lip gloss in hand.

"Hey," Sasha said.

Juliet tossed the lip gloss into her makeup bag. "So, you think people are jealous of witches?" she said, disdain soaking each word.

Sasha did, but it was clear that answer would invite even more snide remarks. She looked at the floor and shrugged. "Skyler was pissing me off."

Juliet picked up her school bag and swung it onto her shoulder. "You know, I've got to meet with a teacher. You should go to the library without me. Maybe I'll see you later."

Chapter Five

Sasha had finished her last bottle of vodka, and she wasn't going to wait for errand day. She put on a dress and called a cab. She asked the driver to wait in front of her preferred liquor store.

She walked through the aisles considering how to restock. While Courtney was not drinking much, Sasha figured she would be by the end of the month. So she got two bottles of her vodka brand and then ventured to the wine section for some of Courtney's favorites. Once paid, she held the paper bag to her body, the bottles clinking against one another, and walked out of the shop.

"Good afternoon, Sasha."

Sasha flinched and whipped her head around. Howie stood behind her on the sidewalk. He smiled. "What do you want?" she said.

"I wanted to inquire after the payment of the ticket from the other day."

"I don't know about any ticket." She opened the cab door.

"A ticket for two hundred and fifty dollars."

She placed the paper bag in the back seat and said to the driver,

"Hold on one second." She closed the door and turned to Howie. "It was for two hundred."

"Now you remember, great. The extra fifty dollars is a late fee."

"Are you kidding me? That wasn't even a week ago."

"If you pay me right now, I can make it two hundred and twenty-five."

"Yeah right." She moved to get into the cab. He grabbed her arm. The driver turned slightly in his seat.

"Please don't make me drag this out, Sasha."

She dug pulled a pen and her checkbook out of her bag. Howie said, "Make it out to me."

"Interesting," she said. "Why don't we make it an even one fifty, then?"

Howie laughed. "Okay, since we are such old friends."

Sasha dug into each pen stroke, as if she could impart some sort of harm into the act of writing his name. She tore the check out, folded it up, and held it out to him. When Howie reached for it, she let the check drop to the ground. "Oh, I'm sorry," she said, keeping any hint of sarcasm out of her voice.

Howie stooped down to pick up the check. When his hand was closing on it, Sasha flicked her finger, jerking the check out of his reach. He glared up at her.

"What? There's a breeze."

He reached for it again and she floated the check above his grasp. He stumbled slightly and she laughed. "Stop," he growled. He pulled himself up.

She couldn't stop laughing. "I'm not doing anything."

His hand shot out. He shoved her, and she fell against the side of the cab. The metal cracked against her back, and she yelped. She heard the driver open his door and say, "Hey!" Howie held his hands up. Sasha saw two women at the end of the block stop and gasp. The one steered the other to cross the street, and they averted their eyes.

"Don't mess with me, Sasha," Howie said. "If you ever perform magic in front of me again, you're done," he snapped.

Howie took a step back, and Sasha walked to the cab door on the other side. She got inside and slammed the door.

Courtney strolled through the grocery store. The day before Sasha called her, screaming and crying. It took several minutes to calm her down to find out what happened and even then, the story was garbled—Howie, the liquor store, the money. Courtney drove over to her house. Sasha was lit up, fueled by rage and vodka. Courtney kept saying, "Slow down, slow down" to get the full story. When it was all told, Sasha had kicked a hole in her living room wall and collapsed on the couch, slightly shaking. Courtney fixed the hole with a quick spell.

Courtney knew Howie was an entity they had to deal with each and every day. His control lingered over their lives, sometimes light enough they could forget it, which was usually when he re-emerged. He only needed the smallest excuse to show up, and Courtney knew this. She chided herself for not considering this with their trip to the high school.

Even before Courtney knew she was a witch, she knew the best way to respond to Howie March was with extreme politeness and caution—the same she did with regular cops. Before she was a witch, if she saw him in town or around the school, she would smile at him and say hello or good morning. Her friends asked once if he was a friend of her parents, which he decidedly wasn't.

And Howie had seemed to take special notice of her. She wasn't the only teenager who was polite to him. But she did appear to be one that he kept an eye on. As one of two black students in their grade, she already stood out, and maybe he couldn't help but wonder if there was something else that made her different.

At the store, she slowed at the rows of tea boxes. She picked up a box of her usual Earl Grey. She was considering the other flavors on the shelf when there was a tap on her shoulder. When she turned around and saw Howie, she suspected he'd followed her into the store. "Hello, Officer. How are you?" she asked.

"I'm doing well, Courtney, thank you for asking. And as always, please, call me Howie."

"Of course." Courtney wanted to start walking away.

"I have a bit of a problem."

Courtney's mind flitted through possibilities. Was he about to say something about Sasha? Could he possibly be about to ask her to help him with an unrelated problem? Something that needed solving with a potion? Just another customer?

He continued, "I haven't received any sort of payment on that ticket I gave you last week."

"Really?" Courtney thought quickly. He probably knew that she knew that he was lying. "Sasha told me she was going to pay it. I'm sorry it hasn't arrived yet. Maybe it's in the mail?"

He smiled. "Well, we both know Sasha can be forgetful."

"I can call her later and make sure she sent it."

"I think it actually might be best if you paid it."

To be so bold! "You know, I don't have my checkbook in this bag."

"I don't mind cash."

"I don't carry that much cash on me."

"How much do you have?"

Courtney had started clutching the box of Earl Grey, without even realizing it. She put it back on the shelf and took out her wallet. She counted her bills, trying to keep her hands from shaking. "Twenty-four dollars."

Howie held out his hand. "I'll take that, and I'll collect the remainder from Sasha the next time I see her."

Courtney couldn't bring herself to hold out the money. It wasn't much, but he was lying. Plus, the ticket had been a power trip in the first place. He reached out and pulled the money from her hand.

"Uh, sure," Courtney said. "Bye!" She wanted to turn and run, but she walked at a calm pace away from him. She rounded a corner, abandoned her grocery cart, and hurried to the exit, smiling and waving at people she knew. She didn't want to make them stare and wonder what she was doing.

She decided she wouldn't tell Sasha about this interaction.

Chapter Six

The girl showed up at Sasha's front door. Sasha didn't recognize her at first.

She was waking up from a nap, still in the fog of sleep, and answered the door more out of surprise than anything else. The girl stood as close to the door frame as she could be to be out of view.

"Wrong house," she said, rubbing her eye.

The girl looked confused. "Sorry?"

"Well, I don't know you, so you've got the wrong house." Sasha shut the door with a lazy wave. There was a tentative knock. She sighed and opened the door again.

The girl toyed with her bracelet. Her generation's was orange. "I didn't know where the other one—Courtney, I think?—lived, so that's why I'm here."

Sasha still wasn't putting it together.

"My name's Marni Cohen. I saw you at the high school the other week?" she whispered.

Sasha gasped and grabbed the girl's shoulder to pull her inside.

She brought her to the kitchen, where they sat down at the table. They looked at each other without saying anything for several seconds. "Shit, what's your name again? Do you want something to drink?"

"It's Marni Cohen. And no, I'm okay."

Sasha ran both her hands through her hair. "I definitely need a drink, and I need to call Courtney, so I'll be right back. She'll take a drink too, even. She hasn't really been drinking. It's so boring. But this is a lot to handle, you know?"

Sasha was up and walking to the living room to try and find her phone. She didn't hear Marni reply, "I know."

She found her phone wedged between the couch cushions and called Courtney, pacing around the living room. "You've got to get over here," Sasha said the second Courtney picked up.

"Is everything okay?"

"Oh my god, is it. That girl from the school is here."

"What did she say? I can be over in a minute."

Sasha stopped pacing. "She didn't say much. Just her name, and that she didn't know where you lived, and that she didn't want a drink. Then I ran and called you."

"Is she definitely there because she's a witch?"

"Why else would she be here? Courtney, get over here. She mentioned you, I told you."

"But she might just want something done? Find out the facts first! I'll get ready, but text me if she only wants some normal help."

Sasha hung up with an eye roll and returned to the kitchen. The girl still sat there, her hands folded on the table, staring into the distance.

"Hi. Sorry," Sasha said. She grabbed three glasses out of the cabinet and lined them up on the counter. She retrieved orange juice from the fridge and a bottle of vodka from the freezer. Juice for all three glasses, and a healthy pouring of vodka in two of them.

"Courtney will be here in a minute," she said, and walked to the table. She curled a finger in beckoning at the glasses, which flew into the air and followed behind her to land on the tabletop, orange juice slopping over the sides. Sasha stared at them. "Ah, I forgot which one was which." She pushed the middle one to Marni. "Let me know if it has alcohol in it."

"Okay," Marni said, but she picked it up and put it to the side.

Sasha stared at her, the other drinks forgotten next to her. "Let's get down to it. You said you were a witch, right? The new witch? That's why you're here?"

"No, I didn't say that, but..."

Sasha raised an eyebrow, ready to throw the girl out of her house, physically if needed.

"Yes, I think I'm a witch."

Sasha leaned back in her chair. "You think?"

"I don't know a lot about all this, but yeah. Little, unexplained things—usually if I'm worked up—but then I'm like, did that actually happen? The pen at school... I would've thought I imagined it, but you saw it too, right?"

"Yes."

It had been the same when she'd first started showing powers. The first time, she'd stormed upstairs mad at her father. She couldn't remember why. She slammed her bedroom door, and a bottle of perfume on her dresser immediately exploded. She froze, unsure if it'd been magic squeezing out in a moment of high emotion or if the force of the door slamming had knocked it over. She didn't say anything to anybody about the perfume bottle. She wanted to be sure.

"Courtney will know what to do next. Honestly, I'm not one for procedure and that sort of thing." Sasha remembered the drinks and pulled one towards her.

They sat in silence for a couple seconds. "I used to see you in synagogue," Marni said.

"Really?" Sasha's parents hadn't been particularly religious as she grew up. Witchcraft had replaced Judaism as something worth practicing for Deborah. David was not overly concerned with their religion either, but he did think it best to at least attend services on the High Holidays in the fall. "It's what's expected," he'd said, and it was the final word.

"Yeah, not that I was watching your family. I guess I knew who your mom was. She was tall like you, right?"

"Yes, she's tall."

"And she was really beautiful. I think that's part of the reason why I always noticed her."

"Yeah, children always seemed to like her." In public, adults had been more likely to approach Catherine, but their children had smiles for Deborah. They'd raise their hands to show her what they were holding—candy, dandelions, little toys. "Wow," Deborah would say without enthusiasm, and when the family would walk away, she'd wipe her hands, even if they hadn't touched her, saying, "Children always have those sticky hands." Once, a little girl tugged softly at Deborah's shirt, and she pushed the child away.

"Your family stopped going," Marni said.

"My father moved out of town when I was a teenager, and he was the one who wanted us to go."

Marni looked around now as if trying to see traces of a father. "Oh, sorry."

Sasha shrugged. "Did you know Catherine?"

Marni shook her head.

"She was the head of our coven. She was wonderful. She died a couple years ago, and we haven't been a coven since then."

"I'm sorry."

"Cancer. It ran in her family." Sasha thought of her own family. Witchcraft ran in it, and some might look at that as a disease. "Her last two years were difficult."

Marni nodded, looking at her hands on the table. "Did she go to chemo?"

"Yeah. Courtney and I drove her to every appointment. She even developed some spell work to try and help the chemo along.

But it didn't work. And then..." Sasha stared out the window into the backyard. "It didn't work. It just didn't."

Sasha excused herself. She walked to the bathroom. Inside, she pressed into the corner, her face up against the green and white striped wallpaper.

One day four years ago, Catherine had asked Sasha and Courtney to meet her at Sasha's house. Sasha had been so young and so clueless that it might be bad news. They sat at the kitchen table, the same one Marni now sat at, and Catherine told them she was stopping chemo. Courtney sat stunned, speechless. Sasha excused herself to this bathroom. She pressed her head against the wall, and then fainted.

Courtney would explain to Sasha later how terrible Catherine's health insurance had been. It'd barely covered anything, but was the only thing she could afford. Many insurance companies charged witches higher premiums, arguing they were harder to treat. It was a stereotype that had been disproved in studies, but still lingered.

For all her talk of community, Catherine did sometimes rail against the non-witches. "All they let us do is fluffy things." She'd made money as a consultant for small businesses in the area, and Sasha hadn't understood then that Catherine didn't have much money. She'd lived all her life in the same house, and her mother had paid the mortgage off before she died. Sasha thought Catherine lived there because she liked the house, not out of necessity.

When Catherine started getting really sick, Sasha would go over to her house and they'd watch TV together. Catherine had always disliked TV, said it made the mind soft. But they'd watch anything. Old sitcoms with laugh tracks, romantic movies about someone from the city moving to the country, even the news.

In what would be the last month of Catherine's life, they sat together, watching a senator tilt her chin up at the camera and elaborate on why there should be a federal ban on witchcraft.

"How can I—or any one of us—trust a witch? We all know their powers of corruptions. I wouldn't feel comfortable if a witch with full powers was working in my husband's office, for instance."

The newscast cut to the senator and her husband attending a black-tie function, smiling for the flashing cameras. Catherine pulled her sweater tighter—she was always cold towards the end—and said, "No one wants to seduce her crusty old husband."

They looked at each other for a beat, and then cracked up.

It felt good to laugh. They hadn't been laughing much. Catherine asked her to change the channel, and they stopped on an old black-and-white movie. One of the main characters was a witch, played by an actress with big eyes. She gazed at the other characters slyly from below shiny eyelids, oozed through the scenes in long velvet dresses. She snapped her fingers to perform spells and drank champagne out of glittering coupes. "I wouldn't mind being remembered like that. Tell people that's what I was like."

Sasha saw the appeal of the character, her irreverent glamor, the actress moving fluidly. But what Catherine projected to the world wasn't to be dismissed. She was solid, and strong. She talked in commands. She walked with her head up, and her eye contact held people in a vise. Sasha was twenty-one years old, and she didn't know how to put into words how she admired Catherine, everything she meant to her. It dawned on her that this was the first time Catherine was referencing a future without her in it, a time when Sasha would have to carry on Catherine as a memory to be imparted to others. She pulled her legs up onto the couch, wrapped her arms around them like a child, and tucked her head against her knees.

"Don't," Catherine chastised her.

Now, with Marni waiting for her, she took several deep breaths, pushed away from the wall, and returned to the kitchen.

She sat down across from Marni, who straightened her posture, smiled expectantly, waiting for what Sasha would say next. Because this was Sasha's house and she was older, she was the elder witch. Various thoughts—swinging between ideas for small talk and potentially wise declarations about being a witch—leapt to her mind and died. The silence stretched on.

"This is a nice house," Marni finally said.

"Thank you," Sasha said woodenly.

They heard the front door open and Courtney called Sasha's name. Sasha ran to meet her in the hallway. Courtney grinned. "Well?"

"She said she's a witch," Sasha whispered, giddy and nervous and raw. They practically ran down the hallway, but before they reached the kitchen, they paused to straighten their backs, and Courtney smoothed her shirt.

"Hello," Courtney said, striding into the kitchen and walking towards Marni. She held out her hand and Marni stood up to shake it. "I'm Courtney Johnson. We're so glad you're here."

"Thank you," Marni said. She sat down again. "I'm Marni Cohen."

Courtney sat next to her, and Sasha rushed to the chair across from her. Sasha pushed the third drink towards Courtney, who acknowledged it with a nod but otherwise ignored it.

"I have some questions for you, if you don't mind. Sasha and I were both born here. Were you?"

"I was born in White Plains, but my family moved here when I was really young."

"Are you an only child?"

"No, I have a sister. She's twenty-three and lives in Philly."

"I take it she's not a witch?"

"Uh, no."

"And when did you start showing powers? Can you describe to us what happened?"

"It was over the summer, two months ago? But I'm sorry, I don't want it to happen."

"What do you mean?" Courtney asked.

Marni raised her chin, but her voice quivered slightly. "I don't want to be a witch."

Sasha's mouth dropped open. She looked immediately at Courtney, who had a similar look on her face. An almost coven. Sasha had allowed herself to hope. Anger rose inside of her. Who did Marni think she was to refuse witchcraft? To refuse Courtney? To refuse her? And she had told her about Catherine's sickness. Personal details about the coven's past that Sasha wouldn't have breathed of to some non-witch.

Sasha stood up. She hissed, "You little—"

Courtney cut her off, "It doesn't matter. You're a witch whether you want to be one or not."

"No," Marni said. She tugged on the orange bracelet again.

"Listen, I don't pretend to be the expert on all things witchcraft, but I have been reading centuries' worth of text by witches since I came into my powers. You can't stop yourself from being a witch. You were a witch when you were born. We all were."

"But I don't want to be one," Marni said. She was pleading, looking from one witch to the other.

"Tough shit," Sasha muttered under her breath.

"We'll be here to help you," Courtney said, her voice softening. She reached to put her hand on Marni's, but Marni shoved away from the table.

"I came here because I thought you could stop it." She shot accusatory glances at both of them.

"It's impossible," Courtney said.

Marni stood up. She moved towards the doorway, and then stopped and held her hand out. Courtney stared at it, then stood and shook her hand. Marni turned next to Sasha. Sasha folded her hands on top of each other on the table. Marni looked between the two. "Well, goodbye."

Courtney showed her to the door. When she returned, she said, "That was not what I was expecting."

Sasha sank back into her chair and pulled her glass to her. "I thought everything was going to be perfect. Why? What an idiot."

CHAPTER SEVEN

W e'll just have to wait," Courtney said. "I'll check the message board and see if other covens—"

"We're still not a coven."

"*Yet*. We're not a coven yet." She carried on, undeterred. "Maybe other covens had similar experiences."

When Sasha didn't respond, Courtney added, "She can't avoid her powers. She can't avoid us."

The next day, Sasha stalked around her house. The walls felt too close, too solid. She complained to Courtney. Over the phone, Courtney sounded far away, although she was likely just distracted by her forum. When Courtney wanted to find out about a topic, she disappeared into research. There was the forum, and then there were the books. Catherine had owned an entire library about witchcraft and their town's covens that had been passed down through generations. She left this library to Courtney. Sasha also owned some books collected by Deborah, but she'd given many of them to Courtney as well.

"I don't know. Why don't you go for a walk?"

Sasha walked down the block. It was okay, she considered. Sort of sunny, and the fresh air felt nice. She walked another block.

When she drove with Courtney, she didn't pay much attention to these neighboring houses. Perfectly cut grass. Trees with their first leaves turning red, yellow, orange. Most of the houses were colonials, as was Sasha's. There was a Victorian-style house on the corner that she had always loved. Did the same people live here as when she was growing up? She hadn't known her neighbors that well then either. She wondered where Marni lived. She walked another block.

There was no specific window of time when a new witch would come into their powers to round out a coven. There wasn't even a guaranteed balance of magic in any given place, as if once Catherine died, there was a vacancy of magic waiting for a new witch to be struck with powers. It could have been a hundred years between Catherine dying and another witch coming into their powers in the town. Marni would've been a witch even if she lived someplace completely different or if Catherine had still been alive. There was no magical minimum or maximum to a place. Another witch could come into their powers the next week, and another one the week after that.

Sasha had always wanted to be a witch. She used to worry, lying in bed at night, that she might not be one. When she was a child, she played at performing spells and making potions. She wanted to do what her mother and Catherine did. She tried to brew her own potions alongside Deborah, sitting on the floor with a plastic bowl from a play set, trying to sneak leftover supplies from the kitchen island. But Deborah would send her away, say Sasha was distracting her. When she became friends with Juliet, they'd play together at being witches, call themselves a coven. Once Mrs. Roth saw them casting their fake spells, Sasha holding a leatherbound dictionary as a grimoire. The next day in school Juliet told Sasha they should only be witches in secret from now on. But she had always thought that it was non-witches who took issue with magic, that anyone who could be part of a coven would jump to it, arms wide.

She walked again the next day, and the day after that. She broadened the scope of her walks. She had little idea where Marni lived. While they had attended the same synagogue, it was the only one in town, so that gave her no clues. She examined each new house she passed, not knowing what she was looking for. She barely knew Marni and she didn't know Marni's parents at all. Sasha considered a modern house with sharp lines standing out against the colonials. Did they have a dog? she wondered as a brown and white Cavalier King Charles Spaniel trotted after its owner towards the mailbox.

Courtney resurfaced, reporting that most stories she read preached patience, as she had originally suspected.

Sasha concocted a new plan.

One of the handful of the books she still had was a thin leather-bound volume, an older book. *On Tracking, On Finding, On Losing* the witch had scrawled on the first page in now faded ink. The date on the bottom of the page was 1801. Most of the spells would be impossible for Sasha to place on Marni because of Marni's bracelet. Of course, Sasha considered, if she had taken her bracelet off, it wouldn't be necessary for Sasha to track her in the first place.

After reading nearly the whole book, she came to a spell for "Finding Someone who Doesn't Want to be Found." It was a potion, and she'd never had her mother's knack for them, but reading through the recipe—littered with blotted out sections— she felt she could do it.

She pulled out the biggest pot in the cupboard, one that hadn't been used since her mother left. She gathered the ingredients. Two eggs and clear liquor—she had on hand. For "wild plants from the target's town" she grabbed a handful of grass from her own backyard. "The target's name written on a piece of parchment"—Marni's name scrawled on the corner of an envelope of junk mail and thrown in the mix. Then, "the witch's own blood, one tablespoon, as she must suffer to obtain the information she wants." Sasha looked down at her hands and arms, kitchen knife and measuring spoons laying on the counter next to the pot. She decided on her left thumb and picked up the knife.

Do it fast. She floated the tablespoon with one gesture and sliced the pad of her thumb down the middle. It was a quick sting and she held it above the spoon, letting the blood drip. It did so slowly. She realized she wasn't going to get a full tablespoon from one cut. She glared at the ingredient list—as she must suffer, after all. She made a cut along her palm. The measuring spoon filled, and Sasha quickly grabbed two bandages from the box she'd also brought downstairs. They immediately soaked through red, and Sasha moved on.

She poured her blood into the concoction. Next, she was instructed to stir the potion rapidly nine times clockwise then immediately set the whole liquid on fire. She had long thin matches from her fireplace. She struck a match and held it in her left hand, with some maneuvering her thumb to comfort, while stirring with her right. She watched the flame flickering while counting. After nine, as the potion swirled—yellow, red, green— she plunged the match in. The liquor caught immediately, the flames jumped over the top of the pot. Sasha stepped back, but regained herself, grabbing the lid and slamming it down. The next step was to speak an incantation, which the witch had written in a language Sasha didn't recognize. Sasha hadn't even performed a spell with an incantation in years. Most simple ones didn't need one. As the fire turned to smoke, she repeated the incantation three times with boldly declared mispronunciations, trapping the smoke within the potion and sealing the entire spell.

Sasha lifted the lid. The potion looked grayish now, as the instructions said it would. All that was left to do was drink it, and the directions promised she would see where she needed to go.

She filled a tall glass and started to sip, then nearly choked. She gulped the entire glass. Then filled it again. Coughs seized her entire chest. Tears streamed down her cheeks. Half the drink down. The directions said to drink the entire potion. She continued.

She slammed the glass down. Her body folded involuntarily in half with coughs, and then a searing heat forced her to straighten. Her kitchen disappeared from her vision. She couldn't even see herself; she no longer was a self in a body. As a consciousness, she watched a scene unfold. It was outside and there was a large group of teenagers. Sasha saw the high school in the background. It was one of the athletic teams on the field.

The players stretched, one bent arm above their head, the other bent by their side, their hands meeting in the middle of their back. Each of their bracelets was visible, even the one young woman with a number of yarn friendship bracelets snaking over the guard bracelet. The bright orange shone through. The guard's official word was how the bracelets, in addition to protecting people from magic, announced non-witches to witches, and always chose a bright color to achieve that visibility. Sasha and Courtney felt that it was to make the absences of the bracelet more noticeable. Marni glowed gold, identified by the spell among her teammates.

The coach blew a whistle and all the players jogged towards her. Sasha watched Marni. Some other players grabbed drinks from their bags while the coach spoke. Marni stood still, arms crossed and listening.

But Sasha knew where Marni went to school. She wanted to see where she lived. With this thought, the scene went black, and a new place drifted out of the dark. It was a house, another colonial like so many of the houses in their town, painted light gray. Next to the front door, the house number glowed gold. Again, black. Then a green street sign glowing softly against a blue sky. Thank you, Sasha thought, and she was yanked back into her kitchen. Back in her body, she crashed into a chair, almost falling over it. She had what she wanted.

. . .

She typed Marni's address into her phone map. She cast a protection spell over herself because she'd be traversing main roads and their blind turns. She started walking, and thirty-two minutes later, sweating in her long dress in the warm fall evening, she arrived at one of the two gated communities in town. She was happy to have an exact address and, once through the pedestrian gate, kept consulting her phone to navigate the maze of streets and similar looking houses.

At the correct house, she walked across the lawn and rang the doorbell. She didn't have a plan past getting there. She heard footsteps on the other side of the door. There was a pause, the person looking through the peephole. Sasha stared at the peephole from her side.

When the door opened, it was Marni. "What are you doing here? How did you know where I live?"

"Magic." Sasha waved a hand. "Can I come in?"

Marni glanced past Sasha, up and down the street. No neighbors were out. She stood aside. "Sure."

Sasha followed her into the kitchen. It was the only room with a light on. A laptop was open on the table with a bowl of spaghetti and tomato sauce next to it.

"Your parents aren't home?"

"No, they're working. They won't be home for another"— Marni glanced at a clock by the fridge—"two hours, maybe three."

Sasha took the seat next to her. Marni pushed the laptop aside and brought the spaghetti towards her. "Did you want anything to eat? I don't have any more pasta, but we have some baby carrots and hummus? Grapes too."

Sasha declined. She didn't know where to start.

Marni watched her with a polite smile. She wasn't going to help Sasha out with this conversation.

"So. You know you're a witch."

Marni nodded, staring down into the bowl.

"You don't think that's exciting?"

Marni sighed. "I don't really want to be a witch. No offense."

"Why not?"

"I've got other stuff going on. I've got my friends, and soccer, and school."

"Soccer? School? So what? You have all that for what, two and a half more years? Being a witch, magic—that's your entire life."

"I want those two and a half more years."

"It's not like you have to drop out of school."

To Sasha, it all seemed so small. But when Marni looked at Sasha, she saw an adult woman who never left her hometown, that rarely left her house and had (as far as she knew) one friend.

"Or," Sasha sighed, "stop playing soccer."

"Things'll change. I know it. And we might make it to State this year," Marni said. Sasha stared blankly at her. "In soccer. Can I not participate? Like, I'm a witch. I have the powers, but I don't do anything with them?"

"Do you know how stupid that sounds? Who would do that? Have powers and not use them?"

"Me! And I bet other people do it too."

Again, Sasha was confounded to have to convince someone the attraction of being a witch. Wasn't it obvious? Having power? Isn't that what all those people frothing at the mouth against witches were threatened by? Why would they care if witches weren't powerful.

When Sasha considered the trajectory of her life, she thought it would have continued the same as it had been going—hanging out with Courtney, sometimes Pooja and Faye, going to the occasional board party. She didn't have to work because she had plenty of money. She felt, I'm spending time with my friends, people I love. But she knew the hours she spent alone, haunting her own childhood home—that her father first left willingly and then her mother, unwillingly—drinking on her own. Floating along. Here was an opportunity for a coven. She wanted it. For herself and for Courtney. She couldn't wait to go to the ceremony to name Courtney leader. She wanted Marni to want it too.

She started parroting Catherine, remembering what she'd said to Courtney when she first came to meetings. "Your power is only limited by your imagination. And with your coven, you work to become even more powerful together. Strengthening each other."

Marni held up her orange bracelet. "Isn't it limited?"

Sasha hated the bracelets, but she wasn't going to dwell on them. "So you can't do magic on other people. Would you want to?" Again, Catherine. But also, thoughts of Juliet egging her to perform spells on Paige Kaplan, who'd always been friendly to everyone.

"No, of course not," Marni said quickly.

Sasha noted if she was considering limits, that meant it was on her mind. She continued, sharing things from the forum Courtney had told her about. "Look, what is it you want to do, really? Anything you've ever thought, I wish I could do that. As a witch, you probably can." It did not occur to Sasha that this tracking spell was the first significant spell she had done in several years. "Even if it's not some big spell. You want to be more of a morning person for school? There's a potion for that you can take before bed. You want a perfect garden? There're spells for that. It makes your life easier, and that's sometimes why I think people are jealous of us. Because at the end of the day, the people who seek to limit us? They're jealous. They wish they could do what we can, and they can't.

"You're part of something in a coven. You're together when you're happy and when you're sad. You call on them when you need help, for anything, and they're there. We're there. You're part of an 'us.'" These were her own thoughts.

She tried to read Marni's expression, if what she'd said connected. Her eyes were blank, and Sasha felt ridiculous, that she'd exposed a piece of her heart to have it considered and placed to the side politely.

"Anyway, it doesn't work the way you want it to. The Westchester Board of Witches will fine you every single year you don't join us, and they'll have to report you to the guard, and I honestly don't even know what they'd do but I can't imagine it'd be pleasant. And before you suggest that Courtney and I not tell the Westchester Board of Witches about you, we can't. In January and February, the board sends representatives to every town and they test for any new witches. Their own sort of witch hunt."

"Why?"

"Well, Ella, she's one of the board members, always makes it seem like they have to do it for us because Courtney and I aren't experienced enough to sense a new witch coming into powers. But I know they do it all over. She's just an asshole."

"So, January, I'll have to be in your coven."

"It'd be *our* coven," Sasha said with some bite. "Sometimes they don't get to us until later, but basically, yes. Or you could join on your own terms."

Marni twirled the fork around slowly. "I could fit in the season," she said. "This is my first season on varsity. I worked so hard over the summer to get here."

"It doesn't work like that." Sasha banged the table with her fist. Marni widened her eyes, and Sasha unclenched her fists, tapped her fingers, remeasured her voice. "I'm sorry, I didn't mean to... Soccer's important to you. Got it. How about you don't have to register yet but come meet with us? We meet at Courtney's house, and people go there all the time to pick up potions from her, so no one'll suspect. Let me give you her address, and our phone numbers."

The next day, Sasha went to Courtney's house for their errand day.

Scribbling her items on the bottom of Courtney's list, Sasha recounted the spell and her conversation with Marni.

"Why didn't you tell me? I would've liked to come see her too."

Sasha shrugged. "You were planning on waiting."

"I'm ready to, but I'm open to reasonable conversation too."

Courtney started re-shelving the books that crowded her desk. They thumped into their spots louder than Sasha thought necessary. Sasha said, "She's dull."

"What do you mean?"

"She's, like, this jock. Keeps talking about wanting to play soccer."

Courtney laughed. "Soccer's probably fun."

CHAPTER EIGHT

Courtney pored over her books, ones she'd read when she first became a witch. She wanted to refresh her memory—not just of the books themselves but of that time in her life. She'd felt uncertain about being a witch at first, but as she started meeting with Catherine, Deborah, and Sasha, and became comfortable with the idea, she walked everywhere with a sense of endless possibility. Catherine began showing her how she could shape her raw power into working for her.

Everything she looked at seemed brighter and sharper, even her classrooms—the chalk on the board suddenly crisper. She'd read everything she could about witchcraft and being a witch, both in print and online. When she read, it tamped down the small part of herself that knew her parents would not be pleased. They wanted her to become a doctor. It had been what she wanted too. But witches didn't get admitted to medical school or even most undergraduate programs.

As it became clear she had a knack for potions, Deborah let her sit with her while she worked. Deborah drank large glasses of red wine while making potions, smacking her lips. Some days, she'd wander off with her glass and never return.

At Courtney's house, Sasha lay on the sofa, half dozing, responding with softer and softer hmms when Courtney read something out loud. Both their phones chimed. Sasha jolted up.

The text said, *Okay, I'll come to meetings.*

"Yes," Sasha yelled, and grabbed Courtney and swung her around, laughing.

"It's really happening," Courtney gushed. She snapped her fingers, and music started playing from her stereo (another hand-me-down from when her parents had moved). "Should we have some champagne to celebrate?" Courtney yelled over the music.

Sasha said, "Yes!"

Marni came to her first meeting that week. She walked in with her bike helmet in hand. "Sorry, I'm late. I had to fill my tires. Took forever."

"Could've used magic," Sasha said.

"I don't know how," Marni said, and she hung her helmet and her jacket on the coat rack.

Courtney began by asking her more questions about her family, family history, and her life. Notebook in hand, she scribbled as Marni talked. Then she brought over a stack of books to show Marni. "With magic, you can help your community," Courtney said. "You're their witch now."

It was something Catherine used to say. "We're their witches." And when Sasha asked what that meant, she would respond, "You'll understand when you're older." But she was older now and still didn't understand. She repeated it on occasion, hoping to catch up to the meaning.

Whatever might appeal to Marni, she wouldn't tear it down. But what about the women who saw Howie push her against the cab outside of the liquor store and hurried to steer clear? They didn't embrace her as part of their community.

Marni looked over an old book, slowly turning pages frail with age and use. She even looked interested in whatever spells she read, but Sasha was determined not to be hopeful again. Marni shut the book and handed it back to Courtney.

"You can borrow any of these," Courtney said, gesturing to the bookcase.

"No, thank you. Though I appreciate the offer."

Courtney flipped through more books, held up illustrated pages and pushed pages full of spell work to Marni, who looked, nodded, closed the books, and handed them back.

An hour passed and Marni said she had to go. After Marni left, Sasha said, "Something about her politeness drives me crazy."

Courtney watched the young witch walking her bike to the end of the driveway, look both ways, then swing onto the bike and pedal away. "There are worse ways to be."

"What do you mean by that?"

Courtney shrugged. "If I had a child, I'd want them to be polite. But I see what you mean. It's like she's keeping us at a distance."

"Wait, you want a kid?"

"Maybe."

Sasha had never even thought of having children. If Courtney had a child, if Courtney were in a relationship, where would Sasha fit in? She pulled herself back from this scenario. Returned to thinking about Marni. She said, "Keeping her distance, exactly."

Later in the week, Marni returned for another meeting. She'd come from practice, out of breath and still in her workout clothes. "We had our first game last night. We won."

"Wow, congrats," Courtney said.

"Great," Sasha said. She kept the sarcasm out of her voice, but there was no warmth or enthusiasm either and Courtney shot her a quick look.

They settled into the living room. Sasha thought they should teach Marni a spell, something simple. Catherine and Deborah had taught them summoning spells their first meeting. If Marni saw that magic could be fun and felt the power flowing though her, she'd warm up to the whole idea, Sasha thought. Stop with the not being in the coven business.

But Courtney wanted Marni to be more comfortable with them first. Comfort was integral to learning magic. It'd been different for them. Sasha learned magic from women she'd known her entire life, one of them her mother. And Catherine met with Courtney several times, inviting her over to her house so they could get to know each other before their first official meeting.

Courtney picked up the large leatherbound book from the top of the pile of books next to her. "This is the history of our coven." She held it out to Marni, who took it in her hands, but quickly passed it back.

"What do we call ourselves?"

Sasha noted the "we."

"There aren't official coven names. Those outside the coven will call it by the town or by the leaders. So, Catherine's coven, or Ella's coven, et cetera."

"Courtney's coven?" Marni said.

"Oh, we don't have a leader because we're not officially a coven," Courtney said. She smiled as she opened the book.

"But yes, Courtney's coven," Sasha said.

Courtney waved her away without looking up. "Anyway, our coven was started by a witch named Bethany Elias who came here from England as a child with her parents in 1689. It must've been a surprise to her. I can't imagine her life—leaving the country you were born in and then to find out you're a witch a few years later. She was lucky. Her family was rich and important in the community, so she wasn't harmed. And when the next witch came into her powers, fifteen years later, Bethany had the town's respect. In another three years, the next witch came into her powers, another daughter from an important and wealthy family, and they had a coven."

"You said harmed," Marni said.

"Yes."

The three sat in silence for several seconds. "There are accounts. Violence, witches killed. Not everyone had the right circumstances to be accepted by a town. Black witches, in particular, were not often accepted by the other witches in their community. They could've been together and powerful and safe, but the white witches more often would accuse the black witch of stealing a white witch's powers. It didn't make sense, of course. Sometimes poor white witches, if the other witches were from wealthy families, could be unwelcome. Or immigrant witches if they weren't from the 'right' country. I've seen accounts of witches disowning other witches because they believed their status sullied magic." Courtney flipped through the pages. "Even in our town, in 1932, a new witch came into her powers, Rebecca Rosen, but she was Jewish and the other witches asked her to leave town."

"Wow," Marni whispered. "Did she leave?"

"She did. The guard started in 1951 and our town was one of the first towns in New York to get one. Catherine told me she heard the coven tried to contact Rebecca and get her to return, to strengthen themselves against the guard, but she didn't. I don't know what happened to her." Courtney paused. "Divisions between witches is the perfect environment for the guard to thrive. That's why, no matter what, we always must stay together. And witches in other covens are our allies, even if we might not get along personally with them."

Courtney returned to the book, reading names and dates and the occasional information that had been jotted down.

"In 1792, Elizabeth Hill gave birth to a daughter. She was the first witch to give birth in our town. It says here that the father had been a man traveling through the town, but there's a good chance that's a lie to protect herself."

"How was she protecting herself?"

"If it was a local man—and a married man, at that—she might've been killed."

"Oh."

Courtney continued flipping the pages and making comments. "It would be over a hundred years before a witch was married to a local. Louise Winston. She was a judge's daughter, a very wealthy man, and her family had lived in town for generations. Or else no one probably would have been interested in her."

"And the man was the son of German Jewish immigrants, wanting to pull up his own social status," Sasha said. "Ephraim Katz, my mother's grandfather."

"But wait. Was that around the time you said the witches sent a Jewish witch out of town?"

"Yes, it seems Louise did not associate herself with her husband's religion," Courtney said.

Marni looked at Sasha.

"I never met the woman."

Sasha's own grandfather, William, had apparently not often referenced his mother being a witch to his children. At her funeral, an eight-year-old Deborah watched as a large group entered and didn't speak to anyone else. Their presence filled the entire church. She noticed people lowering their voices, glancing at them. Catherine was part of the group, a black ribbon tying back her blond hair, a young woman. They sat in the front pews, and the reverend eyed them nervously. Who were they? Deborah asked her father afterwards.

"Unimportant, unserious people," he'd responded. He died before Sasha was born.

"The witches in Louise Winston's direct line—herself, her granddaughter Deborah and her great-granddaughter Sasha—are our town's only multi-generational witches."

Several more witches later, there was Catherine. Below her

name, birth date, and year of coming into powers, was Catherine's own handwriting, bold cursive with large loops.

"Louise passed away and seven years later, her granddaughter Deborah came into her powers and there was a coven again. Catherine became coven leader in—"

"That's enough," Sasha said.

Courtney's head snapped up. "You're right. That's a good place to stop for today." She closed the book.

"Are all witches women?" Marni asked.

"There are some that are men. I've met some cis men and trans men—as well as trans women—on the witch forums I'm on, and some non-binary witches also. And there are records of male witches in the past, although none in our town. Some witches theorize that there were and are more men that are witches, but they hid it. I can see that being possible in the past, but once the Witches' Guard began, I don't see how anyone would be able to hide powers."

Marni nodded. Then she asked, "Why me?"

"What do you mean?" Courtney asked.

"Sasha or her mom—it's in their family. But it's not in my family. And was it in yours, Courtney? Why us then?"

"We don't know," Courtney said. "People ask all the time, but we just don't know yet."

Yet. Courtney was always saying yet, Sasha thought. She was always looking to the future, what else there was that could happen, that could be learned.

"No point wondering why," Sasha said. "You can't change it."

"I actually disagree," Courtney said. "It'd be a fascinating topic to study."

"I'd like to know," Marni said with a shrug.

Courtney said to Sasha, "It's different for you. You knew you'd probably be a witch. But for instance, Louise had two children. Why didn't either of them become witches? We don't know."

CHAPTER NINE

Marni came back. And she came back again the week after that.

A student from Marni's grade lived down the street from Courtney. After the girl spotted Marni biking to the witch's house several times, she walked up to her at school. "Why are you going to Courtney the witch's home?"

"I'm just getting some stuff from her, some potions," Marni said. Marni shut her locker and walked away. The bell had rung, and she had class. She had scored the winning goal in the game the night before. She'd been feeling good. The other girl stared at her. She walked after Marni. "Multiple times a week?"

"I need a lot of it." And then she said, "It's none of your business" at the same time the girl said, her eyes wide, wide, wide, "Are you a witch?" The girl didn't keep her voice down. Some other students heard and turned.

Marni quickly said, "No," and walked away again. But it was out, the thought of it. Marni Cohen had always seemed so normal. She did sports but wasn't one of the stars. She did fine in class, was friendly but not overly chatty with people outside of her friends and teammates. But maybe that was it—she had purposefully cultivated normalness, a middle-of-the-road, non-stand-out style to avoid attention. When some big shift happens, people always look for clues in the beforehand, reassess their thoughts to point out that they always thought something stuck out about a person or situation.

And Marni had begun to enjoy the meetings.

She noticed people whispering, looking at her, looking away when she met their stare.

She changed for practice alone. Her friends weren't in the locker room, and the players who were only nodded and said a quick "hey" before turning away. She pulled on the team-issued joggers and jacket.

Outside, she took several deep breaths to steady herself. The season would be done in less than three months. They were training to reach State Championships. She jogged to join her friends on the field. Before she could, one of the captains, a junior named Amelia Vitale, came up to her and said, "Is it true?" She looked at Marni's bracelet. "Are you a witch?"

"I'm not," Marni choked out. Amelia stared at her for several seconds; Marni's feet nailed to the ground. Amelia shrugged a shoulder and walked away. Marni bolted across the field.

As she passed pairs and groups stretching together, players turned to watch her. She joined the circle of her friends, mumbled a hello.

"Hey," said Sylvie Walsh, her best friend both on the team and at school. The group continued stretching, but their usual chatter was gone, some of the girls counting their stretches quietly to themselves. After a minute, Sylvie said, "We're actually done. We got out here early, but, uh, come sit with us while Coach makes her announcements." No one talked to Marni for the rest of practice except the coaches.

When practice broke up, Marni tried to walk with Sylvie, but she smiled at her and said, "I'll see you later, okay?"

That evening, Courtney texted her to ask how her day had been, and Marni hid her phone under a couch pillow. Even seeing Courtney's name pop up on her phone screen made her throat tighten.

She wanted to text Sylvie, but it suddenly felt unnatural to do so. They talked every day. Sometimes Sylvie texted her before they even got home from practice. She tried to remember Sylvie ever saying something about witches.

"I hate them," Marni whispered, standing alone in her living room.

The next day, the principal called her to his office. The guidance counselor was also there, and she gave Marni a supportive smile.

"I am going to ask you a question, Miss Cohen, and I think it's best if you answer me truthfully." Marni didn't think he'd known her name before today. "Are you a witch?"

Marni looked down at her lap. She nodded.

The principal said she was required to register. He said he would alert the guard and that she could do it that weekend.

Instead of returning to class, Marni went to the library and sat down in the back corner on the floor. She breathed deeply, pressed her hands over her face. She became aware of someone standing nearby and removed her hands. It was Amelia. She bored a hole through Marni's eyes.

Amelia cleared her throat. She said in a quiet voice, "I used to wish I'd grow up to be a witch." Amelia stared at the wall, as if Marni had disappeared. She started to walk away, then turned back to Marni. "If you tell anyone I said that, I'll make your life miserable."

"I won't. I wouldn't," Marni said. Amelia walked away, through the stacks. The library was completely quiet. It was like they were the only two people in the building, like they were deep in a forest, and Amelia was leaving her behind.

I am her witch, Marni thought. The thought took her by surprise.

Marni stood up and followed after Amelia. She reached out for her shoulder. Amelia turned around, surprised. Marni said, "It's going to be okay." She wasn't even sure what she meant by it, but when she touched Amelia's shoulder, she felt like a pebble thrown down a dark, deep well. Amelia pulled back her fist and slammed it into Marni's nose.

Marni didn't mention her two-week detention to Courtney or Sasha. When they met next, Courtney asked, "What happened to your nose?"

"I fell off my bike." She paused. "And I'm ready to register."

Sasha cocked her head to the side, "Because you fell off your bike?"

On Saturday morning, Courtney drove them and parked right in front of the Headquarters. They walked in, each older witch on one side of Marni.

The Witches' Guard Headquarters was a plain building, both outside and inside. Catherine had said the building used to be a hardware store. The front room had several chairs along the wall—who did they expect to sit there? Sasha wondered—and a tall under-watered plant in the corner. The reception counter was behind a glass barrier.

The man behind the counter pushed out of his chair quickly when they walked in. "How may I help you...ladies?"

Howie wasn't there. Sasha considered this a good omen, as good as a trip to the Witches' Guard could be.

"We're here to register a new witch," Courtney said.

The man nodded. "Okay," he said, looking around and shuffling papers on the desk. "Okay," more to himself. He turned to a filing cabinet behind him and opened the bottom drawer, removing a manila envelope. He slipped a packet of paper from the envelope and set it down on the desk. "Name?"

"Marion Cohen," Marni said.

Next, he asked for her date and place of birth, her parents' names, and any siblings' names. Marni provided her answers. Precious, personal facts of her life. Marni said them as if she were holding them cupped in her hands. Watching, each older witch remembered standing where Marni stood, telling the guard about themselves. Sasha had given her answers as if they were on ribbon she was pulling out from her throat and wrapping tightly around her fist. Courtney had given hers as if they were punched out on a typewriter, ringing brightly with each letter struck. The guard wanted facts stripped of emotion, and the witches didn't want to give their emotions to the guard. But their names, their family's names could not exist as formal facts without feeling. The part of the ribbon with Sasha's father's name would have gone inside her fist and her mother's name on the outside next to Catherine's—a name the guard hadn't asked for in relation to herself, but one Sasha would place on any list she'd ever make of family.

The man turned to the next page and was silent, continuing to write. Sasha moved closer to the glass to try and get a look at the sheet. He noticed and moved the paper closer to himself. He turned to a separate sheet and retrieved a book-sized contraption from a desk drawer, which revealed itself to hold an ink pad inside. He wet the pad with a wipe. Then he pointed at Sasha and Courtney. "You two step back."

They took several steps back.

"As if he doesn't know our names," Sasha muttered. But would she really want him to address them by name? A name stands for everything within a person, and would Sasha really want this man engaging with the representation of their selfhood?

Courtney shushed her.

He took a key from his pocket and turned it in the brass lock on the glass barrier, sliding the glass open and placing the ink pad in front of Marni. He instructed her to press each finger first onto the ink pad and then against the paper. The right hand, then the left hand. As she pressed each finger, he said something to her that Sasha couldn't hear. When she asked Marni later, she said it was, "Press a bit harder, please."

Finished, he placed the papers back into the manila folder and began writing on the outside. Sasha and Courtney stepped forward again to be next to Marni.

Marni stood with her hands stretched in front of her. "Do you have a wipe I could use?" she asked, holding out her fingers, stained pink with ink.

The man didn't look at her. "Wait here," he said and walked through a door behind him. He returned seconds later, not with a wipe but with a bolt cutter. "Hold out your left arm."

Both of her hands were already held out, but she stretched her left arm through the open part of the glass barrier. He hooked the cutter onto Marni's bracelet and snapped it. The bracelet fell to the counter, and he added it into the manila envelope.

Sasha and Courtney smiled at each other.

The man sat down. "Okay, you're done."

"Oh, okay," Marni said.

Outside, Marni rubbed her bare wrist. Ink smeared on her skin. "Here," Courtney said and held out her own hands. She ran her hands over Marni's, and when she pulled away, they were clear of ink. She held onto her wrist for several seconds, then it too was clean. It thrilled Sasha that they were doing magic on the Witches' Guard's doorstep, even if it was a small spell. "How do you feel?"

Marni considered the question. "I don't know. Weird. My wrist feels weird. Tingly?"

Sasha had always felt the bracelet was a weight, from when it was placed on her at age ten to when it was removed at age seventeen. Sasha had worn her wrists bare of any jewelry every single day since.

Back at Courtney's house, they sent Marni to the living room. The older witches bustled around the kitchen, giggling and banging into each other as they readied everything. Courtney put the cake they'd bought on a tray. She snapped her fingers in a circle over the cake, creating floating bursts of sparkles. Sasha poured the sparkling cider into flutes. "I wish you'd gotten some real champagne," Sasha said.

"You know Marni's underage," Courtney said.

"Well, I'm not." She pulled a flask from the folds of her dress and poured its contents into one of the flutes.

"There're pockets in that dress?" Courtney asked.

Sasha hovered the glasses in the air to follow them and held one side of the tray with Courtney.

They walked into the living room and with a swish of her hand, Courtney lowered the lights. "Congratulations!" Sasha and Courtney chorused.

Marni smiled. "Thank you. You two didn't have to get me anything."

They placed the tray in front of her. Marni went to take a flute from the air. Sasha grabbed her wrist. "That one's mine." When Sasha touched her, Marni was shot through with a swirling so intense it nearly made her dizzy. A swirling laced with sharp teeth, all of it covering something small and raw. Sasha let go. She looked down at her hand and gave Marni a searching look but decided to drop it.

Courtney cut three pieces of cake and placed each on a dessert plate. The plates had a green border with etched gold leaves.

"The bracelet cutting is a sort of ceremony, but it's their ceremony, and we wanted to do our own," she said.

Marni took one of the plates. "That makes sense." She ate quietly. Her wrist felt empty. Did she feel empty? she wondered. She'd thought her life was marching in one direction, and now?

Her wrist certainly looked empty. She cut off another piece of cake. "These are nice plates."

"Thank you. My parents left them for me."

"Oh, I'm sorry. I didn't know your parents had passed away."

"They haven't; they moved. This isn't the house I grew up in. When my mom retired, they sold that home. But I asked that they leave me with some reminders of family."

"That was nice of them. What did she do?"

"She was a literature professor. And my dad was a dentist. Dr. and Dr. Johnson. They're both retired. They wanted me to be a doctor too."

"And you didn't?" Marni asked.

"You know what? I did. I wasn't sure, either an OB-GYN or a dermatologist."

"Will your parents visit for the holidays?" Marni asked.

"Maybe," Courtney said. "I owe them a video chat to catch up on all that."

"Tell Norman and Dorothy I say hi," Sasha said.

"I'll make sure to. How about a toast?" Courtney said, holding up her flute.

The glasses, Sasha remembered, were also from Courtney's parents. Sasha met Dr. and Dr. Johnson twice. The second time was at their high school graduation, right before the doctors moved. There was a framed photograph in Courtney's office of her and her parents on graduation day. She held her diploma up to the camera, her bare wrists exposed. Sasha had taken the picture, Catherine standing next to her. The doctors shook Catherine's hand when she offered it, and said thanks to her congratulations, then politely excused themselves and Courtney.

Sasha and Marni raised their flutes also. "I'll leave the speech making to you, Courtney."

Courtney gazed at the drink, thinking. "Today is a special day, to be followed by many more special days. When I read accounts from witches in centuries past, despite what their neighbors thought, they considered themselves to be blessed. To Marni, to our new coven, and to being blessed."

"Cheers," Sasha said.

The three brought their glasses together. And Sasha would never wish it all away.

Chapter Ten

Marni walked into school on Monday with bare wrists. She tugged at the ends of her sleeves, but people noticed. They were looking for it.

She showed up crying at Courtney's house in the afternoon. "They've kicked me off the soccer team. The parents made a formal request. They say I'm dangerous." Amelia's mother had led the way, Amelia avoiding eye contact behind her.

Marni sunk to the floor, sobbing. Sasha knew that "fuck them" wasn't the appropriate response. "Do you want a drink?" she asked. Courtney went to embrace Marni, and eventually Sasha joined, patting the young witch's shoulder.

"We have this big game on Saturday," Marni said through sniffles.

"What if we went somewhere ourselves on Saturday? Get out of town to somewhere no one knows us," Courtney suggested. Sasha considered how the "we" of the soccer team that Marni used was no longer an accurate "we." Courtney's "we," the coven, was.

"You know, Catherine used to take me apple picking in the fall," Sasha said.

Marni wiped her cheeks with her sleeve. "As long as it isn't near Briar Cliff. That's where the game is."

"Not Briar Cliff. Easy enough."

On Saturday, Courtney drove them an hour north. Along the highway, the green of summer peeked through the swaths of fall's flames.

The orchard wasn't where Sasha used to go with Catherine, but she looked out over the fields of pumpkins and the tall apple trees in the distance and smiled.

They all wore long-sleeved tops.

They decided to each get a basket. Sasha rushed forward to pay for them. "It's my treat," she said.

They walked towards the group of people waiting for the next truck to pick them up. Marni banged her basket against her right leg as she walked. The crowd was arranged in a loose line. Sasha was not often in crowds of non-witches. And this wasn't their town. She didn't know this town's attitude towards witches. She knew not everyone in their town liked witches—the parents of Marni's soccer team, for instance—but at least she knew how they felt. She was on steadier ground there.

A person in front of them shifted their weight, and then another did. One person rubbed their companion's shoulder. Another person rolled up their sleeves, a gesture both so subtle and so vigorous. This shuffling amoeba made Sasha uneasy. She rose her hand to scratch an itch on her face, but froze, aware of her movements as joining this unconscious dance.

Behind her, someone said, "This is our coven." It yanked her out of the group's susurrations. Her neck prickled and she turned around. She saw Courtney slightly turn her head.

The speaker was a middle-aged woman talking with the two teenagers she was with, possibly her daughters or her daughter and a friend. She caught Sasha's eye. "It's a joke. I'm not a witch," she said with a stilted laugh.

"We have no problem with witches," Sasha said and turned back around. She saw Marni tug at her sleeve.

Courtney cleared her throat softly. "We got lucky with weather today."

"We really did," the woman behind them said, although Courtney hadn't spoken loudly. "Where are you girls from?"

Sasha hated being called a girl. She was in her twenties, an adult. Courtney turned slightly to answer with their town name.

"That's a bit of a drive. No good orchards down there?"

"We wanted to go on more of an adventure."

The woman smiled. "An adventure's always fun."

The truck rumbled up the dirt path, a wagon attached to the back with haystacks in rows. Sasha steered Courtney and Marni to the front of the wagon—where there were only a few spaces left on the hay benches—to be free of the woman and her questions. Sasha sat by herself across from Courtney and Marni.

The truck brought them to the trees. The coven and the rest of the group stepped off to join the crowds already reaching for McIntosh, Gala, Golden Delicious, and Honeycrisp.

"Here're some good ones." Courtney pointed to a lane to their left.

Sasha grabbed a perfect red one from the tallest branch she could reach.

"I don't think I've ever been apple picking before," Marni said. She picked apples indeterminably, not even glancing at the other side before placing them in her basket.

"Really?" Sasha said.

"Well, my parents are busy a lot." Marni alone in that quiet house, eating her meals for one.

Sasha stretched for more apples on a high branch.

"Look. Are those nuns?" Marni said. She pointed to a group further along.

"I think only one of them is a nun," Courtney said. "The others must be aspirants."

The witches walked in their direction. The nun was a middle-aged white woman, wearing the traditional long black robe and headdress. There were five young women with her, wearing white shirts, buttoned up, and long navy skirts. The group chatted happily among themselves, showing each other the apples they'd picked.

Drawing even with the group, Sasha said, "Hello, Sisters," not understanding what Courtney meant was that they weren't technically Sisters of the Order yet.

The nun turned around and smiled at her. "Good afternoon," she said.

Some of the aspirants also stopped to smile at the witches as they walked past them. The witches smiled back.

"Enjoy your day," Courtney said, as they continued past, and the nun nodded.

"You as well."

Courtney threaded her arm through Sasha's and pulled her along. "It's a beautiful day and there are apples to pick. Anyone up for a friendly competition?" Courtney suggested.

The competition: which witch could fill their basket fastest.

They were off, dashing through families, tearing apples from branches and laughing as they raced along after one another. They pushed aside leaves and thin branches. While Sasha could reach higher than the other two, she didn't want to lose sight of them, and she ran to the next trees as they did. A giddiness enveloped her and when she teasingly pulled Marni, Marni still felt the swirling, but now it was a sweet, singing swirling, and she felt buoyed forward by its ecstasy. When Courtney touched Marni's shoulder, she felt a rigid beating, with a faint static underneath.

. . .

In the end, Marni won. Sasha and Courtney were out of breath. Marni ate one of her apples in the back seat in the parking lot while Courtney regained her breath standing next to her car.

"You know what? I feel a little old," Courtney said to Sasha with a laugh.

Sasha nodded in agreement. Leaning against the car she took out her flask and took a quick swig. It burned pleasantly, first in her throat and then in her chest.

"Sasha!" Courtney gasped, checking around them.

"What? No one's around. And anyway, it's a parking lot. What are they going to do? Do you want some?"

Courtney shook her head and glanced around again. Sasha tucked the flask back into its pocket and grabbed an apple from her basket sitting on the ground, gave it a quick check for bruises, and bit into it. She crunched up the moisture and the bitterness, a nice pairing with the sharp and hollow cleanliness of the vodka.

They drove south again. Winding through their familiar roads, the ponds and lakes glittered in the late afternoon sun. Yellow leaves turned golden. The beautiful town they lived in.

CHAPTER ELEVEN

I can't make it Wednesday night," Marni said. "It's Rosh Hashanah."

Courtney made a note of the holiday in her planner, then tucked the book back into her desk drawer. "Do your parents have a celebration planned?" Courtney asked.

"I don't know if they'll be around. They might have to work late."

The year before her parents divorced, Catherine said, no, she wasn't going to come over for Rosh Hashanah. It was a night for family, and she wasn't, she'd said sternly, part of the Hoffman family. David said he had a headache, and he and Deborah went upstairs. Sasha cut up the apples and poured honey into a small blue bowl, performing these traditions for a sweet new year. She ate alone sitting in front of the TV.

Sasha thought she could have Marni over. She'd buy the apples and cut them. Buy the honey. She could even go to synagogue, if that's what Marni wanted.

After goodbyes, Marni slung on her backpack and walked to the front door. Sasha followed her. "Hey," she called out.

Marni turned around, surprised. "Yeah?"

"Do you want to celebrate Rosh Hashanah together? You could come over to my house."

"Sure. I'll see you Wednesday."

On Wednesday morning, Marni called. The call woke Sasha up. "Hey, Sasha. I'm sorry, but my parents are going to be here for tonight after all. They have the day off."

"Oh."

"Yeah, but I'll see you later."

"Right, yeah. See you."

Sasha burned with humiliation. She thought she'd done it all correctly. She'd invited someone over for a holiday. She'd bought the food. She'd printed out the relevant Torah passages from online. It wasn't that she wanted Marni's parents to be gone, but if she considered the thought deeply, that was exactly what she wanted.

She opened a new bottle of vodka and poured a healthy serving into a glass.

She brought the drink outside. Several birds sat on a branch on a tree close to her house, staring at her. She concentrated on the branch and snapped it in half. The birds flew off in a flurry of wings and settled on another tree. Stared at her again.

"Stop it," she shouted. It left her lips, and she spun around, self-conscious. But no one was there to hear.

Sasha went inside for her next drink. What was she doing, she thought, picking fights with birds.

It was early evening, and the room was beginning to get dark. She lay down on the floor in the living room. She rolled the empty glass away from her, then summoned it back. Rolled away, summoned it back. Summoning it back, she was a heavy touch, and the glass smacked into her forehead.

"Ow!" she screamed. Clutching her head, she picked the glass up and threw it blindly. It broke somewhere. She stayed still on the ground, hands plastered to her forehead, until the ache dulled. She mumbled a second "ow."

She stared bleary-eyed at the ceiling in the dark. "I'm just going to go," she slurred.

Getting dressed took half an hour, most of which was spent standing in front of her open closet doors, looking from one dress to the next. She finally chose a black velvet dress with batwing sleeves.

She took a wrong turn walking, but arrived eventually. She put one hand on the door to steady herself and rang the doorbell three times. The house seemed as silent as the first time she'd been.

When the door opened, she stumbled through, catching herself from completely falling. "Aha," she said, mostly to herself.

Marni was dressed nicely, a plain navy dress with long sleeves.

"Hey," Sasha exclaimed, pointing at Marni. "You! I'm here for dinner, celebrations."

"Are you drunk?" Marni whispered.

Sasha threw her arm around Marni's shoulders and pulled her in. Again, Marni felt the swirling overtake her, fast and high-pitched. "No, no, I'm fiiiine."

"Hello?" A woman's voice rang out from the next room. Sasha let go of Marni. The woman walked into the foyer. "Marni, is this a friend from school?"

"Yes," Marni said, looking at Sasha very briefly. "This is my friend Sasha. She's a senior. Sasha, this is my mother."

The woman strode forward and held out her hand. "Jane Cohen, it's a pleasure. I'm sorry we didn't realize you were coming, but we can put together a setting for you."

"It was last minute," Sasha said. Jane looked at her, waiting for the rest of the explanation. Marni swooped in. "Sasha texted me earlier saying her father wasn't able to get off work, and I invited her over. I'm sorry I forgot to tell you."

"Your poor father. Sounds like a lawyer," Jane laughed. "My husband and I are both lawyers, but I'm sure you know that from Marni."

"He's in finance," Sasha said.

"Ah, another profession that keeps you busy. Well, follow me, Sasha. Come meet everyone else."

Sasha smiled at her, but once Jane walked into the next room, Sasha swiveled to Marni. She looked pointedly at her wrists, the long sleeves covering them. But she was wearing long sleeves too, wasn't she? Nice to try and slip in. They would hardly know she was here. She just wanted to be here, not alone in her house, always there, alone.

"There hasn't been a good time yet," Marni protested in a whisper. "They always get home after I'm asleep. Honestly, I didn't even think they'd be here tonight. You know that."

Sasha gave Marni a light slap on the shoulder. "I forgive you. This time."

"Gee, thanks," Marni said.

They followed Jane into the dining room, where three other adults sat talking. The man sitting at the head of the table looked quizzically at Sasha. "Marni invited a friend of hers. Everyone, this is Sasha." The candles were already lit. They had been about to start.

"Hello," Sasha said.

"This is my husband, Saul, and our neighbors, Nate and Brooke Adler. They've just moved to town."

"Hello," the neighbors said.

"Let me get a setting for you, Sasha."

"I can do that," Sasha said. She raised her hand to summon the dining ware. Marni knocked her hand down. "No! Uh, no. My mom's got it."

"Yes, that's very sweet of you, but you're our guest. Saul, can you bring another chair to the table?"

"Of course," Marni's father said, and he and Jane both excused themselves.

Marni sat down at the table.

Sasha leaned against the wall. "God, your parents are polite." She remembered that the other couple was still there and smiled at them. "Welcome to the neighborhood."

"Thank you," Brooke said. "We moved up from the city. You know, more space in the suburbs, for when we start our family."

Sasha realized they were probably only a couple years older than her. "Sure."

"You girls like the high school?" Nate asked.

"Eh," Sasha said.

"We like it," Marni said at the same time.

Sasha shrugged.

"And Marni, your parents told us that you're on the varsity soccer team? That must be fun."

"But—" Sasha stopped as Marni shot her a look. "But I'm not. I'm not on the soccer team or any other team. And I...still manage to live my life. A life without sports for me, I guess," Sasha laughed, aiming for casual and achieving hollow and slightly frantic. She stopped.

"Yeah, it's fun," Marni said.

Nate and Brooke continued to smile. They're barely listening to us, Sasha thought.

"So, girls," Brooke said conspiratorially, "is there a coven here? My mother always used to say it's bad luck to have children in a town without a coven."

Sasha laughed genuinely. Nate did too. "That's an old wives' tale," he said.

"There is a coven, so no bad luck here," Sasha said.

"I knew it. The realtor was sort of flaky on the subject, but I knew it."

"Interesting," Sasha said.

"I guess some people have a problem with witches," Brooke

continued. "So if she can't tell how a client feels, better to say you don't know. That's what I figured. But I don't have any issues with witches."

"Marni and I don't either," Sasha said.

Nate turned to his wife. "I like how you say that as if I do have an issue with witches."

Brooke laughed and playfully pushed his shoulder. "I don't mean it like that. He just didn't grow up with witches," she explained.

"I'm from near Philly," he said with shrug. "We don't have witches there."

"Pennsylvania, yeah. They were one of the more recent states to ban," Sasha said.

"The year before I was born, actually. My parents said the ones who lived in our town moved when it happened. But we all managed fine without their luck."

"Yes, their bad luck"—Sasha's head swam, moving through the wording as if it were a math problem—"was your bad luck too. Or wait...not your bad luck? Their bad luck, though."

Jane and Saul walked back in, Saul huffing while carrying a heavy chair and Jane balancing the wine glass and utensils on a plate. Sasha beat back the impulse again to whisk everything out of their hands with magic and set it in place herself.

Thoughts of luck lingered in her mind. Was she lucky? All those years ago, with Juliet, other witches would have been punished, exiled, and she was still here. For a second, Marni's parents turned their back to her to set the place and they could have been Juliet's parents. Sasha had had dinner at their home hundreds of times. But Jane turned around and smiled at her, and luck and the Roths were swept from her mind.

"Thank you very much," Sasha said, taking her spot between Marni and Jane.

Saul stood at the head of the table and lifted his wine glass. "We're pretty casual about the holidays here. Don't tell my parents"—he paused to let Nate, Brooke, and his wife laugh—"but if there's one thing we are strict on doing, it's the drinking." More laughing.

He walked around the table and poured wine into everyone's glass. Sasha held up her glass before he finished pouring for Marni. Saul noticed and laughed, "Don't be shy, Sasha."

She looked down at the table. Everyone else chuckled. When Saul returned to his seat, they all raised their glasses and drank. Sasha had forgotten how sweet and syrupy kosher wine was.

Saul said a brief blessing over the challah bread, and everyone broke open their round challahs and dipped the pieces into the honey.

"Oh, girls, I left the apples in the kitchen. Could you grab them for me?" Jane asked.

The two witches stood up. Sasha followed Marni into the kitchen. There were two plates with apple slices arranged in a spread. Marni picked up one. "You could chill out with the wine."

"I'm fine," Sasha said, picking up the other plate.

"It's just a little obvious that you're drunk."

"I am totally fine. And what would you want me to say, anyway? Hey, Saul, thanks, but I already had a couple before I got here?"

"Yeah, I guess not," Marni sighed. She moved to walk back into the dining room.

Sasha grabbed her by the elbow. "Hey, we're good luck, didn't you hear?"

Marni shook her off. She pushed the swinging door open and walked through without holding it and the door swung back hard at Sasha. She threw a hand up to catch it. The smack of the door against her open palm drew a raised eyebrow from Marni's parents.

Sasha laughed. "There's some bite there, Marni."

There was another blessing before they ate the apples, finished with "may it be Your will to renew for us a good and sweet year."

Jane said, as everyone reached for apple slices—Marni handed

Sasha the first one she picked up, a gesture she performed naturally, piercing through to Sasha's heart—"Sasha, Brooke, Nate, we have a tradition in our house on Rosh Hashanah. We say one thing we are grateful for from this past year and one thing we are looking forward to in the new year." She gestured to Nate and Brooke. "Please, if you'd like to start us off?"

The young couple looked at each other and smiled. Brooke squeezed her husband's hand, which was resting on the table. "The thing I am so grateful for is our new home. We loved our apartment in the city, but we're excited and we feel so lucky to have found our home among such kind neighbors. Neither of us were able to take time off from work to go home for the High Holidays, and we really appreciate that you've welcomed us into your home."

"It's our pleasure," Saul cut in.

"And what I'm most looking forward to in the coming year is the unexpected. We've made a lot of changes. We're continuing to make a lot of changes in our life and...yeah, looking forward to everything that brings."

Nate smiled at his wife. "I'll echo a lot of what Brooke has already said. The most exciting thing this last year was buying our house. Neither of us has bought a home before, so we've taken a lot of new challenges this year, and I think we're stronger for having gone through them together."

Murmurs of agreement rounded the table.

"And I am looking forward to... Well, I'm actually on the job hunt right now, trying to find something closer to home, cut down on this commute time."

"Good luck," Saul said, and Nate raised his drink in acknowledgement.

Marni went next. "The most exciting thing from this last year was when I made the varsity soccer team." Jane and Saul beamed. "And the thing I'm most looking forward to in the new year"—Marni glanced at Sasha—"is having a really good sophomore year."

Sasha snorted involuntarily and turned it into a cough to cover.

"I love that," Jane said. "It goes back to the unexpected. There are so many exciting things just around the corner that you don't know about yet when you're young. Sasha, why don't you go next?"

"Okay." She mentally rifled through the last twelve months. Mostly she spent her time by herself. Went over to Courtney's each week, gone out with her and Pooja and Faye. "I enjoyed all the time I spent with my friends this last year. And I look forward to more of these times, including with Marni. Since we just became friends."

"How sweet," Jane said.

Dipping an apple slice into the honey bowl, Brooke said, "Marni, your parents were saying that you're starting to think about colleges?"

"Yeah, I still have awhile before I begin to apply, but I'm starting to look at different programs. Mostly in the Northeast."

"And where are you hoping to go to college, Sasha?" Saul asked. "You're probably nearly done with your applications."

Colleges, Sasha thought quickly. What were some college names. Where had Juliet wanted to go? "Uh, New York University?"

"NYU. Great school. A lot of our friends went there," Nate said.

"Right, NYU. That's the one I'm interested in."

"Well, good luck. I bet it'd be fun to go to college in the city. Are you mostly looking at schools in the city, then?" Jane asked.

"Yes."

Sasha pushed back her sleeves to dip another apple slice into the honey bowl. Jane looked at her with wide eyes. "Sasha, dear, where is your bracelet?"

"What?" Sasha looked down at her bare wrists. Everyone stared at her. Marni's mouth was agape.

"Your bracelet. Why aren't you wearing it?"

"I-I don't have one. I'm a witch."

They were all silent.

Sasha stood up. She gripped the apple slice, honey dripping on the tablecloth. "I'll leave. You're uncomfortable."

"No, no, it's okay," Jane said.

Sasha pushed away from the table. She half ran to the foyer. No one followed her. Rushing out the front door, she tripped and fell down the front steps, landing hard on her side.

She pushed herself up, realized she still held the apple slice and tossed it onto the front lawn. She stumbled up the front path, brushing dirt off her dress, tears threatening to run down her cheeks. When she hit the sidewalk, careening towards where she thought the front gate was, a man was walking towards her.

It was Howie. She stuttered back, gasping. But wiping at her eyes with the back of her hands, still reeling backwards, she saw it wasn't. Just a man that looked like him, a similar height, same style of glasses, taking his dog for a walk. Sasha walked onto the road to pass them.

Later, their neighbors gone, Jane walked down the hall to Marni's room. Marni put down her phone. She'd been looking at her social media—her classmates' posts about school, sports, TV shows they were watching, some showing off their holiday outfits and writing *l'shanah tovah*, the Hebrew good year greeting. Her mother leaned on the door frame.

"I wish your friend had stayed," Jane said. "We don't have a problem with witches."

Marni nodded but didn't say anything.

Jane made a movement towards walking back to her room, then paused. "But did she...guffaw when you said you wanted to have a good sophomore year?"

Marni's stomach fluttered. "She has a weird sense of humor."

Chapter Twelve

S o, did you tell them?"

Sasha stood facing Marni. She had just walked into Courtney's house, and this was the first thing she said. Courtney looked up from the book she flipped through.

"No," Marni said. "It isn't the right time."

"Now they know that you associate with witches. Seems like a good lead-in."

"What happened?" Courtney asked.

"I went over to Marni's house for Rosh Hashanah and her parents found out that I'm a witch, but they still don't know that their own daughter is one." She had woken up sore, a large purple bruise on the side of her hips from her fall.

"I don't know what to say," Marni said. "And I don't know how they'd react. You had it easy. Your mother was a witch."

"You know what, I'm actually sick of people saying that to me. I haven't even seen my mother in seven years, and I may never see her again. How is that easy?"

"Easier to tell them you're a witch, I meant," Marni shot back.

Courtney placed the book on her desk. "Enough of this. It's

not easy being a witch, period. Marni, tell your parents when you're ready. Sasha, leave it alone."

"But—"

"I said, leave it alone."

"Fine," Sasha snapped. She stormed into the kitchen. She leaned against a corner hidden from view from the doorway. She strained to hear if they were talking about her, but didn't hear either of them.

After the meeting was over and Marni left, Sasha sat on the couch. "Why aren't you taking my side about the parent thing?"

"There aren't sides to take. It's what's best for Marni. You can't control other people's situations. Especially with regard to their families."

"I'm not a controlling person."

"No, you generally aren't. But right now, that's how you're acting, demanding she do things at the pace you want them to be done."

Chapter Thirteen

When the three met again, Marni told them someone had written *WITCH DYKE* on her locker.

"I'm not even a lesbian," she mumbled.

Courtney gave Marni a hug. The younger witch seemed more shocked than upset. "There needs to be a complaint made to the principal," Courtney reasoned. "Have you told your parents yet?"

Marni looked at Courtney with big eyes.

"You still haven't told them?" Sasha asked.

"They've been working a lot."

Marni's house, sitting with her in the quiet, the one light on in the kitchen, a cocoon of life in a large, empty house.

"I'll write the complaint," Courtney said.

"Thanks," Marni said with little enthusiasm.

Courtney pulled a large book from a pile on a side table. "Right," she said with a perky definitiveness, as if she could wipe away Marni's thoughts of the problems at school. "How about we do some magic?"

Courtney held her hand out, reaching towards a small pillow on a chair across from her. It flew into her hand. "We'll learn a summoning spell today. Easy and useful."

After Marni left, Courtney sat down to write an email to the high school principal. "What if he doesn't care?" Sasha asked.

"Dr. Nilsen was always a very fair man, even with...us." Sasha noted the pause, an "us" she knew was meant to be "you."

"Maybe he's reconsidered his fairness since then."

Courtney's hands hovered over the keyboard. "What am I supposed to do? Not write a complaint? Let it go that someone's targeted her?"

"No. But I think we should have a plan B."

Courtney turned in her seat with a raised eyebrow. "I don't mind having a plan B."

Courtney called Sasha the next day and read the response email she'd received from the vice principal. She paused after finishing the brief note. "It's polite, I suppose."

"She basically said, 'Who cares, she's a witch.'"

Neither spoke for several seconds. Then Courtney said, "Do you think she regrets it?"

"Writing that email?"

"No, I mean Marni. Do you think she regrets registering and taking off her bracelet?"

"She would have had to do it eventually."

"I know. But maybe we should have let her take more time?"

"It only would've been a couple more months."

"You've always been the type ready to dive into your fate," Courtney said.

Sasha considered this. "Maybe. I always figured I'd be a witch, though."

"Yes, that makes things different."

A thought Sasha had never considered occurred to her. "Do you wish you weren't a witch?"

Courtney laughed. "It's hard to imagine. Everything would be so different."

"Is that a yes?"

"It'd be so different. I don't know that I could imagine it. Sometimes I wish...my life were different. But I'm sure I'd feel that way at times even if I weren't a witch."

"Well, I'm glad it was you," Sasha said.

"Me too."

After a pause, Sasha said, "I think the next step is to take this into our own hands."

"Remember, we're not supposed to go near the school."

"We won't have to."

Sasha explained her idea. It came from her tracing research. One spell she'd seen involved turning inanimate objects into "watchers" that a witch could make change if a specific person passed by them, making a rock change color or a candle in a window bigger. And Sasha thought, why not make an object into even more of a watcher. "We'll turn a pebble into a camera for Marni to have and pair it with a rock that we keep to see what's going on."

"Like a baby monitor. We can each have a rock," Courtney mused.

"Do you think you can figure out the magic?"

"I'll look around online."

Courtney found that a lot of witches experimented with turning innocuous objects into cameras, usually for watching their own residence. Sasha and Courtney combed Courtney's backyard for an appropriately small pebble, and the next time Marni came over for a meeting, they presented it to her. She looked down at the pebble. "Is this another ceremony?"

"It's a camera," Courtney said.

"We made it so we can watch what's going on around your locker. We've paired it to rocks that we have. Tape it to the inside of your locker, right against one of the slots, so we can see out."

"I'm just hoping that no one does it again," Marni said.

"This is in case they do, because the school's not going to do anything about it."

"Did they clean off the writing?" Courtney asked.

"Yeah, yesterday it was gone." Marni tucked the pebble into her backpack's front pocket.

Sasha put her rock on her living room table. And when she went to the kitchen, she carried it with her.

For the first two days, she couldn't stop watching. It was only kids walking past and standing at their own nearby lockers. Had one of them written the message? Or did they know who had?

The students didn't know they were being watched. At least not by the witches. They seemed constantly conscious of being watched by their peers. She wondered if she had so thoroughly radiated this anxious awareness of her own body moving through the space of the school.

Sasha watched students shuffle by. One tucked a binder into their backpack while darting their gaze at the students passing. Another craned their neck around at a shout behind them, but it wasn't for them, so they ducked their head and kept walking. Sasha started to recognize some students who walked by Marni's locker often. Some of them were never alone, always the center or the periphery of a group. Two girls always walked together, as Sasha and Juliet had.

When Marni walked up to her locker, she looked right at where she knew the pebble was. Sasha noticed that other students stared when Marni had her back to them. Some completely, baldly, and others by stealing glances at her. Courtney noticed this too, her rock following her around the house, whether reading, working on spells and potions, or eating. When she had an appointment with a customer, she put the rock in her desk's bottom drawer, keeping the drawer slightly open.

As Marni expected, no one approached her locker again.

"I can help you with that," Marni said, reaching out a hand to the stack of books that Courtney was re-shelving in her office. Sasha, sprawled on the love seat, glanced over.

"No," Courtney gasped, spreading out her arms to cover the books. "I mean, thank you, but no."

Sasha barked a laugh. "Trust me, Courtney is too anal with her books. She would never let someone else organize them."

"I'm not too anal about it. There's just a system I have, and it'd take a while to explain, so it's better that I do it myself."

Sasha laughed, and when Marni joined in, Courtney smiled a bit. "I know, I know," she sighed. "Doesn't everyone have at least one thing they're very exact about, though?"

It had been a week since the person had written on Marni's locker. Sasha and Courtney still toted around their rocks with them, watching, but the atmosphere had calmed. While they didn't like someone writing on her locker, the older witches had to admit that it probably could have been worse. "She wasn't attacked," Courtney said in private several times. And once, "Do you think she'll be attacked?"

"No," Sasha had replied quickly. But she reflected to herself that she had no idea. No one would have dared to write something on her or Courtney's lockers when they first registered. That was when Catherine and Deborah were still around, and no one would have dared to insult any witch in the town. And Catherine would never have received such an indifferent response from the school. Someone graffitied Marni's locker and the school sent a response to Courtney's complaint that was the written equivalent of a shrug of indifference. Would someone physically attack Marni next? Sasha wished that she could prevent it with the strength of her hopes.

Courtney picked up the next several books on the stacks,

looked at the spines for the title, or inside for the older books. "Oh, Marni, you might find this one interesting," she said and held out a slim volume. Marni took it from her, quicker and with more genuine interest than when she first started coming to meetings.

Chapter Fourteen

ourtney called Sasha. She was sick and couldn't make it to that night's meeting.

Sasha lay on her couch drinking a vodka cranberry.

Marni sat in the chair across from her, talking about school. "The principal is watching me. He called me into his office and said Courtney's email was a 'stunt.' And he told me he wouldn't tolerate me using magic on other students."

"You haven't been using magic at school, right?"

"No, but he said I'm on high alert for bully potential. Like, I'm the bully."

"Even after your locker was written on?" Sasha asked.

Marni shrugged. "Yeah. Well, something happened right before I registered." Sasha raised her eyebrow. "It kind of got out that I was a witch."

"How?"

"Someone saw me going to Courtney's house, and she asked me about it."

"Ah."

"Anyway, someone from soccer, she said something to me

about it. And she sort of... Well, it was a weird interaction and she ended up hitting me."

Sasha felt there were some missing parts in the story, but she didn't pursue them. She had had the occasional weird interaction with her peers after they knew she was a witch. "Okay."

"So, I got in trouble because of that, even though I didn't hit her back or anything."

"They put it like you provoked her, I bet. You got hit. Your locker gets vandalized. But you're the aggressive one. You're asking for it."

"Right. So, it's like now there's a history of me causing trouble. None of the teachers have said anything to me about my locker."

"Spineless," Sasha said and took a sip of her drink.

"Yeah, maybe." Marni paused. "And then there's my friends. Ever since I became a witch, I'll walk into a group and they'll all of the sudden have to be somewhere else."

"That happened to Courtney also. Some of them half stuck around, but once they went to college, she stopped hearing from them too."

"You and Courtney weren't friends when you were younger?"

"No, we were in very different groups. But it's funny. We used to sit next to each other when we had classes together because of alphabetical seating—Hoffman and Johnson. We didn't really talk much. I kind of thought she was annoying. She was such a teacher's pet."

Marni smiled. "I can see that. The teacher's pet, I mean. What happened with your friends?"

"I stopped hanging out with them. Some stuff happened." There were holes in her own stories.

Marni considered this. "I don't want that to happen to me. They're all so different towards me now. It's why I wanted to wait."

Sasha slowly tilted the last bit of her drink around the bottom of the glass. "Now you know who they are."

"I guess," Marni said.

Sasha swung her legs to the floor and placed the glass on the table with more force than she meant, but she was done with the conversation. She let the clang of glass be the punctuation. "Why don't we go to a bar?"

Marni's eyes widened. "I'm not even sixteen yet."

"That doesn't matter at the right bar."

There was only one witch bar in Westchester County: Gargoyles. It was Sasha's favorite bar. The drinks were strong, only witches were allowed, and everyone came out in their best outfits. Marni was wearing her usual off duty jock outfit, as Sasha thought of it, of jeans and a T-shirt. Sasha found a black velvet jacket in her closet that fit the younger witch. "It elevates your look," Sasha said approvingly. She called a cab.

The cab sped along the winding roads through the darkness. On the road south, they passed a sprawling lake, visible through a thin line of trees. The moon sat plump over the surface. Sasha reached towards it, thought that maybe one day she could touch the moon. Her fingertips hit against the cab window. She'd had a couple drinks before the vodka cranberry.

Gargoyles was a stone building with no sign. The heavy oak door was the most efficient of bouncers, with a spell on it to only admit witches, age irrelevant.

A set of stairs led down to the two subterranean rooms that made up the bar. Wrought iron lanterns lit the rooms with a warm glow. Witches flitted underneath, shadows gracing their faces.

They walked past the bar, where two witches made drinks. Sasha recognized Matilda, her hands flying as she summoned small bottles of different liquids. The drink in front of her glowed blue. "If you want something special, order at the bar," Sasha said. "Otherwise, you summon it yourself. We'll pay at the end of the night."

"And it's okay for me to drink?"

"Yeah, no one cares."

Sasha led Marni to the second room, where she always liked to sit. She stood on the threshold, scanning for a free table. Then she spotted Pooja and Faye waving to her. "I hang out with these two all the time," Sasha said to Marni, waving back. She sashayed to their table in the corner.

Sasha had first really met Pooja and Faye at Gargoyles. It was Courtney who got to know them initially, meeting them at a board luncheon that hadn't been well attended (Sasha slept in that morning) and then continued to bond with them at later meetings and at Gargoyles. Sasha had had a brief fling earlier in the year with a male witch that burned down around her and hadn't been in the mood to meet anyone new. Courtney had to convince Sasha over two months to come talk with them. Since becoming friends with Pooja and Faye, Courtney would point out that if Sasha gave other witches a chance, maybe she would get along with them too. Sasha waved her aside, forgetting her early reluctance.

"You look fantastic, as always," Faye said and gave her a hug.

"Thanks." Sasha made introductions, Marni said hi, and the other witches smiled at her.

"You're a coven now. Congratulations," Pooja gushed.

"You're so young, Marni. And I love your shirt. So sporty!" Faye said.

"Thanks," Marni said.

"Have you ordered yet? You really should try one of Matilda's cocktails your first time here," Pooja said. She raised her own drink, a bright green liquid.

Marni looked to Sasha. "Go ahead," she said, and Marni made her way back to the bar.

"You haven't heard who's your leader yet, have you?" Pooja asked.

"No, not yet, but I know it'll be Courtney."

Faye nodded. "Yeah, she's leader material. You know what's weird? She'll be the first coven leader in our age group. All the other leaders now are much older."

Marni returned with a big grin and a martini glass full of silver liquid trailing smoke behind it.

"How are you liking being a witch?" Pooja asked.

"It's been…okay, I guess." Marni sat down and took her first sip of the drink. Smoke engulfed her, covering her face. She brought the drink down, coughing.

"Marni's had some issues at school," Sasha said.

"Ah yeah, we both dealt with some stuff back then too," Pooja said. "As if being a kid didn't already have its own difficulties."

"Well, I'm not a kid," Marni said. She swirled the drink as the smoke began to die down.

"Of course not. I meant, being younger, being in your parents' home, and having to follow their rules, and all that."

"Sure," Marni said.

"We're part of the Bronxville coven. We'll give you our numbers. If for whatever reason you need another hand or any advice, we're here," Faye said. She pulled out her cell phone and so did Pooja, and Marni recited her own phone number.

Faye and Pooja urged Sasha to have another drink when she was finished with her first and then another after that. They drank red wine and poured some into a wine glass summoned from the bar. Wine drunk was different from vodka drunk for Sasha. With wine, one thread tethered her to a conversation, a face, whatever, and the rest of her swirled gleefully, occasionally bumping against the frame of her body keeping it all inside. With vodka, she sank inside herself, disappeared down a dark hole. Even Marni was cajoled into a second and third drink. "I have school tomorrow," she whispered.

Sasha waved that aside. "Don't go," she said.

Marni cocked her head to one side. "They'll be mad that they can't push me around."

"So?"

"I like that." Marni smiled in a way Sasha hadn't seen before. It was sharper, as if a thin layer had been peeled off her face. Sasha laughed, but she wasn't sure she liked that smile.

At one point—midnight?—Sasha said, "Are you a good witch or a bad witch?" and Faye snorted. Where was Courtney again? Courtney should be here.

Another shot, why not. Marni told jokes about her classmates reacting to her being a witch. "I bet they never think of me, thinking what I think of them."

Pooja held a finger up. "Or? Are the others always preoccupied with what we witches are thinking of them?"

"No," Sasha said. "They see us as a shell over raw nerves and a collection of all the bad ways of being, meanness, selfishness, greed, trickery. Corrupting and seducing." Her voice dripped with derision.

Sasha tripped walking back from the bathroom. She caught herself on the wall.

Sasha's mind unwound, honing in on a point and then spiraling away from it. Words loosened themselves. Each vowel traveled longer. Words were not physicalized the way spells were. But didn't words have their effects also? Oh, Sasha thought, over and over, drink after drink, that's what I want to tell Marni.

Pooja and Faye laughed through it all. Sometimes they grabbed Marni's arm. In Sasha's mind, a touch transported magic from one to another. Neighboring witches added wisdom.

Would it even matter at the end of the night, two, three, four, or more (as Sasha had lost count of her own drinks, she didn't know how many Marni had had (had had had) but she was aware that after the first drink, Marni had (had had had had) summoned her own) what was said to Marni. A solid strong tone. W I T C H C R A F T. W I T C H E R Y. It had nothing to do with drink, just sometimes it was sealed with drink.

Dancing in the front room when the bartenders put on music. Screaming, good-natured, all trying to get their thoughts heard.

Gargoyles had no official closing time. The night felt done. Sasha looked around. The bar was almost empty. Pooja and Faye edged towards the front door, waving, Faye yelling, "I need a cigarette" over and over.

Yawning. Suddenly.

Chapter Fifteen

After ringing the doorbell and knocking on the door for two minutes, Courtney used her key to come into the house. The school had called her to inquire where Marni was, Denise Petrini sounding apologetic over the phone. It struck Courtney that now that the administration knew Marni was a witch, they had bypassed her parents, and put the coven in their place as responsible parties.

Marni was passed out on the couch, Sasha curled in a chair, stirring.

"What the hell, Sasha?" Courtney said. She pulled the curtains open to flood the room with light. Sasha held up a hand to shield her eyes. Marni groaned and turned her head into the cushions.

"Did you bring Marni out drinking last night? She should be in school," Courtney said.

"They're probably happy I'm not there," Marni mumbled.

Sasha waved the curtains shut. "It's one day."

Marni turned over on the couch, adjusting her body. "They only want me there so they can make me feel how much they don't want me there," she said, her voice scratchy and dry.

"And what sort of environment is that for a young witch?" Sasha said.

Courtney pulled Sasha off the chair and dragged her into the kitchen. "What are you doing? What sort of example are you showing to Marni?"

"I was showing her how to have fun and introducing her to other witches. Something you used to like to do too, if I remember."

"Having fun doesn't have to involve being drunk."

"She wasn't drunk."

"Really? Because you both seem pretty hungover to me."

Sasha didn't have a response. "It's good for her to be around other witches," she finally said. "Pooja and Faye were there. It's much better bonding than those stuffy Westchester Witches get-togethers."

"We can meet up with our friends like that on the weekends. Even you got your high school diploma."

"Even me? Gee, thanks. I'm glad to be the low bar for young witches."

"We're all responsible for our own actions, aren't we? And the perception we give people about ourselves."

"That's rich. Did you read that on some dumb forum? I bet even the other witches on your forum get out from time to time. And you're just there on your computer, posting at midnight and waiting patiently for replies that won't come." Sasha became aware she was shouting.

"I go to sleep before midnight, first of all. And secondly, I get a lot of good information from those forums, including—oh, I don't know—spells to turn rocks into a video camera. Something we did so we could ensure that Marni will have a harassment-free high school experience."

"They don't have to be writing shit on her locker to be harassing her. It's an attitude."

"You think I don't know about peoples' attitudes in this town?

People being weird or downright rude? Even before I was a witch, I stood out so visibly from the rest of this town because of the color of my skin."

"Who wouldn't want a day off from that?" Sasha argued.

"You can't take a day off from being different. You just have to keep going. If you don't show up, they win." With that, Courtney walked out of the kitchen.

"They win no matter what," Sasha screamed after her. She heard the front door open and close. Sasha turned and kicked a chair. It clattered to the floor. She left it there. When she stalked back into the living room, Marni was gone too.

Chapter Sixteen

Sasha had known the date of the board Halloween party for months, but she hadn't planned an outfit. She flipped through the dresses in her closet frantically. "I should've bought something new," she said.

Courtney sat on the bed, thumbing at her phone screen. She wore a frothy dress made of layers of tiered gray tulle, which she'd accessorized with light blue acrylic nails and stacks of thin silver bracelets. Her hair was in a voluminous high ponytail. Sasha had shrieked when she'd opened the door, "You look like smoke billowing out of a cauldron!" And Courtney had done a little twirl.

It had been over a week since their fight, and it was a topic they both had avoided cracking open further.

Courtney read through the black witches of New York forum. Scrolling, she said, "I wish I'd realized you'd forgotten. I would've sent you a reminder."

"I didn't forget. I just wasn't thinking about it."

Sasha pulled out a long black column dress and held it out. "You wear that all the time. Do something else," Courtney said. It was returned to the closet.

Sasha forcibly pushed all the dresses she'd already flipped through to the left to access the far corner of her closet. She grabbed a dark green velvet dress.

"Yes, that's it. That's the one," Courtney said putting down her phone.

Sasha nodded. She picked up her glass from the night table and took a drink. She shrugged off her bathrobe, tossing it to the closet floor, and stepped into the green dress. It was a long-sleeved dress that flared out from her ribs into a train trailing behind her. Drink in hand, she looked at the mirror. "Are you sure you don't want a drink?" she asked.

"No, I'm okay. Maybe I'll have a little champagne at the party, but I don't need to pregame."

Sasha shrugged and finished her drink.

"This is the one. You look like a witch who's a hermit in the middle of the forest and her house is covered with moss and ivy."

"Sounds kind of nice," Sasha laughed.

"Wear that gold necklace Catherine gave you."

The necklace had been a gift on Sasha's twenty-first birthday, several weeks before Catherine died. She rarely took it out of the jewelry box on her dresser. The gold curled and danced on her collar bone, a circlet of flowers and leaves.

"Yeah, it is perfect," Sasha said, half to herself, looking in the mirror. Courtney stood up and it snapped her back to focus. "Okay, one shot and then I'm ready. You're sure you don't want one?"

They were out the front door, walking towards Courtney's car when Sasha stopped and turned towards her neighbor's yard. She held up her dress and ran onto their property. "Where are you going?" Courtney called.

Sasha pointed to the large tree in their front yard. "Ivy!" she yelled back.

"You are not!" Courtney tried to whisper-shout. But she couldn't help laughing. Light spilled from the neighbor's windows. Sasha didn't look at them. She reached up on the trunk and snapped off a long piece of ivy with dozens of small dark green leaves jostling each other, then dashed back to Courtney with a mad grin, holding up her treasure.

"They won't notice, I've never even seen these people outside of their house," Sasha said. She twisted the ends of the ivy together and held them tight for a quick binding spell. She placed the resulting crown atop her head. "Now I think I'm ready."

The Board Headquarters were completely redecorated for the Halloween party. The lights were off. Hundreds of white candles floated along the edges of the rooms, casting shadows against the walls. Tables were set up with trays of food and drink, but every other surface was covered with grinning pumpkins of various sizes, their faces cut out severely, their smiles sharp and gaping. A blanket of smoke churned over the floor, and a spell had been cast on the ceiling and walls to resemble a dark sky with small stars twinkling.

"It looks great," Courtney whispered. The flickering candles seemed to call for hushed voices.

Sasha scanned the room for familiar faces. "I'm going to look for Pooja and Faye. Wanna grab some champagne?"

"Sure," Courtney said, and they set off in different directions.

Sasha walked through some of the smaller rooms, pushing smoke silently before her. In one room, moss-covered stones were stacked to the ceiling against one wall. Sasha thought of Courtney calling her a witch in a house covered in moss and ivy, and she smiled. Then she spotted her friends, laughing about something in the corner. She sauntered over, greeting the duo.

"Sasha, I love your outfit. I feel like you fit the theme," Pooja said.

Sasha struck a pose, one hand to her ivy crown.

"Are you suddenly in line with the board's thinking?" Faye teased.

Sasha rolled her eyes. "I would never. You two look stunning."

Pooja was in a glimmering light yellow floor-length dress and gold eye shadow, and Faye wore a black lace mini dress with dramatically flaring trumpet sleeves.

"She just got this," Faye said, pointing at Pooja, "and she almost didn't, because she didn't think she'd have enough places to wear it to. Can you imagine?"

"Yeah, you could wear it to Gargoyles, why not? But let's go into the main room. Courtney's grabbing champagne."

The three winded their way back, Faye and Pooja occasionally stopping to hug someone, give compliments, or say they'd catch up with the other witch later. There weren't many people Sasha greeted. Some witches she didn't know, and others she didn't like.

In the large room, Courtney chatted with a middle-aged witch with windswept hair, who wore a stack of necklaces and scarves. She laughed and patted Courtney's hand with emphasis as she spoke, bangles sliding up and down her own arm.

The three joined them, and while Courtney hugged Faye and Pooja, this witch reached out a bangle-clad arm to Sasha. "Sasha, dear, it's so good to see you."

Sasha looked from the woman to Courtney and back again. "I—"

"Dear, it's okay, it's okay, I haven't been to one of these parties in ages. North White Plains is a little out of the way for me and I don't have a car anymore. It's Joyce Goldberg. Do you remember? When I met you, you weren't even a witch yet!"

Sasha still couldn't place her. The low lighting didn't help. Sasha reached out to one of the champagne flutes Courtney had put on the fireplace mantel.

"We used to visit the lake. Of course, that wasn't what it was called. Let's see, the official gathering name was 'A Place for

Family,' I think. I was telling Courtney—who I have just met, and gosh, what a doll!—about how great it was. Dillon and I went every year to the lake, and we loved it. Sasha, you and your mother and Catherine—you were only there two years, correct?"

The lake. Now Sasha remembered her. The two-week upstate getaway in the summer for New York witches with children. Dillon had been one of the few sons—everyone noticed him. He and Joyce introduced themselves the first morning over breakfast, which they ate at picnic tables. Joyce held a ukulele and went on for what felt like an uninterrupted fifteen minutes about how good it was to see new faces. Catherine and Deborah agreed to come join them later, and then the mother and son made their way towards the small pier on the lake. Various children chased each other around on the grass lawn, shrieking in joy, and Joyce laughed and waved at them.

Deborah said, "Wow." And then, "Everyone saw the ukulele, right?"

"She seems well-meaning," Catherine chided. "And her son looks about your age, Sasha. We'll take her up on her offer of company."

Joyce turned back to Courtney. "Dillon and Sasha were the only teens, so they became quick friends. Thick as thieves by your second year there. But that was the last year of the program."

"How come they stopped? It sounds like a good program," Courtney asked.

"It was. Gosh, it was the best thing ever. But not many witches have families. Between that and...well, there were negative feelings both inside and outside our community about it. But it was simply idyllic while it lasted."

"I had no idea," Sasha said. She enjoyed the time there, being with her mother and Catherine while Deborah wasn't constantly dashing off to be with Sasha's father. And when they'd had enough of their mothers and the other witches, she and Dillon would sneak into the woods. They joked about wishing they had a flask.

The second summer, when they peeled away from the group, Sasha brandished hers, the silver glittering even in the dim light of the woods. Dillon smiled and reached inside his jacket and held out his own flask. They both laughed and ran further into the woods, bouncing off each other, and stopped only when they were out of breath from laughing. They leaned against the trees, they leaned against each other. Dillon laid out his jacket for them to lie on the ground.

The next summer, Sasha's parents were going through their divorce. Their divorce, as if they held it cupped in their hands together, their last shared event. The last thing they made together.

Sasha and Catherine couldn't get Deborah out of bed for a walk around the block. Deborah sat in the dark in her bedroom, smoke swirling around her. It came to sit as a solid presence, so that Sasha had to suppress a cough whenever she walked in. She had figured they wouldn't return to the lake but had never realized it wasn't even an option.

"Sasha, your mother and Catherine used to gush about you, absolutely gush when you weren't around. How excited they were for you to become a witch, and what a great witch you would be—"

Courtney smiled and squeezed Sasha's shoulder. But Sasha said, "My mother did?"

"Of course."

Sasha's throat tightened. She clung to this idea, something to turn over again and again. But she would not remember this part of the conversation in the morning; several glasses of vodka drinks before the party, it slipped through her mind before the end of the night.

"And now look at you, this lovely young woman. I wish I'd made it down to Westchester more often to catch up with you. And I really relished the time I was able to spend with Catherine. I mean, wow, what a witch. Catherine Darley was not only a talented witch, but a true leader."

"Absolutely," Courtney said. Sasha touched the gold necklace.

"Being a leader was as much in her blood as being a witch, and you know what else..."

Sasha was nodding along when something struck her. "Wait, you said there were negative feelings inside our community. What do you mean?"

Joyce adjusted her scarves. "I don't want to speak out of turn."

"Other witches were against it? That's what you mean?"

Joyce looked around. "No one's ever going to always agree on a point, and some witches in the state felt resources could be better spent."

Across the room, Sasha saw Ella walk in, her hair down and slicked back, highlighting her gray streak. "I wonder if Ella was one of them," she said.

"Ella Chow?" Joyce said. "I can't recall. Ella has always seemed very community minded when I've talked with her. Our county board event planner loves her too, and I see why she praises her work. This party is such a delight. I may have to hire her if I throw some big shindig."

"Where do you live again?" Sasha asked.

"New Paltz, dear. I was explaining to Courtney how all our boards invite a representative from the other counties in New York to come to gatherings to stay connected. Ella is particularly invested in this aspect of the gatherings. That's what I mean—community minded. Our Ulster County Board event planner, Susannah, usually likes to represent us at as many gatherings as she can make it to. She came down with a bad virus unfortunately, and when the board put out a call for another representative I said, why not? And I can't wait to report back. The food, the décor—I love it!"

"Ella's great at what she does," Courtney agreed.

Joyce launched into more thoughts about Ella's work, the ambience, the spell work, and Sasha shifted to see who Pooja and Faye were talking to, rolling her eyes at all the Ella praise.

Faye was showing Pooja and another witch something on her phone. "And I saw that if I switched the spell up slightly—" Sasha joined their group and downed her champagne in one go.

"Let's get drunk," she said, interrupting Faye. Faye and Pooja and the third witch all laughed.

While Courtney continued to talk to Joyce, they found their next drink.

They migrated from room to room to taste the different drinks on offer. The third witch, a young witch from the Mamaroneck coven, tagged along. Sasha kept forgetting her name through the night. Aside, Sasha said to Pooja, "She's a bit of a drip."

"No, no, she's fun. You just have to get to know her first," Pooja said.

"Who has time to get to know someone new?" Sasha said, grabbing a bright green drink. She tapped the side with her fingernail and brought it towards Pooja's face. "Have we had this one yet?"

Pooja squinted at it. Sasha moved it to right in front of her eyes, and Pooja rested her forehead on it. "Hmm, I don't think so. I don't feel that I know this drink."

"I guess I have time to know a new drink," Sasha said. She and Pooja cackled, garnering glances from some of the older witches in the room.

After Joyce excused herself to catch up with some board members, Courtney tried to find her friends. She stopped to talk with other witches she saw, and only then would inevitably see Sasha, or Pooja, or Faye, leaving the room. At one point, Sasha's ivy crown was gone.

Courtney decided to keep still in one room. Her dress was heavy, and she had been walking from one room to another and back again. She sunk into an armchair and was about to pull out her phone when she saw one of her favorite witches, Liana Williams from the Mount Vernon coven.

"Courtney!" Liana shrieked when she saw her, and Courtney immediately jumped up from the chair to hug her.

At twenty-one, Liana was one of the younger witches in Westchester. She wore a pink leather catsuit, and her signature long braids were an ombre pink.

"You look fabulous," Courtney said.

"Girl, you too. I saw your post on the board earlier and it looks even better in person." Liana was also active in the black witches of New York forum. Her posts were always strewn with bright emojis —stars, hearts, rainbows, flowers, sparkles, and more.

"I feel like I haven't seen you in forever. Were you at the fall brunch?" Courtney asked.

"No, I actually had to help my mom out with something that weekend, so I couldn't go. But oh my god, that was your birthday, wasn't it? Dang, I'm sorry I missed it."

"It's okay," Courtney said, waving her apology away.

"We should do something sometime. I've been going to the witch bars in the city. They're a trip."

"Really? They're legendary. The spells they have on display...I know it's just for flashiness, but I appreciate some aesthetic work."

Liana laughed. "You're too much, Courtney! Always nerding out over magic."

"And why not? Isn't it incredible what we can do?"

"I'm teasing you. But yeah, it's a good time. I'm thinking about going tonight, maybe in half an hour, if you wanted to come with?"

"Isn't it almost midnight already?"

"Don't get elderly on me."

"Another time," Courtney said with a laugh. "I'm probably leaving soon. Have you seen Sasha?"

"Yeah, she nearly knocked me over when she gave me a hug in

the big room a minute ago. She probably won't even remember seeing me, she's so far gone," Liana said with a shrug.

"Weird," Courtney said. She stood on her tiptoes to look into the main room.

"Is it?" Liana asked. "She's always partying hard. You used to keep up with her, but I know you're cutting back on drinking now. I saw your post. That's fun too."

"I guess I'll go find her," Courtney said, and gave Liana a distracted hug. She didn't used to black out when she drank. Did Sasha? Had she not noticed?

When she found Sasha in the big room, she saw what Liana meant. Sasha was half perched on a pumpkin, sipping out of a tiny punch cup with her pinkie out. Courtney didn't see where their other friends had gone to.

Sasha said to no one in front of her, "I like this one because it is fancy."

"Okay," Courtney said, "time to go."

She hoisted Sasha from the pumpkin. Had she done this before? Picking her friend up and letting her lean on her? It happened so fluidly, despite Sasha being taller by several inches, Courtney wondered if it was some sort of muscle memory. Had Marni had to support Sasha the other week at Gargoyles? They walked towards the front door and Sasha suddenly jerked to a stop, throwing her hand to her head. "My ivy crown!"

"You lost that hours ago."

"But—"

"And you can make a new one at home."

"But it wouldn't be mine," Sasha said with a sigh.

Courtney packed her into the passenger side of the car, and then got into the driver's seat. When she turned on the car, Sasha started fiddling with the radio.

"Did you have fun?" Courtney asked. Courtney remembered being picked up by her mother or father when she was a teenager, going to the movies with her friends, before she was a witch. They would always ask that as she bounced into the car.

"Oh yeah, oh yeah. It was good. We had so much fun, didn't you think?"

Did you know I wasn't with you most of the night? Courtney wondered. What she actually said was, "It was really great to get to know Joyce. I didn't realize witches from other counties came to our gatherings."

"Yeah, Joyce Goldberg, yeah. I did not expect to see her ever again. Or maybe... I don't know. Yeah, she's nice."

"And you were friends with her son? 'Thick as thieves'?" Courtney looked at Sasha with a small smile.

"Yeah, yeah, Dillon. Yeah. He was fun."

By the time Courtney reached the highway five minutes later, Sasha was asleep, her hand curled around the gold necklace.

CHAPTER SEVENTEEN

The weeks passed by. They had their meetings. Sasha arrived at Courtney's house first, then Marni. Then Marni and Sasha left together. Sasha and Courtney still hadn't talked about the fight, and Sasha wasn't coming over other than for meetings.

She thought they'd had a nice time at Halloween. But when she thought that she remembered Courtney saying, "even you" and every time she did, it was louder and snider in her memory. Across town, when Courtney picked up her phone to text Sasha something interesting or funny, she remembered trying to track Sasha through the Halloween party, her dress heavier and heavier each time in her memory. Sasha didn't remember this part of the night; Courtney figured she didn't. She would put down her phone.

One meeting, Marni told them she told her parents about being a witch. Sasha lifted her mug of tea, one of the orange ones from Courtney's parents. "Mazel." There was a thin frost over the front lawn when they left, and Sasha stomped on it, tipping her head back with a maniacal grin with each crunch. She'd begun drinking at noon, and since Courtney still wasn't drinking regularly, she'd brought her flask to the meeting. She started tilting towards the ground and felt herself jerked up. Marni had grabbed her.

"Are you okay?" Marni gasped.

Sasha brushed her grip off of her.

Sasha usually spent Thanksgiving with Courtney, but this year Courtney didn't say anything about getting together for dinner. Sasha didn't say anything about it either. She bought a microwaveable personal pizza. She ate one slice and left the rest sitting on the counter. She carried a full bottle of vodka and a full bottle of orange juice to the living room and turned on the TV. The bottles emptied inch by inch.

Courtney made a Cornish hen (she'd never liked turkey) and also spent the holiday alone. After dinner she called her parents. Her brother and his family were at their house. Everyone jostled to fit in the cellphone camera frame to shout greetings at her. She stored her leftovers in Tupperware to eat for the rest of the week.

The first snow of the season came at night. Sasha walked into her backyard, drink in hand. The sky seemed light pink. She walked slow circles. Tiny snowflakes landed on her hair, her hands, in her drink.

She was brushing her hair out of her face when she tripped on a root. Her face and shoulder slammed against the ground. While the glass didn't break, the drink splashed out, soaking the top of her dress. I should just stay here, she thought, the ground swirling before her eyes.

Her muscles relaxed, she closed her eyes. A gust of wind roared through the yard, and she tensed.

Sasha clawed at the ground, the hard dirt, the wet snow, pushing herself up. She slinked back inside and fell asleep on the living room couch. She woke up several hours later, shaking in damp clothing—her drink, the snow on the ground—her whole body gripped by each shake.

A box showed up on Sasha's front step. It was the first day of Hanukkah. Courtney had suggested they not meet that week, to allow Sasha and Marni to celebrate, as their meetings often went until it was dark. Hanukkah wasn't even a major Jewish holiday, and Sasha knew that Courtney knew that.

The box was from her father, his yearly gift. She floated the box over to the kitchen table and left it there.

On the fourth night, a night Sasha actually remembered to light the menorah, she sat in front of the window and the darkness outside, watching the candles drip wax. The menorah went in the window for the light to be shared.

She put down her drink and tore open the box. It was a square emerald pendant on a silver chain. There was a handwritten note from her father and stepmother. *Happy Holidays, Sasha. Love, Dad and Kerri.*

Holidays. They didn't celebrate Christmas, but then, Sasha didn't know what traditions her father may be following now with this wife. Sasha threw out the card, but she did like the necklace.

Sasha hadn't been planning on going to her father's wedding. When Deborah saw the invitation for the wedding in the mail, she swept her arm across each shelf of glassware, crashing to the ground each wine glass, champagne glass, aperitif glass. She slumped to the ground. Sasha pulled her up.

She dragged her mother to a dining room chair and went to call Catherine. "Don't tell anyone," Deborah murmured when Sasha returned.

Sasha checked Deborah's arms, pulling out several small shards of glass. Catherine arrived and looked at the cuts Sasha showed her. Several weeks before, Courtney had come to the house to perform a similar task. There was less blood this time.

"Minor," Catherine declared. She showed Sasha a spell to put the glasses back together.

"Hey," Deborah called from the chair, "don't act like I'm not here."

"I would never," Catherine said over her shoulder.

The glasses repaired, Catherine asked Sasha to give her a minute to talk to Deborah alone. In the hallway, Sasha listened at the door.

"Help me understand why you are acting like a child," Catherine said.

"You don't get it," Deborah said between weak sobs. "I'm nothing like you. You've never been in love. You're shriveled up and old."

Sasha cringed. Even if it was true, it was cruel to say to someone that cared about her.

"You're right. You are nothing like me." That was Catherine. She took insults and flung them back sharpened.

There were not even sobs in the silence.

"He used you, Deborah. For your magic. He's a sneaky, despicable man that only thinks of himself. He's done you the favor of getting out of your life. You'll see that eventually, but in the meantime, you have to pull yourself together. You have to be an adult. And if you can't do it for yourself, do it for your daughter."

Sasha crept away before Catherine came out of the dining room and met her in the living room. They walked to the front door together. "We're doing fine here," Sasha said.

Catherine looked at her, hand on the doorknob. "Of course. You will be." Catherine stepped outside.

Sasha asked, "Should I go to the wedding?"

"He is your father."

"Yeah, but..." Sasha searched for how to sum up the situation.

How things had been since her father had left. How things had been when her father had still been there. "You hate him, don't you?"

Catherine looked at her. "As far as your relationship to your father goes, it doesn't matter what I think."

"I wanted to know what you think."

"I think you'll regret it if you don't go."

Sasha brought the invitation up to her room.

Courtney came over one afternoon and saw it on her desk. "Is this your dad? When are you leaving for the wedding? Should we meet Thursday instead of Friday that week?" Courtney took her planner out of her bag.

"No, we're still good. I'm not going."

"Really? Why not?"

"Why would I?"

Courtney looked at the invitation again. "I'm sure it's important to him that you be there."

"You wouldn't say that if you knew him." Sasha looked to the door and lowered her voice. "Anyway, I don't think my mom would be happy if I went."

"You can tell her you're staying over at my house."

Sasha raised her eyebrow. "Courtney Johnson? Lying? I've been a bad influence."

Courtney started writing in her planner. "Lie is a strong word. Bending the truth, maybe? You don't think your mom would call my mom to check in, would you?"

"She would never think to do that."

"And anyway, it's lying for a good reason. For your good and your mom's."

"I thought you said it wasn't lying?"

When the day came, Sasha took two trains down to New Jersey, transferring in Manhattan, and then took a cab to the venue. She was early. David told her to wait in the front row in the room where the ceremony would be. She sat there, appraising the decorations. The minimalist wooden chuppah with yellow roses clustered at the corners. The gold flower stands at the ends of each aisle, with more yellow roses. She took a photo of all the flowers and sent it to Courtney along with, *Gee, I wonder what will be in her bouquet.*

She heard people talking in the ballroom across the hall, and crept in. The catering crew, setting up. She hid behind a column and, when the bartender walked away, summoned a bottle of wine.

She slipped into the bathroom and went into a stall. The wine was heavy on her tongue. When she heard the door open, she jumped onto the toilet seat, steadying herself with a hand against the stall.

A woman's voice said, "It's not too late for you. My cousin had a child in her early forties."

"I know, but I've honestly never been interested in having kids."

"Really? I didn't know that about you."

"I'm fine with other people's kids, and I am looking forward to getting to know Sasha, but I'm not interested in the whole parenting thing. David doesn't want to do it again either." It was her father's fiancée. Her nearly stepmother.

There was a pause. "She's a witch, right?"

"Yes, and I really don't have a problem with that, but please don't mention it to anyone else. You know how people can be."

"I won't. But David's family knows, right?"

"Most of them don't, no. His parents were hoping that she wouldn't take after her mother."

The taste of the wine soured in Sasha's mouth. She barely knew her father's parents and only spent time with them when accompanied by her father. She had thought that was normal.

"I went to high school with this girl that ended up being a witch," the other woman said. "She kept it from her parents for a couple years apparently. I can't imagine how!"

Sasha heard Kerri and the other woman each walk into a stall.

Sasha jumped off the seat and as she did the wine bottle slipped out of her hand. It smacked against the tiled floor and Sasha froze. "What was that?" Kerri called. "Are you okay?"

Sasha unlocked the stall door, wine gushing onto her shoes, and dashed out of the bathroom.

She ran out of the venue. Once she saw no one followed her, she walked, and looked up directions to the train station on her phone. By the time she arrived, she had blisters on both of her heels and on the side of her right foot, limping slightly.

She sat with her head leaned against the window on the trains. Whenever someone went to sit next to her, she looked at them and raised her left hand to her temple, revealing her wrist, bare the bracelet. They kept walking, until a woman carrying a baby cocked her eyebrow as if to say, "So?" The woman had gray shadows under her eyes. She swung her bags below the seat in front and sat down, shifting her baby's weight.

Fine, Sasha thought.

She felt as if she would be on a series of trains for the rest of her life. Walking through Penn Station, she nearly cried. On the Metro North riding through Westchester, she watched a man get off the train, pick up a half-smoked cigarette from the ground, and put it to his mouth.

She took a cab to Courtney's house. She would spend the night there, after all. Once the two young witches walked up to Courtney's room and shut the door, Sasha started crying. "What happened?" Courtney asked.

She asked several times, but all Sasha would say was, "I ruined my shoes. I'm just really upset that my shoes are ruined."

Courtney gave up questioning her and hugged her. Sasha sank against Courtney's shoulder with a fresh bout of sobs.

Chapter Eighteen

Several days after the Hanukkah present arrived, Kerri called Sasha.

"Hi, dear," her stepmother chirped.

After brief pleasantries, Kerri relayed that she and Sasha's father would be coming up to Westchester for a birthday party one of her former colleagues was throwing that weekend, and they wanted to invite her. "It's Saturday, which I know is sort of last minute."

"Seems a little weird to go to a birthday party for someone I don't know."

"No, no, it won't be like that at all. He always has these huge bashes, which kind of become birthday slash holiday celebrations. There'll be over a hundred people, no one will notice you're even there—"

"What a compliment."

"—and no one will mind if they do, is what I was going to say."

Sasha didn't respond, moving her phone to her other ear.

"It would mean a lot to me and to your father. It's been, what, a year since we've seen you?"

"I haven't been counting," Sasha said with a yawn.

"Well, that settles it. We're overdue. I'll email you the location and time."

The night of the party Sasha put on a sparkling navy dress. She told herself she didn't have to go, but she called a cab, and then the cab dropped her off at an enormous house in Purchase.

Sasha walked up the driveway lined with a long row of parked cars. The house was lit up, white Christmas lights covering the facade and every light turned on inside. Sasha could see guests through the windows, laughing and drinking, putting their arms around each other. Sasha didn't think anyone could see her, even as she neared the front door. She was a smudged shadow, the quiet night pushing against her, against the cheerful hum of the house.

She could keep the night between her and the house. She closed the distance.

When Sasha opened the door, the people standing in the foyer looked over, but then returned to their own conversations. The house was so loud with talk that she couldn't make out any of what they said.

She passed into the family room where a Christmas tree at least fifteen feet tall stood. Gold and silver ornaments winked from the branches.

There might have been a hundred people in this room alone. Sasha pressed against the wall, scanning for a way to get through. She took out her phone and texted Kerri that she'd arrived. The sooner she saw them, the sooner she could leave.

Sasha spotted a doorway on the far wall that opened onto a kitchen, and she threaded and pushed through the crowd to get there. She was sweating when she arrived. In the middle of the kitchen was a large granite island and on it a stacked pyramid of champagne glasses. Sasha took one coupe, downed it immediately, then exchanged it for another.

She moved through rooms, periodically checking her phone for a text from Kerri or her father. She thought she was moving in a circle but kept finding herself in new places. Mostly, the other guests paid her little notice. In one room with low lighting, two people sat very close to one another, very quietly facing each other, and when Sasha walked in, they both turned and glared at her.

"Sorry, sorry," Sasha said, hurrying through.

She'd finished her drink and was convinced she was walking through a never-ending string of rooms when she returned to the kitchen. She let out an audible sigh and was about to beeline for the drink display when someone called out, "There you are," and touched the top of her shoulder.

She turned and there was Kerri, holding her arms out. Sasha let her hug her, patting her back once in return. David Hoffman materialized behind his wife, and Sasha had to get another hug.

Kerri wore a long dark red column dress, and David was in a black suit and a tie that matched his wife's dress. David stepped away, and Kerri swept her up, taking her arm with a conspiratorial glint to her eye.

"Let's walk around. Let's introduce you, Sasha." She tried to protest, but Kerri patted her arm. "We have so many friends here, and you've never met them!"

Who cares? Sasha thought.

The introduction tour began. Charles, Lloyd, Mary, Tanya. The names came fast one after another. Each time, Kerri introduced her as "our daughter" and then "Sasha's a witch."

"Oh, how nice. Our daughter just started a new job in the city. She has three roommates," one couple responded. And then Kerri and David asked, where was she living, what was the new job. Her witchness was trotted out as a fun fact, glanced at by her father's friends and acquaintances. She hated when people raised their eyebrows after noticing her bare wrist, but this blunt repetition hollowed her out. At least with the raised eyebrows, the stares, the witchness was hers, and now Kerri had yanked it away, flattened it out, and made photocopies to hand out.

Sasha felt sufficiently wrung out by the time they let her sit down. They'd made their way back to the tree room. Her father sat down on the couch next to her. "You look well," he said.

Sasha shrugged. "I guess."

"We're glad you were able to join us tonight, I know it was last minute," he said speaking as if reading a pre-written script from an index card. "How's Catherine?"

She put a hand to her forehead. David took a drink, watched people walking by, waved at someone. He'd only asked after Catherine to say something. Sasha felt as if she'd been stabbed in the stomach.

She said, "I am not drunk enough for this."

He looked at her. "What? It's not a bad party."

"Catherine's dead. So, she's...fine? Not fine? I don't know, how are people after they've died?"

David considered. "Not for us living to know, I'd say." He didn't look embarrassed at not knowing.

"Who was Catherine?" Kerri asked.

Who had Catherine been to Sasha?

David said, "A witch, like them."

Sasha sighed and stood up. Kerri tried to take a hold of her arm, but she was already moving.

"Don't leave," Kerri said.

"I'm getting another drink." She meant to slip out, somehow, but when she reached the foyer—empty, finally an empty room— and looked around, Kerri and David were right behind her. She was taken by the hand again and led back into the maze of the party. More introductions began.

"Please, I need another drink," she said. A drink was put in her hand, and she gulped at it, stuck between her father and stepmother.

CHAPTER NINETEEN

When Sasha returned home from the party, she went to text Courtney, yawning. But then she remembered Courtney was only talking to her about coven business. She sighed and put her phone face down on the kitchen table.

Without going to Courtney's house regularly, the pattern of Sasha's life was wafting away like smoke.

She woke up, and since she didn't have anything to do, she'd have a drink. She'd text Pooja and Faye (she'd created a new group chat for the three of them without Courtney in it) and see if they wanted to get together, but they were usually working, so eventually she stopped asking them.

By the time weekends crawled around, she'd convinced herself that they must have a group chat with Courtney and were making plans to hang out without her, and slinked around the house with a glass of wine. She swayed, dancing with herself in her empty dining room, and told herself that she preferred this. The dusty chandelier swam in her vision.

She drank some more and went online shopping. Sometimes she forgot she'd ordered something until it showed up on her doorstep. She bought twenty new dresses in the month of December, reorganized her closet, cramming her dresses together to make room for the new.

She went to coven meetings, but her mind wandered as Courtney taught Marni simple spells. She jerked to attention one day and she was alone in the living room. She found Courtney and Marni in the kitchen, the orange tea kettle beginning to steam. The way they looked at her when she walked in—she was too dazed to read it. Had she fallen asleep?

Courtney told them she needed to take a break for the week of Christmas, and they agreed.

Sasha barely even noticed when she ate, but eventually her fridge and pantry were empty.

She walked to the supermarket in the last hour before it closed. She could see her breath in the air and kept her hands balled in her pockets. Inside, she pushed a cart, squinting against the harsh lights.

She was considering different boxes of pasta when a woman's voice said, "Sasha?"

She looked blankly at the woman. An older woman, blond hair with streaks of gray pulled into a low ponytail, holding a basket with a few items in it. She smiled at Sasha.

"You probably don't remember me," the woman said. "We only met once, at Catherine's service."

"You're...?"

"Her younger sister, Margaret." She held out her hand and Sasha shook it. "It's a pleasure to meet you more properly."

Sasha could see the resemblance now. Margaret was shorter, her face narrower, but the eyes were the same and so was the smile.

"What are you doing here?" Sasha asked.

Margaret laughed a little. "I shouldn't be laughing, but if you don't laugh, you cry. That's the saying, right? Another funeral, unfortunately."

"I'm sorry."

"Thank you. A high school friend. She'd been sick. Of course, it doesn't make it any easier, knowing."

"I'm sorry," Sasha said again.

Margaret looked at her watch. "Would you want, if you're not busy, to grab a drink? I could really use one."

"Me too," Sasha laughed.

"Let's see," Margaret said, "Catherine would have been around sixteen, and she thought she was this total expert at magic." She took another sip of her beer. "She said she could fix the oven. I don't know if you knew this, but our father didn't come back from the Korean War. Well, he did, but to another woman. Here I am, laughing again at things that aren't funny. Anyway, Catherine didn't want our mother to have to spend the money on a handyman, and while our mother really wasn't familiar with magic, Catherine just... She got her way, even then. So Mom said okay. But Catherine didn't know the right sort of spell and ends up blowing the damn thing through the wall."

Sasha gasped, also laughing. "No!"

Margaret laughed loudly now. "And Mom and I are huddled in the corner completely shocked, middle of winter, this huge hole in our kitchen wall. Magic was so, so new and mysterious and wild to us."

Sasha's drink was almost empty, and the waitress came over. "Ma'am, do you want another screwdriver?"

"Yes, please get another?" Margaret said and Sasha agreed. When the waitress walked away, Margaret leaned in. "I can't believe she called you 'ma'am.' You're not even thirty."

"It's because I'm a witch, I think."

"Interesting. Well, anyway, that day, Catherine—she doesn't look over at us. Her back stiff and chin up, she walks right over to the phone in the hallway and calls up Helen. 'Yes, it's Catherine. I need some help.' Oh my god, she couldn't even say what she'd done, she was so embarrassed. But Helen came right over and fixed it up."

Helen Bertram, who had been covenmates with Catherine and Sasha's great-grandmother Louise, a coven for less than a decade before Louise died, and then formed a new coven with Catherine and Deborah. In Sasha's memory of Helen, she was an eternally old woman, always offering Werther's candy from a cut glass bowl. "I'm surprised that Catherine would do that—perform a spell without fully thinking it through."

"She probably thought she had fully thought it through." They both laughed some more. The restaurant emptied around them. The waitress brought Sasha's next drink. "She was like that," Margaret said, more to herself, probably thinking of other incidents far in the past. "We all make mistakes when we're young, though."

"Sure, but some are bigger than others," Sasha said in a quiet voice. She wouldn't have said it with anyone else. It's something she would have only said to Catherine. Margaret and Sasha—they were what was left of Catherine, and talking together, they had conjured her up, and it'd brought the thought out of Sasha.

Margaret took a contemplative sip of her beer. "Catherine told me about what happened with your friend when you were young. I hope you're not holding it over yourself still."

Sasha sighed. "Most people's mistakes aren't scarring their best friend's entire face."

Margaret downed the last of her beer. "Yes, well, that's true." She fixed her gaze on Sasha. "What happened that night?"

Sasha sighed, pushed her drink around the table. "I don't even totally know. I was really drunk. We'd been arguing a lot. She had a crush on this guy, but he had a crush on someone else, and Juliet wanted me to use magic to curse her or to put a spell on him. Once my powers came in, she kept wanting me to do magic for her. My mom was kind of losing it around that time because my dad was getting remarried. The way Juliet went on about this guy, it reminded me of the way my mom was about my dad, like nothing else mattered." Sasha paused. "My dad... He used to ask my mom to do magic for him. Stuff to help him at work. Whenever he was in the running for a promotion. She had this persuasion potion she used to make. Apparently, it was really good because she used to sell it for a lot of money. I don't know if Catherine knew my dad was using it at work, and my mom used to tell me not to tell her."

"She wouldn't have taken that lightly, magic being used to get ahead at work."

"Yeah. Anyway, we were at this party in someone's basement. It was a couple weeks after my dad's wedding. We'd pregamed at her place. I guess her parents weren't home? The guy she liked was there, and she kept going on and on about him and dragging me over to hang out with him and his friends. I kept going to get drinks and trying to hang with anyone else, but she kept on coming back to get me. I don't know why she was clinging to me so tightly when it felt like she barely liked me then. And I was kind of in and out, browning out, you know? And one of those times I came back in, I was yelling at her, 'Stop talking about her. You don't know anything.' And I don't know what she'd said to me first, but there was so much hate in her eyes, and she yelled back at me, 'Your mom is a useless freak. No wonder your dad left.' And I lost it."

Margaret closed her eyes.

"I didn't mean to do a spell, but I did. I had had a lot to drink. I scratched my hand through the air, and her face cut open and started bleeding. I swear I didn't mean to do it. And then the Witches' Guard siren went off. I was just standing there. I didn't know what to do, and the other kids were trying to help Juliet. A bunch of drunk teenagers. Some people I didn't even know were yelling at me about what a horrible person I was, which, honestly, mind your own business. Then the guard showed up. There were so many of them when they came into the basement. And they carried this thing, a long metal rod with a collar at the end." Sasha half lifted her hand to her throat, then put it down, not wanting to mimic it. "They used it to drag me out of there."

"Wow," Margaret said. "You must have been scared."

"Yeah. Sobered me up. Afterwards, there was this guy at the party that I had some classes with. We'd never been friends, but he was always friendly, so I tried asking him about what happened, what I didn't remember. He hadn't been near us, but he said suddenly I'd slapped Juliet, and then she started yelling at me. He didn't know what she said." Sasha stopped to take a drink. "Sometimes I don't even feel bad about it. I think, whatever, she's fine. Her scars probably aren't even that bad."

"You don't know how they make her feel, faded or not. It probably completely changed her, not just physically."

"Maybe for the better. She was a selfish brat."

"A lot of us are when we're teenagers. Have you ever reached out to her?"

Sasha shifted in her seat. "No." Why were they talking about Juliet? Hadn't they been talking about Catherine?

"You could," Margaret said. Sasha felt chastised, but Margaret eased into another story about Catherine when they were girls. And when the waitress brought their check, Margaret waved Sasha's wallet away. "It's my treat, my absolute treat to be here with you, talking about someone we both loved."

"Here, here," Sasha raised her glass, emptied it.

Chapter Twenty

Sasha was sitting in her living room when she saw the guard car pull into her driveway. She stood up and ran outside. Howie got out of the driver's side. There was another man in the passenger's seat.

"Get off my property," Sasha shouted.

"Calm down, Sasha. I'm just here for a chat."

"Don't take a step closer."

Howie put up his hands in a mock show of friendliness. "What is Margaret Darley doing back in town? How long is she staying?"

Margaret had told her that in addition to the funeral, she was taking care of some things on Catherine's house, which she now owned, and rented out to a couple. "Why's that any of your business?"

"It's my business to be aware of visitors to this town and their intentions. Plus, she's an old friend."

Sasha did realize that Margaret and Howie would have grown up at a similar time in their town. She didn't generally think of Howie as having grown up, though, but more as a creature that had sprung forth fully formed. "Ask her then."

"Fine," Howie said with a smile. He took a step back to his car. "Her last name is still Darley, isn't it?"

"I have no idea."

Howie shrugged. "Two sisters, neither got married. Kind of unusual, don't you think?"

"Not really," Sasha said.

"She left town in quite a controversy when she was young. You should ask her about it."

Sasha glared at him as he got back into the car.

The night Sasha attacked Juliet she was brought into the Witches' Guard Headquarters. The guards brought her to a room that was empty except for a table and two chairs facing one another. Howie walked in and sat down in one of the chairs, papers in hand. "We can lose the collar," he said.

A guard stepped forward and unbuckled the collar, pushed her into the other chair.

Howie smiled at her. "I can't wait to see what Catherine and your mother will say." Still smiling, he looked down at the papers in front of him. "Hoffman, one N, correct?"

She didn't answer.

"I'm pretty sure. We'll go with that." He began writing slowly. "Here's what's going to happen: The guards will bring you up to one of the cells, where you'll be overnight. Don't worry, there's a cot." He smiled again. "And then in the morning I'll have your sentencing ready, and then...we'll go from there."

Two guards stepped forward and forced her up; Howie returned to writing. "Am I about to go to exile?" She felt tears at the word "exile" and fought them back.

Howie kept writing. The guards pulled her to the door. As they walked her out, Howie looked up and she thought he gave her a sad smile.

Lying on the cot, she stared at the ceiling. She was going to be sent to exile. And she would spend her entire life there. In cells like this one? She didn't know what time it was, how much time she had left until morning. She cried. She wondered if Courtney knew. Her mother and Catherine must, the way Howie had brought them up. And Courtney must have heard the siren. She cried some more. She tried to stay awake. She was jolted out of sleep by keys unlocking the cell door.

"Get up," the guard yelled at her.

She pushed off the cot and tensed, ready for him to come into the cell and grab her. Instead, he stood to the side of the open door. She realized he meant for her to walk out on her own. When she was out of the cell, he pointed, and she walked down the hallway. She looked behind her. He wasn't following.

When she got to the door at the end of the hallway, he shouted, "Go through."

When she did, she was in the front lobby, where she'd been to register as a witch. There were no guards there. The second hand on the wall clock ticked softly. She shifted, standing in the middle of the room. She took two slow steps to the front door, looking around, waiting for Howie to appear. She quickened her steps. She was at the door. She was out the door. She started towards the sidewalk when a car horn whipped her head around. It was Catherine. Sasha ran to her car and got into the backseat out of habit. Courtney was there and grabbed her into a hug. Sasha began to whimper. Catherine started the car, and Sasha pulled away from Courtney.

"Where's my mom?"

"We'll talk about it when we get you home," Catherine said.

Courtney put a hand on her shoulder. "Where's my mom?" Sasha whispered.

"Um, Catherine will tell you."

Sasha dropped her head into her hands. She jumped from thought to thought and soon she was hyperventilating.

They brought her home, and once inside, Catherine drew Sasha into a hug. Sasha could feel her taking deep breaths. She stepped back, keeping the young witch in her grasp. "She's gone. I'm sorry. They were going to send you to exile, and she made a deal to take your place."

"How do you know they would have sent me to exile?" Sasha said, fresh tears running down her cheeks. "How do you know? Maybe she didn't have to do that. We could still get her back?"

"He told me. I went to try and see you last night and he told me."

"Maybe—" Sasha started, her voice a shriek.

"No," Catherine said. "It was going to happen."

Catherine steered Sasha into the living room, Courtney following close behind. The two younger witches sat on the couch, and Catherine walked to the kitchen, saying she'd be right back. Courtney put her arms around Sasha.

"I'm so sorry," Courtney whispered. Sasha lay her head on her shoulder, exhausted.

Catherine and Courtney stayed for the rest of the day. The house, her parents' home, which had become her mother's home, now belonged to her. Catherine started to explain the legal passing down of a witch's assets when she went into exile, but at Sasha's blank face and swollen eyes, she said, "We'll talk about it another time."

They ate dinner, mostly in silence. Sasha took two bites of the spaghetti Catherine made. The food was heavy, swallowing diffi-cult. She'd ate at their table hundreds of times without her mother, over a thousand probably, but now she knew she would never sit here with her mother again. Exile was a life sentence. Sasha dropped out of her chair onto the floor.

"You need to eat," Catherine said. Sasha grabbed the plate and brought it into her lap. She ate with her back to the table.

After dinner, Catherine asked if she wanted them to stay overnight. "No," Sasha said.

"Okay. But call me any time of the night if you need to," Catherine said.

Sasha nodded.

Courtney hung back when Catherine walked out. She gave Sasha another hug. "I'm so sorry about your mom. But I'm glad you're still here."

When they were both gone, Sasha lay down on the living room floor. Cocooned in her crying, she was relieved to still be there too.

Chapter Twenty-One

Sasha was surprised when the envelope with the official Westchester Board of Witches seal arrived at her house, instead of Courtney's. Ella had sent Courtney and Sasha a text the week before saying that the board had begun their deliberations and should have an answer early in the new year. The envelope contained the name of the coven leader.

Sasha called her fellow witches and put the envelope on the table to wait for them. She poured herself a drink, and two non-alcoholic drinks, so they could all have something to celebrate. She couldn't sit still, and pacing around the house led her back to the envelope in the kitchen.

Courtney and Marni arrived. The three stood around the table in Sasha's kitchen. "You should open it," Sasha said.

Courtney smiled. Her hands shook slightly as she slowly tore open the flap and took out the square card. Her brows furrowed. She looked up at Sasha. "Um. It's you. You're the coven leader."

Marni looked between the two, each staring at the small piece of paper still in Courtney's hand. When neither spoke, the youngest witch broke the silence. "Wow. Congrats, Sasha."

Sasha stood stunned, unable to say anything. Courtney

handed her the card, but even seeing her name printed out seemed unreal.

Courtney cleared her throat. "Congratulations, Sasha." She stepped forward and hugged her, but it was a hug like they didn't know each other very well. She whispered, "Excuse me," and slipped outside.

Sasha followed her into the backyard. "It should be you," she said, grabbing Courtney's arm. "We'll call them and get it changed."

"It's a final decision," Courtney said, choked, yanking her arm away. She turned from Sasha. "Leave me alone. Please."

Courtney could barely speak, her throat was so tight. How could this happen? Everyone always told her she was a natural leader. She thought she had done everything right. She went to all the board gatherings, forged connections with each of the individual board members, learned and brought up personal details to show she cared—this one's love of impressionistic painting, this one's beloved Pomeranian, another's hiking trips.

The trees in Sasha's backyard spun in her vision. Courtney put her hands on her knees. Her forehead was slick with sweat. Whether Sasha was still behind her or not, she didn't know. Sasha might have been speaking, she didn't know.

But this was not the first time she had been passed over. When trying out for middle school plays where the promise was every student had speaking roles, each time she was given the role with only one or two lines, no matter how many times she practiced her audition with her parents. She joined the high school paper as a freshman, went to every meeting, wrote articles each issue, established a science and medicine column as a sophomore. A white girl in her same year joined the newspaper the second half of their junior year, with solid writing skill for a beginner, wrote articles that were assigned to her, and was voted editor in chief when they were seniors. She had thought the board was different. She had told her parents the board was different.

She threw up on the frozen ground.

Sasha was required to appear before the Westchester Board of Witches. Every time she had visited the Board Headquarters before, she had been with Courtney. She took a cab south.

There were thirteen witches on the board. Sasha walked along the line of them, shaking their hands. She only knew a few of them by name, including Ella, who gave a weak smile as she shook Sasha's hand. They all knew who she was. The oldest witch, a short witch with her gray hair pulled into a chignon who introduced herself as Rita, said, "Your mother would be very proud, Sasha."

"Thank you."

After introductions, the board sat down. Their chairs were arranged in a semi-circle with one chair for Sasha facing them.

"We're very pleased to have you as a coven leader, Sasha Hoffman," Carol Smith, the Board president, whom Sasha had met once before, said. "You join a long and proud line of witches."

"Thank you," Sasha said. "It's an honor I'm not sure I deserve."

Carol smiled. "We elected you as leader. The consideration is a closed affair, but we are confident in our choice. Now, Ella?"

Ella stood and approached Sasha. She held out a black jewelry box. Her eyes were ice.

Inside the box was a pin. Sasha recognized it. "This was Catherine's," she said, picking it up. It was an old bronze pin with the moon and the sun intertwined. The year 1671 was inscribed on the moon.

"It is the board's. It belonged to Catherine while she was coven leader, and now that you are the new leader, it is yours."

For another thirty minutes, Carol read speeches and statements, and then Sasha agreed to uphold the rules of leading a Westchester coven and signed several documents.

When the ceremony was done, Ella immediately walked

towards the front door. Sasha followed her. Ella summoned her coat and had her hand on the door.

"Wait," Sasha said.

Ella stopped. The other board members were chatting in the room behind them, soft laughter floating into the foyer. "It shouldn't have been me."

"Well, that's one thing we see eye to eye on."

"Can't I give the position to Courtney?" Sasha begged.

Ella turned around. She folded her arms. "Unfortunately, no."

"I don't understand why they picked me."

"Don't be dense. It's because your mother was a witch. Even though most witches aren't descended from witches themselves, there's still a belief that someone with a witch relative must be a better, more powerful witch. And frankly, witches of color have had to fight for decades to be recognized as valid and equal witches. How many witches of color do you see on the board itself?"

"Just you."

"Exactly. They stick with what's comfortable, who they're used to seeing in power, which is someone white. Combine that with your heritage and here we are."

"They're idiots then. You couldn't tell them that Courtney would be better?"

"I tried. This was the longest deliberation I've been part of in my twenty years on the board, because I kept arguing my case. But I was overruled."

Sasha leaned back against the wall, suddenly exhausted.

Ella pulled on her coat with jerking movements, brusquely shoving her arms through. "I'd appreciate it if you didn't embarrass me. As the board representative from our part of Westchester, your failures will reflect poorly on me. Furthermore, it'd be nice if you didn't embarrass witches to the general public."

"You've never liked me," Sahsa said.

Ella stared at her, face blank. She opened the door and left.

. . .

The three witches—a coven now, officially, Sasha's Coven—started meeting at Sasha's house. Courtney insisted on it as Sasha was leader.

"What spells do you want to do with Marni today, Sasha?"

Sasha stared at Marni, hoping the young witch would present some answer. She stared back at Sasha.

"Summoning spells?"

"We finished those."

After the meeting, Sasha watched Courtney and Marni talking together as they both got into Courtney's car. Marni laughed about something Courtney said.

Chapter Twenty-Two

Sasha invited Margaret to come over to her house for a drink and take-out.

She gave Margaret a tour of her house, showing her the rows of leather-bound books, and the several paintings that Deborah had collected.

"How beautiful," Margaret mused, standing in front of a blue and white abstract painting. "Your mother has great taste. How often do you hear from her?"

Sasha started. "I don't. She's in exile."

"Darling, I know. I meant how often does she write?" Margaret asked. She wasn't looking at Sasha, but was still admiring the painting, moving closer to examine the brush strokes.

"What do you mean?"

"How often does she write you letters?"

"She can't," Sasha said. "Can she?"

Now Margaret faced her. "I thought...but no, you must be right."

Margaret started turning away. Sasha grabbed her by the upper arm. "You know witches that have written from exile? Has my mother written to you?"

"No, Sasha. We weren't close. And no, I don't really know any other witches."

"But you know other people have gotten letters from witches in exile?"

"Someone once said they thought witches could write from exile. But it must have been a rumor if you don't know anything about that. Or maybe that's the way things used to be."

Sasha loosened her grip on Margaret's arm. "Maybe," she said. She needed to put a hand on the wall.

"I'm sorry I even said anything. I have no idea what I'm talking about. It was just a passing comment someone made about it, an acquaintance. You might not know this, but people have this way of talking about witches. They—you—fascinate people. Rumors are always getting spun. I don't even tell people I don't know that my sister was a witch or they're bombarding me with questions."

"You know what? I'm fine, but I'm tired," Sasha said. "I'm going to lie down."

"Are you okay? Let me get you a glass of water."

Sasha walked upstairs and settled into her bed. Margaret brought her a glass of water, knocking on the door.

Sasha took the glass of water with a sigh. Margaret started picking up the empty glasses on the bed side table. "That's okay. You don't have to clean up."

Margaret held the two glasses she'd already picked up. "Okay. You'll call me? We can do dinner tomorrow."

"Sure."

Margaret walked backwards out of the room, closing the door behind her. Once Sasha heard the door shut downstairs, she grabbed her phone out of her pocket and called Courtney. They hadn't talked in several days, the last time a brief text exchange about meetings. When Courtney picked up, Sasha said, "Did you know witches could write from exile?"

Courtney paused. "Yes."

"And you didn't tell me."

"Who knows why she wasn't writing? Maybe she was sick. I thought—"

"You don't have to think anything about my mother. That's for me to be doing," Sasha said. "You should've told me."

"I thought it would just hurt you."

Sasha hung up.

The next day around noon, the doorbell rang. Sasha opened the door with the chain still on. She eyed Marni though the gap. "Did Courtney send you?"

"No. I told her I was coming by, but I wanted to come see you."

Sasha sighed. She shut the door, undid the chain, and let Marni in.

"Have a drink with me," she said. She poured several shots each into two glasses, topped them off with orange juice.

Sasha took a long gulp, nearly finishing the drink. She considered the rest of the glass and finished it off in a quick swig. She unscrewed the vodka cap to start again.

Marni watched her. "You know, I don't know what you and Courtney fought about, but why don't you talk to her about it?"

"I'm sure she'd love that. She thinks she's my damn keeper, holding back, making decisions for me for years. And you know what? It's not like she talked to me when she was upset about not getting leader."

Marni shrugged. "Maybe she was more upset at the board for that."

"She talked to you about that?"

"No, I'm just guessing."

Sasha put a hand over her eyes. She liked Marni, she reminded herself. She lowered her hand and took another drink. Cool.

Clean. Sharp. What had they been laughing at getting into Courtney's car the other day? she wondered. She had wanted to text them the next few days to suggest going to dinner that weekend. Had picked up her phone to do so. But she'd imagined Marni wouldn't want to spend her weekends with them, and then Courtney would have some excuse. It'd stopped her hand.

Marni said quietly, "Some of my friends have been avoiding me since they found out I was a witch. I wish it could be fixed by having a talk."

Sasha hadn't looked at the rock in weeks. Was anyone talking to her at school anymore?

"How have your parents been dealing with the whole witch news?"

"Okay. They're definitely getting used to the idea. They just want to know what it means for my future."

Sasha raised her eyebrow. "What do you mean?"

"You met my parents. They're pretty big on college education and that sort of stuff."

Sasha scoffed. "Who needs that?"

"I think I might be interested." Marni took another drink. "That's what I wanted to tell you about."

"You're going to leave town." If she left, how much longer would they have to wait for another witch.

"No, I was thinking a school in the area. I'd be a commuter student."

"And what would you study?"

"I actually really like math. It's always been my best subject."

"Interesting," Sasha said. "I was never much of a student, but there must be some witches with college degrees."

"Yeah, Courtney's going to do some research, ask around her forums."

"Of course. Courtney and her research," Sasha said.

"Will you consider talking to her?"

Sasha sighed. "Yeah, I will."

Marni smiled. "I'm glad to hear it. I gotta get going. I've got an essay due Monday."

"Especially if you're going to be a college student one of these days. But first"—Sasha raised her finger—"I insist you finish your drink. It's an order."

Marni laughed. "I can do that." And Sasha raised her glass too.

CHAPTER TWENTY-THREE

Margaret's time in town was winding down. They met at one of several pubs in their town. Homey feeling with over-stuffed cushions at each booth. The type of restaurant that only had booths.

Sasha'd had several drinks at home before she came to meet Margaret and tapped her fingers on the table energetically. Their drinks arrived quickly. Sasha wondered if Margaret knew any of the other people dining with them. Sasha didn't.

While they looked over the menu, the talk turned to Catherine again.

"When Catherine was younger, she always had dates, every weekend. She lost some interested suitors, as my grandmother used to say, when she became a witch," Margaret said.

"Do you think she cared?"

"I don't know. We didn't talk about it much as we got older. But when we were growing up, we'd whisper about which boys we thought were the cutest when we were supposed to be asleep."

"Were you ever married?"

"No."

Sasha thought of what Howie had said. Two sisters, never married. Was that so unusual, though?

"I've been with Bill, my boyfriend, for several years. He's wonderful, and he's wonderful to me. I almost can't believe we've only known each other for a couple years. That's how completely we know each other. Every day I've been gone, we start the morning with a telephone call while we have our coffee."

Sasha snorted and quickly caught herself, "Sorry, I didn't mean—"

"No, it's okay. We fully embrace our corniness. We were both single for a long time before we met. He'd been divorced for over a decade. We sort of thought the romantic parts of our lives might be behind us. I bet you would like him." Margaret beamed. "You should come up to Boston, and then you could meet him."

"That could be fun," Sasha said, but she kept her voice flat. She wasn't used to making these sorts of plans, fitting into someone new's life.

"And he's fine with witches."

Those words, "he's fine with witches," made Sasha's mouth taste like metal. Margaret wasn't a witch, even if she was sister to one. What made her an arbiter of how someone was with and towards witches? "Would you want me to come visit soon?"

"Yeah, why not? I leave in a few days. You could drive up with me then?"

"Really? I can't drive, you know."

Margaret laughed. "That's fine. It's an easy drive for me to do myself."

Sasha took a drink. What else was holding her here. She could go for a few days. "Okay, let's do it. I have some stuff to take care of first."

As they walked out of the restaurant, a woman approached them. She waved at Sasha, and after the shock that a townsperson was greeting her, she realized she knew this woman. It was Marni's neighbor Brooke.

"Hi, Sasha, how are you?"

"I'm okay."

"Listen, I wanted to say I was sorry about the things my husband said on Rosh Hashanah."

Margaret smiled at her with a look of polite confusion. Sasha tried to remember how she'd felt about this woman that night, before the couple had realized they were talking to a witch.

"You don't have to apologize for your husband."

"Well, I want to. There are certain things he doesn't know about life. I know I'm the same in other ways, so..."

"So, you try to be generous," Margaret finished.

"Exactly, thank you."

Sasha thought, Why should your generous forgiveness towards your husband's thoughts on witches mean anything to me? You're not a witch; of course it'd be easy for you. However, the woman did exude a comfort with witches, and not in a way that she wanted to show she was okay with witches, but that she had spent time with them before. It made Sasha like her, but she didn't have to agree with her. But Margaret was looking at her, giving her the sort of look Catherine used to give her that communicated that a certain politeness was expected.

"That's an interesting thought. I'll think it over," Sasha said, knowing she probably wouldn't.

Brooke smiled. "I'll let you two get going. It's cold. I hope I see you around, Sasha."

They exchanged goodbyes.

"She seemed nice," Margaret said.

"Hmm," Sasha said. Again, she was reminded Margaret wasn't a witch.

"Just so many people in this town," Margaret said, "that are walking around with their heads up their own asses. Their priorities are all messed up."

Sasha laughed so hard she had to stop walking. Margaret cracked a smile. "She didn't seem like that. How do you know her?"

"She's Marni's neighbor. What do you think peoples' priorities are around here?"

Margaret gestured a hand in the air above her head. "Money. Not just money but having it so you can show it off. Have I told you about the couple renting Catherine's house?"

"Not really."

"They're this young couple and they moved here from out of town. They've been renting it since she died and I've watched them change in these few years. The husband was wearing this watch when I first stopped in this time. I didn't even say anything about it. He pointed it out to me. 'Isn't this something? April got it as a present for my promotion.' And she was all, 'Oh, it was the least I could get for him after he got me a diamond necklace for my birthday.' They weren't like that before. Plus, I hardly know these people. Why are they going on about all the presents they're getting for each other?"

Sasha glanced behind them. She couldn't see Brooke. "She's probably rich too. Don't you have to be to live here?"

Margaret sighed. "It used to not be like that."

Sasha asked Margaret to drop her off at Courtney's. It was late, after ten o'clock. Courtney opened the door, sleepy-eyed and confused. She was in her matching-set pajamas and had her hair wrapped.

"Sorry I didn't call first. I was out with Margaret," Sasha said.

"Who?"

"Margaret Darley. She's Catherine's sister. Can I come in?"

"Oh. Yes, of course."

Courtney led her to the living room, rubbing her eye with her fist. "I remember meeting Catherine's sister at the funeral. Younger, right? Short woman with wavy blond hair?"

"Yeah, that's her. She's in town for another funeral. We've been spending time together. It's been nice." They both sat down.

Silence stretched between them. "And that's how you found out about letters from exile."

"Yes."

"I'm sorry. I really am. I thought I was protecting you, but you're right. I should've let you know." Sleep still dripped from her voice.

Sasha stared down at her hands in her lap. "It's okay. It sucks. She's never written to me. Either she doesn't want to, or she's dead. They're both pretty shitty possibilities."

"It's probably not that she doesn't want to. Your mom was never expressive. And maybe she's forgotten your address," Courtney suggested.

"I live in the house she lived in for twenty years. You don't have to make excuses for her."

Another silence.

"I'm sorry about the board picking me for leader. I know we can't do anything about it, but you deserve it. You'd be the better leader."

Now it was Courtney's turn to stare at her lap. "Yeah," she said quietly.

"I wish things were different."

They sat with their disappointments.

"I went to this party my dad and stepmom invited me to a little while back. He didn't even know Catherine had died."

Courtney closed her eyes briefly, imagining absorbing a conversation like that. Their silences were warming. "I know it's always a lot when you see your dad," she said.

Sasha shrugged. "At least it's not that often. What have you been up to?"

"Working mostly," Courtney said. She leaned back on the

couch, pulled her legs up underneath her. "It's nice to have you here again."

Sasha smiled. "I'm glad to be here. I'm actually going to go to Boston for a couple days with Margaret, but I'll be back before Wednesday meeting."

"That should be fun."

"I think it will be," Sasha said. She stood up. "You probably want to get to bed. I'll talk to you tomorrow."

Courtney stood up also. "You know you'll have to get a pass from the guard. Since you're driving through Connecticut."

Sasha groaned. She so rarely even left their county that she'd forgotten about that rule. "I hate the thought of Howie knowing where I am. We'll just be driving through. What are the odds someone stops us?"

"It's a big risk."

Sasha knew she was right. The rule stated that a witch traveling to or through a state where witchcraft was banned needed a pass from their local guard. The potential punishment for being caught without one was exile. They reasoned if you didn't want to tell the guard where you were, then you must be trying to infiltrate the banned state. Maybe some guards even believed that.

Sasha was not as lucky as they had been when they'd brought Marni to register. Howie was at the guard headquarters when she walked in. He smiled broadly and told the officer at the front desk that he could personally help Sasha. She rolled her eyes. "I need a pass to drive through Connecticut."

"Really? And why are you driving through Connecticut?"

"I'm visiting Boston."

"And why are you visiting Boston?"

"Is that really necessary information?"

"Sasha, would I ask for unnecessary information? I need to

make sure that you're not visiting Boston for inappropriate reasons."

Sasha knew that Howie had no interest in sending her through a banned state without a pass. He didn't want her exiled. He wanted her in town, always nearby for a harassing visit. And she knew that he knew that there was a decent chance she'd go anyway if he didn't give her the pass. "As Massachusetts is not a banned state, I'm free to visit without your permission. I provided my reason for traveling in Connecticut. I don't have to provide anything else."

"Sounds like someone's been reading up on our rules and regulations," Howie chuckled. "Boston. Any chance you're visiting Margaret Darley? I believe that's where she lives."

She remained silent.

Howie went to a filing cabinet and pulled out a sheet. He wrote several things and then signed. He pushed the sheet through the opening in the glass. "Sign and write your name here."

The sheet was a generic State Pass for Witches. Howie had filled out the blank lines to show the banned state she'd be traveling in and the amount of time the pass allowed. He'd given her five days. It was enough. She signed below his signature and wrote her name out on the next line. She hated seeing her signature next to his, but this was a small consequence for something wonderful.

"So, has Margaret told you yet why she left for Boston in the first place?" Howie asked as he ripped the top sheet at the perforated line. He handed her the sheet she'd signed and went back to the filing cabinet with the yellow carbon copy.

"People move for lots of different reasons, and I don't see why you think you know what hers was."

Howie turned back to her and smiled. "I'll take that as a no."

Sasha folded her pass and put it in her pocket. She turned and walked to the door.

"Have fun, Sasha. Send me a postcard if you see one I would like, will you?"

"No," Sasha said, and she didn't even look back at him.

CHAPTER TWENTY-FOUR

Courtney stood in line at the post office. When she'd walked in, a woman at the front of the line gave her a small wave, while the rest of the patrons stared at her, briefly or for an extended period. She shifted the package from under one arm to the other. The line turned away.

Then Marni walked in. "Hey," she called out, waving. The rest of the line stared at Marni even longer as she joined Courtney.

Courtney remembered a couple months before, how Marni didn't want to have her bracelet removed, didn't want to engage with their coven history, the politeness that had grated on Sasha. Would she have greeted Courtney so openly and warmly in town then? Maybe, to be polite.

Marni also had a package in hand.

"What are you sending?" Courtney asked.

"My parents wanted to send my sister a care package, stuff from stores around town that she always liked. She's in law school now."

"Another lawyer. Must run in the family," Courtney said.

"Yeah, it's a whole thing." They laughed. "Anyway, what are you sending?"

Courtney held out her own package. "Birthday present for my mother. I always agonize over picking the perfect thing," she said.

"She'll probably love it no matter what."

"Maybe. I think so," Courtney said. Sometimes she took a whole year picking out presents for her family, starting to consider the next one the day after their birthday. They did enjoy her presents, but she always worried this would be the time they wouldn't. "Are you close with your sister?"

"Yeah, I always looked up to her like crazy, and she spent a lot of time with me when I was growing up. You have a brother, right?"

"Yeah, he's older as well. We were close when we were younger, but he lives in North Carolina now and is married and has two kids. He's a teacher, so he's pretty busy."

"Aw, Aunt Courtney."

"Yeah," she said with a smile. She took her phone from her jacket pocket. "I have some pictures of them, hold on." She placed the box on the ground and flipped through her family group chat, photos sent of her niece and nephew, four and one years old. Her niece trying to hold her younger brother while Courtney's brother supported him, Courtney's mother with both children sitting on her lap, all three grinning. Norm and Dorothy watched the children often, having purposefully moved down the street to be close. Courtney found one of her favorites, her father and her brother, both wearing their glasses and her niece—who may one day need glasses—wearing fake toy glasses to match them.

"They're really cute," Marni gushed. "Your niece looks like your mom."

"Yeah, you can tell they're family."

"When's your birthday, Courtney? I don't think I know."

"Late August. Sasha's is in May. Yours is in March, right?"

Marni nodded.

"We'll have to celebrate."

"Yeah, definitely. Are you and Sasha big on birthday celebrations?"

"Sasha sort of hibernates in May." It was the month Deborah had been exiled. It was the month Catherine had stopped doing chemo. "She's one of those people that doesn't like to be reminded of her birthday." Even though Catherine had waited until after Sasha's birthday to tell them, Sasha associated the two. "But I do reach out to her to see how she's doing, tell her something I like about her or respect about her, that sort of thing. It's important, I think, to tell someone what they mean to you. You never know what'll happen."

Courtney wrote a long letter to Catherine after that day in May, about how much she appreciated what Catherine had taught her. She slipped it in her mailbox. Courtney still had the letter Catherine had written in return.

You are a talented young witch, and I feel honored to have been your coven leader and your covenmate. One day, you may be coven leader yourself. Be strong and be patient. It might just be you and Sasha for awhile. When I see you two together, I see how deep your bond is already. I'm very proud of that.

Marni nodded. "That's a really nice thing to do."

Sasha didn't even like coming over to Courtney's home during May. Lounging and drinking cocktails in the backyard. Their errand days. There had been one notable exception to Sasha's May hibernation. Two years before, a customer began spreading that she'd been displeased with a potion Courtney made her. Courtney noticed a dip in orders throughout the town and tried to reach out to the customer to see if anything was wrong. She received polite answers that everything had gone well. Sasha went to the woman's house and demanded to know what the issue was—because Sasha could be blunt in a way that would get Courtney labeled as "having a bad attitude" or "being aggressive," which could lose her even more business.

The potion had been to disappear freckles across the woman's nose. And it worked, but without her freckles, the woman didn't know herself in the mirror. "So the potion worked exactly as it was supposed to. The problem was your choice in seeking it out," Sasha said, and with further poking the customer admitted that Courtney had talked with her before taking the order to make sure this was definitely something she wanted.

Courtney mixed up a potion to reverse the first potion—a particularly effective general counter-potion Deborah had devised—and when the woman's freckles were back, Sasha sat in her living room while she called and texted every one of her friends and neighbors to recant what she'd said about Courtney and add glowing reviews.

Once they'd both paid to send their packages, Courtney and Marni walked out together. It was a gray day. "Oh, look. Isn't that Sasha?" Marni said, pointing across the town square. "Who's that woman with her?"

"That must be Margaret," Courtney said, "Catherine's younger sister."

They'd been talking more like they'd used to since Sasha had shown up on her doorstep. For nearly a minute, Courtney watched Sasha. Watching her without her knowing she was being watched. She thought Sasha had a smile on. Her arms hugged her coat tightly against her body, her shoulders hunched, but she kept turning to face Margaret, listening, nodding.

Chapter Twenty-Five

They started driving early. The air was crisp. Sasha couldn't stop smiling.

She had a flask in her jacket pocket and took a swig during their first rest stop in central Connecticut, stepped off to the side of the restroom. With her back to the parking lot, she stared at the bare trees, their bare branches. She hadn't left New York in years.

Back in the car, Sasha ran her tongue over her front teeth, for the last flavor of the liquor, thrilling at her visit and luxuriating in Margaret's company.

"It's a prettier drive in the fall."

"I bet," Sasha said.

"You know why they made these highways originally?"

Sasha didn't like when people asked questions they planned on answering themselves, but it didn't bothered her now. "Why?"

"It was for people to get out of the city on day trips. Rich people and the new middle class. I can't help but think about it. I'm seeing something nice, but it was made that way for people with money."

Sasha, who'd had money all her life, pondered this as she looked out the window. "But now everyone can enjoy it."

"Can they? First you need a car. Even renting a car for a trip isn't cheap," Margaret said. "I don't want to dampen the mood. Sometimes I can't help thinking about this sort of thing."

"Why?"

"God, power is all around us. As you get older, it's difficult to not see."

Sasha thought of the guard, the travel pass she had in her wallet. Had to have.

They were about to cross over the Massachusetts border when a cop car parked on the side of the road pulled out and flashed its lights. Margaret glanced into the rearview mirror and pulled over.

Rage built inside Sasha as the cop approached the car. "How does he know?" she muttered.

Margaret put her hand on Sasha's arm. "Stay calm. Don't give him an excuse to give you trouble," she whispered.

She lowered the window once the cop was standing there. "Is there a problem, sir?"

He pointed a finger at them. "Either of you ladies witches?"

Sasha took her travel pass from her wallet and handed it to him along with her ID. Margaret pulled out her own driver's license and he nodded, as non-witches had licenses and IDs a different style than witches did. He looked at the pass for what felt like a long time. Sasha knew she was following the rules, but still her heart pounded.

"Step out of the car, miss."

She opened the door. The cop walked in front of the car to meet her. When they were facing each other, Sasha could tell the man was not much older than she was, early thirties maybe, and this made her resent the "miss" even more.

He stood with his hands on his hips, looking her up and down. He pointed at her pocket. "What's in there?"

She jerked back and he grabbed for his gun. "What is that?" He yelled.

"It's a flask," she hissed.

"Why do you have that?"

"Why do you think? It's perfectly legal to have a flask. I'm over twenty-one."

The man hadn't yet removed his hand from his gun, although he'd relaxed. "Alcohol is one of the one hundred and six banned substances for witches while traveling."

"It's not," she said, although she didn't know.

"It is. I can bring you to the local guard and you can argue with them in a cell overnight if you'd like."

"Fine, fine," she snapped, darting a look behind her. She unscrewed the cap and poured the vodka out onto the ground. The flask had been nearly full. They stood in silence as the liquor streamed out. Sasha gave the flask a final shake. "There. Now I no longer am traveling with a banned substance."

He paused, as if he wanted to object. She slipped her flask back into her pocket. It was her favorite and she didn't want it to be confiscated.

The cop handed back her ID and pass. She returned to Margaret's car, the passenger side door still open, and he started walking away with a nod. Then she stopped. "How did you know?" she asked.

He turned back to her. "An older woman and a girl traveling together? It's not that common."

"We could be relatives."

"You don't look alike."

"Do you look like all your aunts and uncles?"

"No. Are you related?"

"No."

"Right."

"Well, aren't you clever," Sasha said, causing Margaret to call her name sharply.

The cop started walking again. "Get going, witch," he said over his shoulder.

Sasha got back into the car and slammed the door shut. "Asshole."

"It could've been worse," Margaret said. She pulled back onto the road.

They crossed the state border. *Massachusetts Welcomes You!*

Margaret asked, "Why did you bring a flask with you?"

Sasha turned to her, surprised. She didn't know anyone would need a reason to. "It's just my flask. You know, that I have?"

Later, Sasha would text Courtney to check in before she went to sleep. She told her about the cop. She told her about the stop, the flask, what he said when they argued.

Back in New York, Courtney lay in bed, under the covers, the heat on. Courtney stared at the words on her screen. Just words on a screen, but they were Sasha. She could see her saying them. Courtney started typing, then erased it. She wanted to say, *Don't pick fights with cops.* She wanted to say, *Especially don't pick fights with cops if you're with me.* And *I'm serious.* Even before she was a witch, Courtney was taught she had to be careful of cops. She'd told Sasha this before. Courtney didn't know if she remembered. Courtney didn't know if Sasha had been drunk when she'd told her and forgot by the next day.

She typed out, *Be careful with cops, okay? They're not the guard, but they're still dangerous.*

Courtney looked at the word "dangerous." It was the right word, but would she come across as too extreme? Dramatic? No. It was the right word. She sent the text.

Sasha responded, *I know, I know. I just get so mad at them. I'm bad at holding it back.*

Courtney sighed and put her phone face down on the bedside table.

.   .   .

Margaret lived on a quiet, short city street in a brick building. They walked up three flights of stairs to her apartment.

"Good, the heat is on," Margaret said when they walked in. The rooms were decorated in red, gold, and maroon. It was cozy and neat. Margaret told Sasha to put her bag next to the squishy red couch, a pull-out she'd be sleeping on. "Come look at this," Margaret said, gesturing for Sasha to follow her into the dining room nook. There was a small dark wood side table and in the middle a cream and pink floral tea set.

Sasha brushed past Margaret. "I know that tea set."

Margaret smiled. "I thought you might. It was our grandmother's. Catherine always loved it, so our grandmother gave it to her before she passed away. And when Catherine died, she left it to me. We hadn't used it together since we were pre-teens."

Sasha picked up one of the cups. Catherine never used it to serve tea, but had the set prominently displayed on the kitchen hutch. Sasha thought of the leader's brooch, still in its box shoved in a drawer in her bedroom.

"You didn't come back to New York often?" Sasha asked.

"No, I didn't."

Sasha realized that this may be skirting towards the reason why Margaret left New York originally, the salacious thing Howie had hinted at. It tugged at her curiosity, her definitive answer, that there really was something that had happened, and it wasn't Howie trying to pull gossip out of the air. Sasha determined not to ask anything further about it. But Margaret continued.

"I'm not sure that Catherine ever said anything to you about my leaving?"

"Honestly, she didn't mention you much." Sasha realized the harshness of the statement. "I mean, I'm sure she did with other people. It just didn't come up much between us."

Margaret shook her head. "It's okay. She probably didn't. I didn't leave New York under the most respectable circumstances." She paused, looked at her hands. "After I finished high school, I was living in town. There wasn't the money for college. I had a job, but I couldn't afford to live on my own, so I still lived at home. I was twenty and feeling a bit bored. I met a man. He was charming and funny. That same old story. Plus, he was in his forties and seemed so much more worldly. Unfortunately, he was also married. The affair lasted for almost a year. When we were found out... Well, apart from the disapproval of the town and the damage to Catherine's reputation, my mother was devastated. Our father had left her for another woman. I don't blame her for feeling it personally. Catherine was furious about that more than anything, I think. She forbade the man from ever speaking to me again. She even threatened him with curses, which of course she wouldn't have been able to do, but I heard that the head of the guard actually encouraged her on that threat. It definitely worked. Then she shipped me off. She gave me four hundred dollars and relocated me to Boston. One of my best friends from high school was here, so I guess Catherine thought that'd keep me occupied. That friend found me a roommate, I got a job, and I've been here ever since."

"Did you miss home?"

"Not then. It was nice to be with people my own age. And living in a city was exciting too. Plus, I was nearly as mad at Catherine as she was at me. Who did she think she was, sending me away? Of course, she was right. When I was older, I did miss home, but I thought Catherine was still angry with me. Even when I saw her, I thought she was pretending that she was happy to see me and happy for my success in Boston. So, I didn't visit often or for long. When our mother died, that's when Catherine said to me that she wished I'd come to visit more, and I realized I'd been foolish. It wasn't even home that I missed, but her. But so much time had passed. We weren't as close anymore. We tried to make up for lost time." Margaret turned away, a hand to her temple. Sasha picked up the other pieces of the tea set in turn to busy herself.

"Another thing. The man I had an affair with? He was Howie March's father."

Sasha's head snapped up. "What?"

Margaret nodded.

Sasha said, "Wow, I really don't think of Howie as having parents."

"After the affair was revealed, his mother..." Margaret paused. "Some stuff happened. She had to go to a hospital for a bit." Stuff happened. Was that the way people talked about Sasha's mother? Easy to step around the difficulties in the lives of strangers and near strangers. Years of pain packaged smoothly into "stuff happened."

But I like Margaret, Sasha thought and pushed down the bitter taste.

"I'm not proud of what I did, but I don't think Catherine and I were to blame for what happened with his mother. At least, Catherine definitely wasn't. I guess he couldn't blame his father or didn't want to blame his father if he could blame someone else for it. And I was gone. But what could he do? He was a teenager. She was a witch. She was *the* witch."

Margaret excused herself to take a shower. First, she insisted on getting Sasha a glass of water and sitting her down on the couch, pointing out some magazines on the table and the bookshelf in the corner.

Sasha thanked her and nodded. She flipped through one of the magazines quickly but tossed it back to the table and walked over to the liquor cabinet she'd noticed across the room. There was a bottle of vodka behind bottles of gin and whisky.

The bathroom door swung open behind her, and Margaret started to call out a thought, then said, "Oh, you wanted a drink?" She furrowed her brow.

"Is that okay?" Sasha asked.

"Yes, you can help yourself. I guess I thought it was a little late."

"Is it? It's been a rough day. I could use a drink."

Chapter Twenty-Six

Sasha woke up and had to remember where she was. It had been so long since she had woken up somewhere outside of her own house. What was she doing here? Seconds ticking by felt like hours, and she was sure Margaret hadn't come out into the living area yet because she was avoiding Sasha, regretting inviting her. The thought gnawed at her.

After Margaret had gone to bed, turning down Sasha's offer to sit down for another drink, Sasha had refilled her flask from the vodka bottle. She could replace the bottle when they were out the next day, she figured. Now, Sasha pulled her flask out from under her jacket and took several pulls. She laid the cool metal against her chest, where it soothed her.

When she pushed up to half sitting, she saw the vodka bottle still sitting on the living room table and picked it up to refill her flask.

She let her flask fall to the bed and walked to the window. It was snowing. A car crawled down the street, windshield wipers swinging back and forth. The buildings across the street were also brick. Sasha couldn't see in the windows, which she liked, because it meant people couldn't see her. She put a hand on her heart, to settle it. She would offer to go home that day, see how Margaret reacted.

Sasha heard a creak on the wood behind her and turned from the window. Margaret was bleary-eyed in the morning but smiling. "Ready for coffee?" she asked.

Sasha followed her into the kitchen, and her plans began to melt as Margaret talked, full of warmth, none of the awkwardness Sasha had expected.

Margaret shook grounds into the coffee maker. "I was thinking we could go to a museum today? Bill said he'd be interested in meeting us too."

"Okay, sure. I like museums." Sasha hadn't been to a museum in at least ten years and had mostly gone to them on school field trips.

"Great, I'll let him know," Margaret said with a big smile. "Now what do you want for breakfast? I usually have oatmeal." That sounded good to Sasha, so Margaret took down two bowls, poured oats and water into a pot, and put it on the stove, talking all the time about the different tourist spots in Boston, what was worth a visit and what wasn't. Snow swirled outside the window, and the smell of coffee filled the kitchen.

The Museum of Fine Arts, Boston was a light gray stone building with columns sitting above the main entrance. Snow continued to fall. Bill was meeting them inside, and Sasha didn't know what to expect.

He was there before them, a man of average height and gray hair, and waved when he saw Margaret. She nearly ran to him, and they hugged for several moments. Sasha hung back.

"Wow, it's good to see you," she heard Margaret say.

"Oh, kid, it's good to see you," Bill responded.

When they finally broke apart, they continued holding hands.

"Sasha, this is Bill, my boyfriend. Bill, this is Sasha, Catherine's friend."

"The famous Sasha," Bill said, stepping forward with his hand out.

"Famous?" Sasha said.

"I've been hearing about you non-stop since Margie's been away, every night over the phone. 'Sasha told me something great tonight.' 'Sasha and I had a good laugh today.'"

"Ah," Sasha said, but she found herself otherwise speechless. Her palms itched. She really needed a drink.

Margaret and Bill consulted a map of the museum while they waited in line to pay for admission, and then they insisted on paying for Sasha's ticket. "How about American Art?" Bill asked her. He absentmindedly massaged Margaret's neck.

Sasha thought maybe she should look away. Maybe she should walk away. She was infringing on their time together. But she said, "Sure."

They walked up a staircase lined with large colorful vases and jars. The stairs led to a quiet and dimmed rotunda, with carvings and murals on the ceiling.

"Have you ever been to Boston before?" Bill asked. The first galleries they walked through were art from the time of the American Revolution. Individual and family portraits in bold oils, and silverware, bowls and plates that still gleamed impressively.

"No," she said. It was an automatic answer, because she hadn't really been anywhere, but then she remembered. "Wait, yes." She had been ten years old. Her father still thought that Sasha may not turn out to be a witch. He wanted her, his only child, to go to an impressive college. David Hoffman had wanted to go to Dartmouth but hadn't been accepted. He had to go to Boston for a business meeting and took Sasha with him. It was the only trip Sasha ever took with her father.

She watched TV in their hotel room the first day while he went to his meeting, eating snacks out of the mini bar, and then the next day they drove up to New Hampshire. Sasha had liked the brick buildings nestled among the trees. But she wasn't interested in the library her father gushed about. David knew a professor, an uncle of a high school friend, who invited them to stop by his office. David grasped the man's hand warmly and pointed out to Sasha all the degrees framed on the wall. Sasha wondered where that professor was now. Probably dead. It was fifteen years ago, and David talked on their drive home about how the man had worked well into his eighties.

"When did you visit?" Margaret asked.

Sasha put a finger on the glass case surrounding a silver etched bowl. "It was a while ago. We were just here for a day. It wasn't a big deal."

"We'll call this your first official visit then," Bill said. They smiled at her. They were reaching out, inviting her into their life. It made her dizzy.

"Okay," she said.

"If you like paintings, we must take you up to the Sargents," Margaret said.

She'd follow them wherever they wanted to go.

They encouraged her to go at her own pace around the galleries. When their back was turned to admire a painting together, she tucked herself into a corner to retrieve her flask. A witch could disappear, in a way. She willed more energy into the rest of the room. Someone looking over the room would completely overlook the corner, so it wasn't that she was gone or invisible, just that no one would take notice of the space. She took a healthy swig, felt her whole body come alive as if flushed and warm. She took a second sip, to smooth the jagged edges that were creeping up within her and returned the flask to her jacket pocket. She told herself Margaret and Bill were happy to have her here, and she would be happy to spend this time with them. She allowed the energy of the room to flow as it pleased again and walked out of the corner.

She strolled among the portraits of American forefathers. There had been witches then. There had always been witches. None were depicted, though. Sasha wondered about these foremothers and fathers. Witches who wrote the volumes she and Courtney had on their shelves.

She turned a corner to the next room and came across something from her other foremothers and fathers. Silver finials gleamed softly in a glass box in the middle of the room. Finials to adorn the Torah scrolls. It'd been so long since she'd seen finials at all. She hadn't been to a synagogue in nearly ten years. She used to like when the rabbi took the scrolls out. She walked the aisles holding the scrolls, Sasha and her family following others to move down the row to touch the Torah, the rabbi walking slowly.

Sasha hungrily read the description: a New York silversmith, a Rhode Island synagogue, finials were called *rimmonim*, which was Hebrew for pomegranates.

Sasha didn't realize she had her hand on the glass box, until a voice said, "Miss, please don't touch the glass."

Sasha's hand jerked into a fist, her knuckles brushing against the glass as she yanked it back to her body. She turned around to see the guard. "I'm sorry," she said.

Back to oils. In one room, Sasha was surrounded by portraits of women. Still no witches.

There was one painting of a woman at a theater. Sitting on the balcony, seemingly alone, she wore a black coat and watched the stage through small binoculars. Women watching. Sasha didn't want to be watched by anyone most of the time. The other spectators were faceless, beige blobs. A man across the theater leaned over his box, his body twisted to face the woman, a slash of black across his face—his binoculars. He watched the woman. His face towards Sasha also. She, Sasha, a woman, a witch, watched a woman watching a performance, while a man watched the woman and her.

When she drifted away from the painting, she saw a woman

looking at her, who quickly turned away. Looking because she could tell she was a witch?

Sasha left the room. The next room was empty, and she took out her flask again, and took a long pull. She went to find Margaret and Bill. "Let's go to the Sargents," Margaret said.

The Sargents were large and lush and announced themselves by lounging back. They hung in a room decorated with fleur-de-lis wallpaper.

In one painting, a young girl stood with hydrangeas bathed in light. When Sasha moved closer, the flowers revealed themselves to be thick stabs of blue, white, yellow, and green paint. Sasha's hand trailed out towards it. She realized Margaret was at her side— watching after her? She pushed away a pang of annoyance. "I like the way you can see the brush strokes," Sasha said.

"Yes, it's an interesting style."

Sasha thought it so much more than interesting. "It's like he's saying, 'Here's the paint, here's how I did it, but I bet you can't.'"

Margaret laughed.

Bold colors, lush flowers, Sasha could enjoy this. She disappeared in a corner again and went to her flask. Sometimes Sasha drank when she was happy; sometimes she drank when she was sad, or bored. Often, the most overpowering and frequent reason to drink was simply for another taste of sharp, clean liquor. The reason of want. She drank to drink more. She was a drinker who cherished the drinking itself. With drinking, she was able to so quickly fill a physical and emotional want: the want of another glass.

The next room was larger, with recreations of American rooms from different periods. One from the 1880s was filled with golden details, Tiffany glass, porcelain. There was an oil painting of a woman in a silk raspberry-colored dress, pulsing to be bitten. It must have been a wealthy family, Sasha thought. And the Sargents also, the large portraits. Those families would have been wealthy.

The little girl surrounded by giant hydrangeas, the girls with the giant vases.

She turned from the recreated room and halted. She stood in front of a tall painting of a woman in a long plain white dress. The woman faced to the side, ignoring the viewer's gaze. The artist had a similar style to Sargent, but there was a hushed quality to the painting, as if it were a secret scene. She seemed to be outside at night, standing against a beige wall. Her arm raised up to her chin, her face lit softly. Sasha approached the label. *Aurora the Witch.*

She smiled, the witch before her. This was her ancestor—with very little information given about her—as surely as the Jews who'd watched the finials glittering while their rabbi read from the Torah in Newport.

Sasha wanted to touch the witch. To be with her. There was no one in the world but Sasha and Aurora, the witch. Who was she? Had she been one of the New England witches, a strong group, which ran into its troubles even before the bans? Sasha reached up. She was tall enough to reach the witch's raised hand. When she did touch the hand, there wasn't a warmth, as she had expected—so convinced she'd been about to touch another person. It was just paint, waxy, dry, smoothed out over the years.

"Miss." The voice sounded as if this wasn't its first call. Yet Sasha couldn't pull her eyes away from the painting. There were quick footsteps and then Sasha's hand was jerked away from the painting. The man, a museum guard, looked down at Sasha's bare wrist in his hand. "There is no touching the artwork."

"I'm sorry," Sasha gasped. "It's just... I just—"

"I'm going to have to ask you to leave."

She felt so tired suddenly. "No. Oh, please, no." He let go of her wrist but moved to guide her towards the exit. She sank to the ground.

"Miss?"

"Please, I won't do it again. Please, I'm here with my friends, but don't tell her."

The guard leaned towards Sasha and took a noticeable sniff. She shrank back. There were a few other museum goers in the room now. Maybe they'd been there the whole time. They stared at her, this crumple of black clothes on the floor. Aurora looking away on the canvas. "You're not in the state to be here." The guard spoke quietly, not unkindly, as if he was suddenly reminded of someone. "Come on, it'll be okay."

"You don't know that," Sasha said with a sigh. She realized she was sweating. Her mouth was dry. She leaned her forehead against the cool floor. She couldn't go for her flask. The guard shifted his weight and cleared his throat. "Okay," she said, pushing off the floor.

She browned out and came to on the museum steps. The snow was now a light chilly rain. She looked behind her, at a guard that was saying something to her as he walked back inside. It was a different guard.

She wrapped her arms around herself and walked down the steps. The bottom of her dress dragged through puddles. She saw she had a missed call from Margaret and called her back. She took a deep breath, and when Margaret answered, put on her cheeriest voice. "Hey!"

"Where are you?"

"I'm here. I stepped outside. It was kind of stuffy in there. I needed some air."

"Are you feeling sick? Do you want us to come meet you?"

"No, no, I'm fine. I'm taking a walk."

"Are you sure?"

"Yeah. I'll meet you back at your apartment," Sasha chirped, hanging up before Margaret could ask more.

There was a café down the street from Margaret's apartment. Sasha bought a cup of coffee and sat in a corner. She put her head in her hand and let her drink go cold.

She bought two more cups while waiting, dragging her wet hem behind her when she walked up to the register, before Margaret called and said they were on their way home. Sasha said she'd meet them there and left her half empty coffee cups behind.

The caffeine made her shake, especially her hands. Margaret kept glancing at Sasha as she took off her coat and hung it in her closet. "Is something wrong?" Did Margaret have to notice everything?

"I just had some coffee."

"Isn't it a little late for coffee?"

Sasha fought down a rush of annoyance. "I wanted it."

Margaret crossed her arms. "I don't mean to be accusatory, but are you drunk, Sasha?"

"I am not."

"Is that why you left the museum?"

Sasha tried to laugh. "I told you I needed some air. The museum was so stuffy."

Margaret frowned. "You stank of it in the Sargent room. I thought maybe... I don't know what I thought." There was this look in her eyes, that she was going to keep pressing on even though she didn't want to.

"What, because I drank some of your vodka? I'm going to replace it."

"Replacing it doesn't matter. This worries me."

"Why? We've gone and got drinks together."

"This is different. Why do you need to have a flask on hand? Do you always have one with you?"

Sasha squirmed. "It's just like..." She didn't know how to finish the sentence. "I wanted this visit to be perfect."

"I'm so happy to have you here visiting. It would be wonderful no matter what. I didn't realize you'd put this pressure on yourself. Was there something I said?"

Blood pounded in Sasha's ears. She muttered she was going to the bathroom. She locked the door and sat on the white tile floor, huddled next to the bathtub, hugging her legs to her body. She scrunched her eyes shut and laid her head on her knees. She wanted to see blackness or further, nothing.

Chapter Twenty-Seven

Sasha fell asleep in the bathroom. She woke up, the softness of the bathmat making way quickly to the hardness of the tile underneath. Her neck was stiff. She crawled to the door, listened for voices. She stood up slowly.

Margaret and Bill weren't in the living room, but their voices drifted through the apartment. The bedroom light was on, and the door open. She walked quickly, picked up her bag and her jacket, and walked to the front door. She only looked ahead, trying to walk quietly. She heard Margaret call her name, so she ran.

Margaret didn't follow her.

Sasha used her phone to look up directions to the train station. She considered calling Courtney. It was dark. She was cold. She wanted to talk with someone who cared about her but didn't want to answer any questions about how the trip was going.

After several blocks, and glancing behind her for Margaret, she stepped into a bar.

The bartender barely looked at her ID—he could refuse her service if he wanted—before handing it back and starting on her screwdriver.

The first sip settled her. The sweet tang of the orange juice, the bite of the vodka. Like a song, like a hug, like a smile from a friend, like home, like all she needed. She texted Courtney that she missed her and Marni and that she was coming home earlier than planned.

She ordered a second drink.

People came and went around her. She didn't notice Bill until he said, "Hello, Sasha."

She nearly fell off her chair. "You followed me," she said, looking around the bar for Margaret.

"No, this is my regular bar. I'm meeting a friend here." He shrugged. "Margaret's pretty torn up, though."

"Well, I'm going home to New York."

Bill nodded. "That's up to you." He kept standing, hands in his pockets. "We'd be happy to have you stay if you want to come back."

"No, I have to get going," Sasha said. She threw two twenties on the counter and pushed past Bill with her bag.

She kept walking. She checked behind her to see if Bill had followed her. He hadn't. Towards the train station, again.

There was an old homeless woman standing tucked in a doorway. She held a blanket wrapped around her and in her other hand shook a large plastic 7-Eleven cup, coins jangling inside.

Sasha knew there were homeless witches because Courtney had read an article about it. It was difficult to tell, as some homeless non-witches didn't have bracelets.

Sasha stopped in front of the woman. She steadied herself against the side of the building. "Are you a witch?"

The woman looked directly at her wrist, although it was covered by her jacket.

"Here's what I think of witches," she said and spat at Sasha's feet.

Sasha gasped and jerked backwards. There was laughter behind her. It was a group of young people. Maybe the woman had done it sensing an audience. "You disgusting old woman, I was going to give you money," Sasha hissed. With a flick of her wrist she caused the woman's blanket to fall to the ground onto piles of dirty snow. Sasha regretted it as her hand moved through the air, and even more so when it elicited fresh howls of laughter from the crowd. Sasha rushed off as the woman leaned to pick up her blanket, her knees bending with difficulty.

Marni was over, an orange mug of tea in hand while she flipped through a spell book. Courtney had taken out her ingredients and was going to let Marni help her make some potions. Then the headache started.

She'd had a lot on her mind the last few days, thinking about the coven, her place in it and in the town. Thinking about Marni and Sasha. She didn't want to leave them—not because then they wouldn't be a coven, as she had a thought creeping at the edges of her mind that she didn't care so much about covens anymore, but because she cared about them and wanted to continue being there with them, learning and thinking about magic. Then there was a fresh round of orders from clients and appointments stacking up for the next few weeks. Courtney thought that was causing the headache at first—her mind being pulled in too many directions. She kept readying ingredients, pulling open a garlic clove. But before they could start, she needed to sit down. Marni followed her to the living room, where Courtney lay down on the couch. Her forehead was damp with sweat.

"Maybe you should head home. I don't want to get you sick if I have something."

"Okay, do you want me to bring you to your room first?"

"That would be helpful," Courtney said.

Marni put an arm around her shoulders and steered her towards the stairs. Courtney gripped the banister all the way up.

Marni held onto her arm while Courtney eased into bed. I must seem so weak, she thought. She pulled the comforter up to her chin. Marni went to the bathroom across the hall and dragged the garbage bin in, placing it next to the bed. "Do you want a glass of water?"

Courtney shook her head. "I wish Sasha were here," she said.

"She'll be back soon."

"I worry that...I don't know, she'll disappear again." Courtney had been keeping these thoughts out of her mind, but being sick always made her think of the worst scenarios. She put a hand gingerly to her forehead, and then her cheek, both warm.

"What do you mean?"

"Sometimes she disappears for a day or two. I don't even know if she realizes she's doing it. You know how she's alone a lot of the time. I worry she'll disappear for longer."

"You live alone too."

"Yeah, but I have clients, a job. It keeps me busy, gets me out of the house. Sasha just found out her mom could've contacted her but hasn't all these years. And honestly, it's not even surprising that Deborah hasn't. And her father is completely free to call and visit, but rarely does. Losing Catherine was hard on her."

"What does she do when she disappears? Just get drunk?"

"I don't know." Courtney looked at her with a furrowed brow. "Do you think Sasha drinks a lot?"

"Kinda," Marni said.

"One of my friends from another coven said something about that. I didn't really notice before. Everyone was drinking, including me, but, yeah, maybe."

Courtney closed her eyes. Marni slipped out of the room and returned with a glass of water she put on the nightstand. She whispered, "Feel better."

CHAPTER TWENTY-EIGHT

Sasha arrived at the train station in southern Westchester county as the sun began to rise. Orange touched the horizon. She'd fallen asleep on the train and felt like a creature freshly cracked open from its egg. In the cab home on the highway, her eyes were still heavy, and she rubbed a finger against the window as she followed the scenery that zipped past. The driver had the radio on low.

She wondered if she'd overreacted to the fight with Margaret. It hadn't even really been a fight. Why had she cared that Sasha brought a flask, was drinking? That was it, though—she cared. Sasha's mind circled around the thought. People who cared about her cared about her being okay. She repeated it—she cared, she cared, she cared. But Margaret misunderstood about the drinking, Sasha considered. Maybe an older generation thing. She thought, I should call her. Later today, once she's awake.

The sun was up, and the sky was a gray blue with thin clouds. They sat at a light, and Sasha realized they were back in town, stopped on Main Street. The first stores were opening up, turning on the holiday lights they hadn't removed yet. She relaxed her shoulders, ready to be back on the streets she knew, the stores she knew, back in her own home. There was a knock on the window.

She jerked to. It was Howie, with a newspaper and his leather pad tucked under his elbow, a smile on his face. He waved and gestured to roll down the window. "Friend of yours?" the driver asked, obliging. Cold air stung her face.

"You're back early," Howie said.

"How do you know this is early?" She hadn't said how long she'd been gone for.

He smiled wider. "I'm not surprised to see you."

He waved again, stuck his hands in his pockets and walked away.

Not surprised? What was that supposed to mean? Had he known? Had Margaret told him? No, she remembered Margaret's story about her affair with his father. But maybe he'd let bygones go for his own reasons. Now her mind circled this new thought.

Sasha rubbed her eyes. "I am so tired," she said.

Chapter Twenty-Nine

Sasha showed up on Courtney's doorstep, looking like she hadn't slept the night before.

"Ugh," Sasha said, brushing past Courtney as she opened her door. "I am so done with Margaret."

"Hello yourself," Courtney said. She'd spiked a fever the night before, now gone, but her energy was still low.

Sasha spun around, a big grin on her face, a notch frantic, too big of a smile, really. "I'm so happy to be back. You have no idea," she said, grabbing Courtney into a hug.

"Did something happen?"

Sasha sighed. She stood with her hands on her hips. "I don't even want to go into it. She's all controlling. I'm an adult. I don't need someone bossing me around."

"Did you have fun otherwise?"

They walked into the living room. "No, I hated the whole thing," Sasha said with a wave of her hand.

"Well, I'm glad to have you home."

Sasha flopped onto the couch. Courtney also took a seat. "If I seem out of it, I'm a little under the weather."

Sasha searched her friend's face. "Yeah, I can see it in your eyes. You look really tired."

Courtney sighed. "Yeah, I'm okay. Marni was over. She put me into bed. I felt silly, like a kid."

"Yeah, Marni's nice like that. Do you need anything today?"

Courtney shook her head. "No, I'm okay."

"You know Marni's going to go to college, though?" Sasha asked.

"Yes. Wow, right? I'm almost a little jealous."

Sasha had never had an interest in college, but Courtney had always been good at school. "Maybe if it works out for Marni, you could go too. It's not just teenagers in college, right?"

"Yeah, my mom once had a student getting her degree in her seventies. It's a little intimidating to start anew," Courtney said.

"What would you want to study?"

"I don't know. I would've done pre-med if I went when I was younger. It could still be useful knowledge. I wish there were a witch school, so I could study witch medical theories and history."

"That'd be something," Sasha agreed.

Courtney sunk into thought. Sasha folded her arms over her torso. They sat together in comfortable silence. Sasha replayed what Howie said that morning and thought about Margaret, if she would try and reach out. Courtney thought about a different version of her life where she wasn't a witch, and she went to college and then med school.

A sudden ringing jerked them out of their reveries. It was Sasha's phone. She took it from her pocket, hands shaking. The thought of it being Margaret gripped her. Excited, scared. "Oh, it's Faye," she said, and picked up.

"Hey, hon. How's life?" Faye chirped.

"It's okay. How about you?"

"I'm good, but listen, something kind of crazy happened. Pooja's met a man."

"What do you mean?"

"Like she met this guy. And they've gone out on dates."

"What?" Sasha spat. Courtney raised her eyebrow in question.

"Crazy, right? They've only been on three dates, but Pooja seems to really like him. Anyway, I called because he's invited me to join them for a night out with his friends. I want to go, but, you know, I don't want to be surrounded by a bunch of non-witches. Would you and Courtney want to come with?"

"Huh," Sasha said, looking over at Courtney. "I'm at her place now. Text me the details and I'll let you know."

"Perfect, it's tonight. Hope I see you!"

Sasha hung up and turned to Courtney. "You got plans tonight?"

CHAPTER THIRTY

The bar was in White Plains. "If it's awful, we can leave and go to Gargoyles," Sasha said while they were in the cab. They slowed down on a street alive with light.

"My heart is beating, honestly," Courtney said.

"Isn't it always?" Sasha laughed.

Courtney waved her away. "You know what I mean. Is that embarrassing?"

"No, you don't get out much lately," Sasha said, nudging her in the ribs to show she was teasing.

Sasha paid the driver, and they rushed out, arm in arm. Music and laughter poured out of the bar.

Inside, she scanned the narrow, dim room. The interior was heavy on wood. Holiday lights still curved around the bar and the windows. Sasha counted eight TVs, showing several different sporting events.

She spotted Faye and Pooja among a group of people standing around two high tables. Faye saw them and ran over. She was resplendent in glittering black silk that billowed behind her as she moved towards them. Several men and women watched her as she went.

"Hey," Faye shouted over the music. When she was in front of them, she lowered her voice. "They're okay. The guy's been friendly enough so far, but, like, the rest of his friends act like they've never even met a witch. It's so boring."

"Maybe some of them haven't," Courtney said.

"That's so boring."

"Which one is the guy?" Sasha asked.

"The tall one with the beard talking to Pooja."

Pooja wore a dress that looked like it was made of black cobwebs gripping her body. She had on gold eyeshadow and dangling gold earrings. The man Faye described stood close to her while his friends chatted with them, and he seemed to glow from Pooja's proximity.

"Let's get a drink first. You'll need it," Faye said. They walked up to the bar. "I've had two glasses of white wine already. Someone told me I'm like their mom," Faye said with a shrug.

"Are you going to get anything?" Sasha asked Courtney.

"Just a soda. You?"

"Thought I might switch it up. Maybe a mojito. I'm in the mood for something sweet and bitter."

"Now, that'd be like my mother," Faye laughed.

A bartender approached, and Faye leaned over to give her order. Sasha thought of how her own mother had liked to drink red wine or champagne. If her mother were a drink, though, she would be something that vanished as you went to drink it.

Sasha ordered her mojito, and Courtney got her soda. They followed Faye back to the group. Pooja gave them both a big hug, and her guy, whose name was Evan, shook their hands. "More witches?" he said with a laugh. "You really travel together."

"I know, right? It's almost like being part of a group is key to the way our community runs itself," Sasha said.

He didn't hear her. He was already watching Pooja again. The way he looked at her actually did remind Sasha of her mother and the way she used to look at Sasha's father.

Faye tapped the back of Sasha's hand, "I thought it was funny."

Some of Evan's friends edged closer to them. One of them leaned over, "Faye, are these more of your friends? Introduce us."

Faye sighed softly but put on a smile and introduced Sasha and Courtney. They shook hands, and waved, and Sasha was nearly done with her drink by the time pleasantries were finished.

"Are there a lot of young witches?" one of the women asked. Sasha thought her name might be Melanie? Melissa?

"Relative to the whole group of us in Westchester?" Courtney asked. "Not in particular. There have been studies kept by witches over the years. It seems that magic, being natural, keeps track of itself, and there's a steady balance of it. There aren't people coming into their powers every generation in every small town, and sometimes multiple people in a generation come into their power in one town, like Sasha and me."

"You do have a very young coven," Faye said.

Sasha didn't want to talk about it in front of these people, these non-witches. Their coven and details about it, even easily discernible details such as their age, were private topics. "Faye, I like your dress. Is it new?"

Faye twirled with a smile. "Thank you, darling. It is. I picked it up on sale the other week."

"Is there a rule that you have to wear black?" one of the men asked. Sasha definitely didn't remember his name.

She rolled her eyes. Courtney, in a dark red dress, took the question as seriously as the other. "No, but it's traditional. I like to wear colors, but I know a lot of witches like to stick to black. And it's always in fashion, so it is always available."

The group nodded along thoughtfully. But they started breaking off into pairs and trios, chatting with one another and checking their phones. Courtney's thorough and logical breakdown of questions seemed to demystify being a witch.

Sasha looked down at her empty glass. "If only we were at Gargoyles, I could summon a new one."

"I know, but we can't exactly bring him along with us." Faye nodded at Pooja and Evan, now slightly separated from everyone else. Evan whispered something in Pooja's ear, and she laughed.

"Come on. I want to stay for a bit," Courtney said.

"Why don't we try and talk to other people around? They may be more interesting," Faye suggested.

"I'm certainly ready to return to the bar," Sasha said.

A group of men was eager to entertain them at the bar and Faye gave them a dazzling smile, but when one of them looked down at her hand, resting on the bar with only a strand of rhinestones on her wrist, and then found Courtney's wrist with only her watch, he nudged his friends and jerked his head to a different part of the bar.

"Have a nice night, ladies," one of them mumbled, and made an almost formal bow.

"They noticed we didn't have bracelets on." Courtney grasped at her wrist. "I should've brought a sweater."

"Why?" Sasha said.

"Come on. You know it's just easier sometimes not to deal with peoples' reactions."

"Would you want to talk with someone who doesn't want to talk to a witch, though?"

Faye swirled her wine thoughtfully. "For some people, witches are a draw."

"I wouldn't want that either," Sasha said.

"Leave the flirting to me and Courtney then," Faye laughed.

"Do you really want to date someone who's not a witch? A man or a woman?" she added for Faye, who dated men and women.

Courtney sipped her soda. "It does feel like a narrow needle to thread. But there has to be some people out there that are open to dating witches, but aren't going to fetishize either."

"Sure, the ones that want to use you for your magic."

"That's not everyone either," Courtney said quietly. She thought about reaching out to squeeze Sasha's shoulder. She wasn't sure if Sasha heard her. "It's just such a small pool to date only in the witch community."

"And that can get messy too," Faye said. She shrugged, "Right now, I'm not looking to date someone, but some flirting? Maybe a kiss or two. Maybe more. Why not?"

"I know they say it never works out, but that can't be true of every time a witch tries to date a non-witch. Pooja seems happy," Courtney said.

"This is only their third date. They could go on three thousand dates and still it'd go wrong somehow."

Courtney held up her hand. "I don't want to argue about this."

Faye looked between the two. "I guess I just can't understand" —Sasha waved her hand at everyone in the bar—"this."

Courtney looked around, at all the people laughing and talking and watching each other, and them too. "People get lonely. And I've never even had a boyfriend."

Faye piped up. "I've dated non-witches, one in high school. He was okay."

"After you came into your powers?" Sasha asked.

"Before and after, yeah. Or during, I guess. He was a bit weirded out by it but was getting used it. I broke up with him, though." Faye put her wineglass on the bar next to Sasha's drink. "I have to go to the bathroom. I'll be right back." She walked to the back of the room, glittering silk trailing behind her, adjusting her rhinestone bracelet as she went.

Sasha took a sip of Faye's white wine. She rarely drank white wine. This one had a hint of citrus.

"What would your mother be like if she was a drink?" She asked.

Courtney looked down at her hand, her fingers drumming a

beat on the bar. "'Sweet and bitter.' Did that seem ungenerous to you?"

"We don't know her mother."

"That's true. I guess my mother would be something serious. What's a serious drink?"

"Cognac," Sasha offered. "I've never seen anyone under the age of forty-five drink it."

"Yes, cognac. That makes sense. What about yours?"

"Smoke in a glass."

Sasha laughed and Courtney laughed too, the way only friends are allowed to laugh about something sad together. "It'd be very dense in the glass too, so that it seems really there, really present, when you're looking at it. But when you try and actually have the drink..." Sasha snapped her fingers. "Gone."

The bartender finally made his way back to them, and each ordered another drink. "Should we go back to the group?" Courtney suggested.

She grabbed Faye's wine glass, and they walked over to Pooja. Faye returned behind them, she took her glass and tipped it towards Sasha, who met her with her own glass. A satisfying click and they each drank.

"How's Marni been?" Pooja asked.

"She's good. She's great," Courtney said.

"She's going to go to college," Sasha said.

"I kind of wish I'd gone to college," Faye said.

"Witches don't?" Evan asked.

The four witches looked at each other. "It's not traditional," Courtney said finally. "And the spells witches learn and do— they're not taught at schools."

"I took a couple classes at WCC, just sitting in—marketing, writing, economics," Pooja said. "Some of the instructors had comments about it. They had these ideas of witches that were very old-fashioned, like we all lived in a hut in the woods. One of them said, good for me for joining the twenty-first century. I finished my classes, but I didn't want to take anymore. It'd be nice if there were witch colleges."

"That's what I was saying to Sasha the other day," Courtney gasped, flinging her hand out. "I'd sign up for classes in a second."

"Same," Pooja said, with a small smile.

"How did you two meet, by the way?" Courtney asked.

Pooja and Evan each gestured to the other, then laughed. "We went to the same coffee shop, and I'd noticed her. She always had this...I don't know, aura around her. I swear the place hushed when she walked in. One day we were standing in line together and I managed to think of a somewhat non-contrived way to start talking to her."

"Which was?"

"'Crazy weather we've been having lately,'" he said, and laughed.

"Has the weather been so crazy this winter?" Sasha asked.

"Not at all. It was pretty bad, but somehow I made it work."

"You're just lucky I had noticed you too," Pooja said.

They continued on with their story. They were beginning to thread together their lives.

Sasha slipped away to return to the bar. She drummed her fingers, waiting. "Sasha?"

She turned, thinking it was one of Evan's friends. She hadn't recognized this voice, but she knew his face immediately. She was rocketed back to summers years ago. Upstate New York, muggy, buggy, wading into murky water, clay between her toes. Sneaking off to the woods. Running, laughing, reaching out for him. Had he been this tall then? His face was older, less soft, and more crystalized. He wore his hair differently and wasn't wearing glasses. He was better dressed, but everyone had been dressed casually for the retreat. Even her own youthful casual looks had been misguided attempts at chic sportswear.

"Dillon." She breathed his name out as if she'd been holding it in for ten years.

He was pale with black hair and dark eyes. She'd always felt they matched. They were similar in other ways, more important than the way they looked. His mother was a witch. Deborah had called Joyce Goldberg "hippie witch" with her long bohemian skirts, her layers of bead necklaces, and her ukulele, and made sure to never have a conversation longer than five minutes with her. But Joyce waved enthusiastically every time Sasha strolled over to their spot on the small expanse of sand that was next to the man-made lake. "I saw your mother in the fall. Did you know that?"

He smiled. "I did. 'That Sasha Hoffman, as beautiful as ever.'"

Sasha blushed. "What are you doing here, anyway? Do you live around here?"

"No, I live in the city. But a couple friends of mine have relocated to the suburbs recently, after getting married, so here I am. And here you are. Of all the bars in all of Westchester County. What is the beautiful Sasha Hoffman up to these days?"

In ten years, she'd come into her powers, attacked Juliet, her mother had gone into exile in her spot, Catherine died. She said, "I'm here. And we have a new coven member, Marni. And I was named coven leader." Sasha glanced at Courtney, still talking with Pooja and Faye and some of Evan's friends.

Dillon put his fingers in his mouth and whistled, "Congratulations. Well deserved." He went to take a drink, then paused, "So, Catherine...?"

"Cancer. A couple years ago."

He closed his eyed. "I'm so sorry. That's awful."

"How about you? What do you get up to in the city?"

"I'm working, like everybody else. I'm thinking of moving, though."

"Where?" Sasha said quickly, nearly a demand.

"I don't know yet. Working and drinking—sometimes that feels like that's all people do in New York."

"People like those things." She pointed to the beer bottle in his hand.

"True. I guess I'm bored with it, though. Call it my quarter-life crisis."

The bartender approached them, and Sasha ordered a screwdriver. "Let me get your next round," she said, putting her hand on Dillon's arm. He nodded.

With their drinks, Dillon stood up and took Sasha's hand. "Let's go sit in the back. There are some booths there."

Sasha followed him. People moved aside for them. She wanted to slow the moment down, but it was over in less than a minute.

At the booth, he took her hand again across the table. She grasped onto his like a lifeline.

"I really want to know what's actually going on with your life. You don't have to smooth anything over for me," he said.

"Honestly? It's boring. My life is so boring. My mom left. Your mom probably knew about that?" He nodded. "It's just been me and Courtney until Marni came along a couple months ago."

"I'm sorry about your mom."

"Yeah." Sasha took a drink.

"You know, there's something about this age, the mid-twenties. I've got tons of friends feeling bored with their lives. Me too, like I was saying."

"Maybe you're right," Sasha said. She noticed her drink was nearly finished. "They barely give you half a drink here. I'll be right back."

When she returned, she held up her drink and let it go. The glass floated in the air between them. "Here's my question of the night. What would your mother be as a drink?" She plucked her drink out of the air.

"Hmm, maybe a cider?"

Sasha laughed. "Yeah, I see that."

"What do you think yours is?"

"A glass full of smoke."

Dillon chuckled, but Sasha was growing bored of her punch line. "What would you be as a drink?" she asked.

"Probably a beer. I mean, that's what I usually drink. You know what you are?"

"What?"

"A double shot of vodka."

She grinned, but thought to herself that he hadn't seen her in years. But then, had she really changed so much?

"Why do people like to do that? Put ourselves into these categorizations? 'Which character from whatever show are you?' 'Which element are you?'" he asked.

"Fire."

"You?"

"Yeah," she smiled.

"Definitely."

He threaded his fingers through hers and rocked her hand back and forth.

She took a giddy sip of her drink.

"Maybe wanting to be part of a group?" she said.

"Probably. 'Look at us. We're all fires.'"

"I feel like you're more air."

He laughed.

She continued, "Maybe people want to describe themselves easily."

"Yeah, it's too easy. It's outside of them," he said.

She had the sudden desire to meld her brain to his. She leaned over the table and grabbed his head in her hands, tipped it forward and touched her forehead to his. "There," she said.

They used to lay on the forest floor, cool in the shade, and her body, exposed, prickled with goosebumps. Once she took a drink from his flask while lying down, and some liquid trickled into the notch of her neck. He licked it up and she squealed.

Her drink was finished again.

. . .

Out of blackness, out of nothingness. Dillon was saying, "Your mother did something completely selfless for you. How is that not love?"

His face swam in front of her, and while she was only returning to consciousness, she launched into her next thought fully formed. "I don't know that it was selfless. My father was gone. Sometimes? I wonder if she was avoiding being alone with me." And how had she formed this thought without consciousness? A thought thought thousands of times before so that it was etched onto her insides, onto her tongue, ready to spring forth.

Dillon scratched at his ear. "Well, I hate to be dark, but if she didn't go away, she still wouldn't have been alone with you. You would've been in exile instead, correct?"

Sasha laughed. She rammed the heels of her hands into her eyes. "Yeah, yeah, you're right. I don't know then. She just doesn't make sense to me. I found out they can write from exile, and she never has. She could be dead."

"Yeah, I know that's difficult."

"You don't know." The room swam, jerking back and forth.

"Sasha, I've never even met my father. He hasn't wanted anything to do with my mom or me since she got pregnant. And for all I know, he could be dead."

"I'm sorry. I'm an idiot. I forgot."

"It's okay."

Sasha disappeared into nothingness again. When she resurfaced—in what could have been seconds, could have been minutes—she had her head on Dillon's shoulder and was crying. He was rubbing her back. She lifted her head, put her hands on both sides of his face, and whispered, "Seduce me." She kissed him.

She sunk back down, resurfaced to still kissing him. She wanted to be in this moment of kissing him forever.

CHAPTER THIRTY-ONE

Who was that guy?" Courtney asked in the cab.

Slumped low in her seat, Sasha looked up at her with wide eyes. "It's Dillon."

Courtney shrugged.

"Dillon Goldberg. For two summers I went to this witch family thing upstate with my mom, and he was there with his mom. Remember, she was at the board party in the fall? Joyce Goldberg? Dark hair? Talks a lot?"

"Oh my god, yes. He was the summer boyfriend!"

"I can't believe he was there tonight. He said he's going to come visit."

"Oh yeah? How do you like the taste of that crow?" Courtney laughed.

"No, no, no, this is different. His mother's a witch. He's part of our community."

"Tangentially."

"I don't know what that means." Sasha felt so tired suddenly.

"He's still a non-witch. I'm just saying. Anyway, I may have met someone too."

Sasha jerked around to face her more fully. "Who?"

"One of Evan's friends. We exchanged numbers, and we're going on a date."

"Was he one of the ones asking those dumb questions?"

"No! He seems sweet."

Sasha opened the window. They were on the highway, air streamed in. "I'll have to meet him. See how he is," she said, raising her voice above the air.

The next morning, Sasha cleaned her home. It wasn't the most impressive feat given she used magic, but a thin blanket of dust had built up on the surfaces.

She felt a push for forward motion. She felt restless, that the day was open to be filled, not just to exist in. She made a Bloody Mary, and drank it standing at her front window, watching.

There was a woman across the street pushing a stroller. She didn't look much older than Sasha. Maybe they could get along. Maybe Sasha could be her witch. She wanted to belong to people. But when she pulled open the front door, the woman was waving to another woman, walking towards her. They stopped, hugged, and began talking with ease. They already had each other. Sasha closed the door quietly, hoping they hadn't seen her.

Chapter Thirty-Two

When Sasha's phone started ringing, she figured it'd be Courtney. But the screen said *DILLON*. She burst into a smile. She didn't generally write someone's name in all caps on her phone. She couldn't remember taking his number, but she could tell she had been excited, that every touch of the keyboard had been a stab of exclamation.

"Hi," she said.

"Hi," he said. "I've been thinking about you."

"Good," she said.

He laughed. "When do I get to see you again?"

"How about tonight?"

"I like that idea."

He took the train up from the city that evening and took her to a restaurant in a neighboring town. Another quiet, small town with large houses and roads carving through the trees. "Nice place," she said, touching the white linen tablecloth. Their table was right by the window, and she looked out at the trees with their spindly branches, shadowy in night.

"I think this is our first official date," Dillon said, picking up the drink menu. "Should we get champagne?"

"Definitely."

Her hand itched to hold his again. But she didn't know how to move like this, inside of this potential linking. He reached out to take her hand and gave it a squeeze, then brought his hand back to the menu, not even looking up.

The champagne flutes were tall and narrow. She watched the waiter pour her drink, pausing for the bubbles to subdue. When the waiter left, she held her flute and said, "To Pooja being into some guy and Faye getting me to come to that random bar."

They drank.

"Do you do this a lot?" she asked.

"What?"

"Go on dates."

He shrugged. "Sometimes. I was seeing someone last year if that's what you're asking. What about you?"

"Come on, you know it's not like that for witches."

"Depends on the witch, though. You're beautiful and charismatic. I can only imagine men throwing themselves at your feet."

Sasha rolled her eyes. "Not my thing."

"I'm glad to be the exception then."

Courtney had read about witches dating on her forums. Witches volleyed back and forth on online dating and whether or not to mention that you were a witch. *Some people are into it*, one witch brought up. *Some people are* too *into it*, another pointed out. One witch warned that her friend had always written that she was a witch on her profile, and it *just led to trouble*.

Courtney had tried online dating before. She had read that black women were the least matched with of every racial group, and her experience showed this. When she wrote that she was a witch, she got even fewer matches. She hadn't stayed long on dating apps any of the times she tried them.

The good thing about meeting Pete in person was that he already knew she was a witch.

She arrived at the coffee shop early, ordered her drink and then wondered if she should've waited. She picked a table by the door and sat in the chair, adjusting the light blue wool sweater she'd chosen for the date. She was worrying if this had been the wrong outfit choice—had it been as scratchy the last time she'd worn it?—when a familiar face walked in. Liana, from the Mount Vernon coven. Courtney jumped up to greet her, surprising the younger witch, who hadn't noticed her yet. Liana laughed when she saw who it was and took Courtney into a big hug.

"Courtney! What are you doing down here?"

"Actually, I'm about to meet a date."

"Okay! Look at you, getting out there. Where did you meet?"

Courtney had talked with Liana before about dating as black witches. Liana dated women and was active on various dating apps.

"At a bar."

"Cute, cute. Are you drinking again?"

"Not really."

"Good for you, sticking with it. Listen, I don't want to mess with your mood before your date, but I heard you didn't get coven leader."

Courtney crossed her arms, feeling the scratchiness against her hands now. "Yeah." She didn't know what else to say.

Liana shook her head. "That's bullshit. I like Sasha as a person, but I don't know who the board think they're fooling with that pick. She's drunk as a skunk at every board function I see her at. It's like they only ever pick one of us if there're no white witches as an option."

Courtney thought of the black witches she knew who were coven leaders in Westchester, there were currently two in the whole county. "You're right. But I don't know what to do."

"Yeah, I don't know either and I'm not trying to put this on your shoulders. They're the ones that did a crappy thing to you. We deserve better."

Courtney nodded. "We do."

"Well," Liana laughed, "there's some serious talk before your date. I gotta grab a coffee and go, but we'll talk more about this?"

"Yes, please," Courtney said, and they hugged again. Courtney went back to the table she'd staked out.

When Liana left, coffee cup in hand, she gave a big wave, and called out, "Good luck!" It made Courtney smile.

Pete arrived, and he was more awkward than she'd remembered. He approached her and opened his arms for a hug at the same time she held out her hand to shake, as if he were one of her customers. Maybe she was awkward too. They both said, "Oh" and she held out her arms, and he put out a hand, then quickly shifted back to a hug. Once he had his drink, they sat down together. They both smiled, and as Courtney launched into a question, he started saying something, and they both laughed.

"Sorry, go ahead," he said.

"I was just going to ask how's your week been?"

"Yeah, it's okay. It's been a little crazy at work honestly. We found out on Monday that the company is planning some layoffs."

"Wow. Do they do that a lot?" Courtney asked.

He shrugged. "I've only been there for a year, but I don't think so."

"Are you nervous?"

"A little. No one wants to lose their job, and since I'm still kind of new, I'm probably in the line of fire. I've got some really good experience here, so if I do get let go, maybe I can find something else with a better salary, which would be nice. But it's still nerve-wracking. I guess you don't really have to worry about getting fired as a witch." He paused. "Is that okay to say?"

"It's fine. I guess no, I wouldn't be fired in the traditional sense, but like anyone else running their own business, I could lose customers."

"Yeah, but who would want to stop working with you?" He looked down after saying it and quickly glanced back up at her to gauge her reaction.

Courtney was about to launch into all the reasons a customer could want to stop ordering from her, when a voice in her head said, He's being flirty, not literal. Instead, she said, "And you and Evan work together, right?"

"Yeah, we started at a similar time. He's a great guy. Pooja's great too. How long have you two been friends?"

"Pooja's wonderful. She's so sweet and a talented witch," Courtney said. "We've been friends for years. She's a bit older than me, and we first started meeting at these official events that our board throws. Then my friend Sasha and I, we got to know Pooja and Faye better seeing them out at Gargoyles, which is this witch bar."

"That other witch that was with you, the tall one? You can keep up with her?" he said with a laugh.

Courtney sat up a bit straighter. "What do you mean?"

He cleared his throat. "It's just that you said you don't drink very much. And she was kind of ordering a lot. But she seemed nice."

Courtney nodded slowly. "Everyone was drinking," she said, but she had seen Sasha going for drinks very quickly after getting her last one, and had thought, Did I used to go so fast also?

"Yeah, totally. I'm sorry. I didn't mean anything against her. She seemed nice," he added again.

"Right."

"Uh, you said you have an older brother. What's he like?" Pete asked, and the conversation lurched into this new direction.

When the date was over, Courtney agreed to a second date, and they hugged again. "I'm really glad we met," he said.

She smiled and said, "Me too. I'll see you later." She wasn't sure how she felt about him, but she had had a good time.

Chapter Thirty-Three

Courtney put her hands on her hips and observed the dining room. Marni and Sasha stood one on each side of her. Sasha wore one of her favorite dresses, a long black silk bias cut dress. Courtney wore a light green collared shirt and a navy pencil skirt with a gold belt. Marni wore a gray wool sweater and black dress pants. There were four places set. The dishes were white with a solid navy lip, and the napkins were navy linen. Courtney examined the crystal goblets she had chosen.

"They don't quite match the plates, do they?" she asked.

"I like it," Sasha said.

Courtney reached out for one of the goblets. "You like for things to not quite match."

"Who wants something perfect?" Sasha countered, and Courtney paused.

"Well, I guess he is your guest."

"Have you seen him since the bar, Sasha?" Marni asked.

Sasha grinned. "As a matter of fact, yes." And now he'd be here with her, and Courtney, and Marni.

Courtney summoned the dishes form the kitchen, the meal

they'd put together of chicken thighs, asparagus, sweet potatoes, and a salad. She began arranging the table.

"You didn't want to invite Pete?" Marni asked Courtney.

"We've only hung out once. We're hardly in love," Courtney said.

"We're not in love either," Sasha shrieked, and the other two laughed.

The doorbell rang and Sasha shot towards the front door. She heard Marni giggle behind her. She didn't care if her enthusiasm showed. Courtney followed behind. Dillon wore all black also—Sasha wondered if he'd done it purposefully to match her—and held a paper bag with two bottle necks sticking out of it.

"Hi," she said.

Inside, he held out his hand to Courtney, who grasped it in a firm handshake. "It's a pleasure to meet you. Thank you for inviting me to your house. I brought this for you." He took out one of the bottles, a pinot noir.

Courtney took the gift. "Thank you. And it's my pleasure. I've always wanted to meet the man that could sweep Sasha off her feet."

Sasha smacked Courtney's shoulder playfully, "Stop! I'm not... It's not..."

But Dillon laughed and moved on to introduce himself to Marni.

Marni and Courtney sat on one side of the table, and Sasha sat next to Dillon. She nudged her chair to be a little closer to him and quickly squeezed his thigh under the table. Courtney offered the salad bowl to Dillon first.

"So, your mom's a witch?" Marni asked.

"Yes. And a musician. She teaches lessons and she even has some customers she makes instruments for."

"Do you play any instruments?" Courtney asked.

"She taught me piano and violin, but I never was as talented or passionate about music as she is."

"What do you think is more important to do something? Passion or talent?" Courtney wondered.

Dillon thought about it. "Passion, I think. Otherwise, you won't stick with it."

"I was going to say talent," Marni said with a shrug.

Courtney started piling salad onto her plate and passed the bowl to Marni. "And what is it you do?" Courtney said.

"I'm a graphic designer. So, we're a family of artists in each of our own ways."

"Is your father a type of artist too?" Marni asked.

"I don't know. I don't know him."

Marni apologized.

Dillon waved it aside. "It's okay."

"Did he leave because she's a witch?" she asked, someone still trying to figure out what it all meant to be a witch, someone who'd been told growing up, in ways spoken and unspoken, to be skeptical of witches.

Sasha bit down on her tongue and Courtney nearly spit out the sip of water she'd taken. "Marni, honestly," Courtney said.

But Dillon said, "It's fine. Probably a lot of people think it when they hear about my family history. My mom doesn't really talk about him much. It might be that. She called him once an 'unserious person' so maybe he didn't want a kid with anyone."

Marni nodded thoughtfully.

Courtney changed the subject. "And you live in the city now?"

"Yeah, makes it easy to visit."

Dillon helped himself to the chicken. Sasha had cooked them, cursing through the entire process, even with the help of magic. "How about we crack open that wine?" he said.

"Sure," Courtney said. She held a hand above the bottle, and the cork flew into her palm. As she poured, Dillon turned to Sasha, "And I brought this for you." He pulled the second bottle out of the bag. It was a tall bottle of vodka. "For some double shots," he said with a smile.

Sasha grasped his shoulder. "You're so sweet. Marni, can you get me another glass from the kitchen?"

Sasha laughed with abandon as she poured another glass of wine, the vodka bottle half empty sitting between her and Dillon. Marni laughed at Dillon's story too, but Courtney only smiled briefly, watching Sasha's wine fill towards the brim. She drank her tea from one of the orange mugs, which she'd brought out to accompany dessert.

Sasha pushed her hair out of her face. "I have to come into the city to meet your friends. They sound hilarious."

"Yeah, we get up to some adventures. You'd all be welcome to come down. My one friend, Adam, he's wild. We went to Atlantic City for his birthday last year, and we're at this bar on our first night. He forms this, like, blood bond with this real tatted up middle-aged guy while playing darts, then tried to convince him to play William Tell with darts. The guy luckily just laughed at him. It was a great trip."

Courtney mumbled, "Sounds kind of dangerous."

At the same time, Marni said, "What's William Tell?"

"He was this guy," Dillon said, "who shot an apple off his son's head for some reason? I can't remember. But that's the game. Like this." Dillon stood up and grabbed Sasha's hands, pulling her up. She erupted into laughter again.

"It's dangerous," Courtney repeated louder. Only Marni looked to her.

"Sasha goes over there," he said, spinning her around and sending her towards one end of the dining room. "And I..." He scanned the table and picked up one of the empty orange mugs and took it with him to stand against the wall, opposite Sasha, who was bent over laughing. He balanced the cup on the top of his head, laying his hand on top of it to keep it steady. "Would stand over here. And Sasha would shoot it off, but obviously we would never—"

Sasha pointed her hand dramatically. "Take that!" and the mug burst into thousands of small fragments with a loud crack. Marni yelped, and Courtney bolted out of her chair. Sasha was still laughing, as Dillon shook his hand, laughing too.

"You almost got me."

Courtney ran over to Dillon and the scattered dust-size remains of her parents' mug, tears at the corner of her eyes.

Sasha caught her breath and joined her, "I'll fix it, Court."

"How?" Courtney demanded, turning to her. "It's not in two or three pieces. It's completely destroyed."

"I'll bring them together in a rejoining spell," Sasha said, holding up her hands to perform the spell, but Courtney knocked them down.

She said, "The pieces are too small, and you'll end up messing something else up."

"I'm so sorry. This is my fault. I'll replace the cup. I can find something similar online," Dillon said.

"These were my parents'."

"At least you still have a couple more," Sasha said.

Courtney gripped her hands into fists, her fingernails biting into her palm. "That is not the point, Sasha. This is inconsiderate of me, of what my family left for me. What if you break another one? What if you take one out into the back yard, start wandering through the trees and leave it somewhere we—you—can never find it again?"

"I wouldn't do that," Sasha protested.

"You just did. People are right. You do drink too much, and you don't pay attention to anything except the next glass."

Sasha stepped back. "So, you don't drink for a couple months, and you get yourself onto a real high horse. Because you're so perfect, you've never made a mistake."

Courtney took a deep breath and closed her eyes. "Get out of my house."

Sasha turned and stomped towards the door. Dillon started after her, "I'm so sorry, honestly…"

"Dillon, come on," Sasha yelled from the foyer, grabbing their coats from the closet, and he drifted her way, head down.

"Wait," Courtney said, and when he paused, she picked up the vodka bottle and held it out. "Take this with you."

Dillon took it. Marni stood up and walked towards Courtney. After the front door shut, she said quietly, "Do you want help cleaning up?"

Courtney shook her head.

In the morning, Dillon traced his finger across Sasha's back and shoulders. "How are you feeling?"

She rubbed her eyes. "Fine. Did you sleep okay?"

"Yeah, I just meant about last night?"

She buried her head into the nook between his shoulder and neck, breathed him in. "What about last night?"

"You don't remember?"

She pushed away and propped herself up on her elbow. "I kind of remember. Courtney was mad about something?"

Dillon ran his hand over his chin. "Yeah, we, uh, broke this coffee cup that apparently belonged to her parents. She was pretty upset."

Sasha put a hand over her face. "Was it orange?"

He nodded.

She squeezed her eyes shut. "Shit."

"Yeah, I felt bad. We left after that."

She looked over to the dresser, to the glittery pink heart Courtney gave her in high school. "To brighten up your day," Courtney had said with a laugh when she handed it to her after a coven meeting.

"I'll have to call her."

He nodded, and she pressed against him again. He wrapped his arms around her. "Let's go somewhere," he said.

"Don't you have work?"

"It's Saturday."

She laughed. "Yeah, let's go."

Dillon grabbed his phone to consider destinations, and Sasha wondered downstairs. She rummaged through her fridge to see if she had makings for Blood Marys. Hadn't they been talking about Bloody Marys the night before?

She heard him walking down the stairs and turned around. He leaned against the wall. "How about Burlington? We can drive up through New York and stay the night?"

"I love it," she said, holding her hand out to him.

Chapter Thirty-Four

Sasha wanted to set off for Vermont and find a place to stay on the side of the road as they drove, but Dillon, chuckling, said they could find someplace online. He booked a room at a bed-and-breakfast before they were dressed. "We don't want to get stuck without a place to stay."

Once they arrived, she admitted that he'd made a nice choice. Entering their room was like walking into a forest. The wallpaper was an abstract pattern of various shades of dark green, and the velvet curtains were a deep shade of blue. The furniture was made up of sinuously curved wood and two tall bouquets of thin brown branches sat bundled in dark gold vases on the fireplace mantel. Later, she would totter out of bed, drunk, the world spinning, to touch the branches, and find they were fake.

Sasha kicked off her shoes and eased onto the bed.

"You're not ready to sleep, are you?" Dillon teased.

"I'm getting a preview for later," she said.

"You want a preview?" Dillon leaned over her, and with a hand brushing her cheek, kissed her. He pulled back, briefly pressed their noses together, and brought their bags to the closet.

They found a restaurant for dinner a block away, decorated

with an emphasis on the rustic aesthetic with exposed wooden beams and juniper and pine wreaths on the walls. The waitstaff all wore buffalo plaid shirts tucked into blue jeans. Once the host seated them and walked away, Dillon said under his breath, "I'm almost surprised they're not all wearing mini maple syrup bottles on chains around their neck."

"What do you mean?"

Dillon gestured. "It screams, 'Hey tourists, you're in Vermont!' But I guess we're those tourists they're trying to reel in."

"I don't mind being a tourist. I never go anywhere. Where should we go next?"

Dillon opened the menu and started reading it. "I thought maybe we could find a bar with some live music. How does that sound?"

"No, I meant, I like being here, somewhere else, with you. I'd do it again."

He looked up at her. "Sorry, I didn't even realize... Yeah, we could...I don't know, go someplace else another weekend."

She couldn't read the tone in his voice. "I know banned states make things more difficult for me. I'm sorry."

He shook his head. "Don't apologize for their bullshit."

She swallowed the rest of what she was going to say. She was touched by his understanding of their situation—of course he got it, having grown up with it—but still she could not decipher his reaction to her suggestion. He seemed to be reading the menu now with a determination not to look up at her again.

Their waiter arrived, introduced himself as Ryan in a chipper voice with a big smile, and took their drink order—a dark beer for him and her screwdriver. Dillon started noting items on the menu that might be good. The center of her palms sweat, and she looked around to see if their drinks were being made. When their waiter returned, she hadn't even looked at the menu. She held her hand out for her drink as he walked up to their table.

"There you go," Ryan said, with a laugh.

At the back of her mind, she noticed that people didn't look at her wrists when she was with Dillon. She wore a three-quarter sleeve shirt; her bare wrists were there to see if someone wanted to look.

"How's the chicken noodle soup?" She asked.

"Hearty!" Ryan answered.

"I'll have that."

Sasha gulped at her drink, watching Dillon make his order. She placed her glass in front of her on the table, but continued to grip it, a shield in order to continue conversation. She didn't know whether to advance the traveling conversation or not but couldn't think of a single topic to shift to.

But Dillon spoke first. "So, what did Courtney say?"

Sasha relaxed her grip on her glass. "When?"

"Haven't you talked today? You wandered off at the rest stop. I thought you were going to call her to talk about last night."

Sasha rubbed her entire face. She had gone to a bench half ringed by trees at the rest stop. But she had just leaned back, raising her face to feel the thin sun. "No, I don't know what to say."

Dillon picked up the fork, tilted it back and forth touching each end to the tabletop. They both watched it. "Yeah, it can be awkward to apologize," he finally said.

"It's not just that. I want to talk to her in person." But the thought of seeing Courtney made her feel lightheaded. When she saw Sasha, would her face fall? Withdraw? She probably wouldn't howl or hiss at Sasha. She might cry though or shake in anger. She didn't remember what happened the night before, how Courtney had felt then was a blank to her, and this separation and unknowing between them pitched her anxiety even higher.

She shook her head. "I'll do it when I get home, I promise. Let's talk about something else."

Dillon nodded, and started talking about work, a new project he'd started, the co-worker that was annoying everyone else, and how his manager almost caught him looking at job listings on his phone that week. They were laughing again. She ordered two more drinks during dinner. She had a perfect early buzz. When they left, she felt as if she barely touched the floor, floating smoothly towards the door.

The host at the restaurant told them a bar two blocks away sometimes had dancing. They found it and Dillon ordered a drink for each of them. Sasha downed hers quickly, watching several couples dancing to the band covering 1980s hits with enthusiasm. She grabbed his hands, guided him to the dance floor. He held her around her waist, and she slung her arms over his shoulders. Sasha felt like liquid, silkily dashing across the floor. A woman with an Irish accent dancing near them started repeating to her companion, "She was fragrant. She was so fragrant."

Once Sasha tripped, but Dillon grabbed her, pulled her up and close to him. "Are you ready to leave?" he whispered into her ear.

"No," she said. "Never."

CHAPTER THIRTY-FIVE

Courtney had not been able to make the mug whole. The pieces were too small or some of them had fallen onto Dillon's hair or sweater and he'd left with them—she didn't know.

She stared out the window of Ella's living room. There was a willow tree in the backyard that she usually loved. Even in the winter it had sweeping, dramatic branches as it held court in the middle of the well-manicured lawn, now a splotchy pattern of yellows in the cold. She watched it with no emotion. There was a shifting in the silence, and she realized Ella had asked her something. Ella, her cup of coffee in hand, her legs crossed at the ankles, watched her expectantly.

Courtney's cup sat on a coaster on the side table, and she picked it up. "What was that?"

"I asked how you've been? It's been a while since we've got together."

Courtney sighed. "I've been better."

"Tell me what's on your mind," Ella said, taking a sip of coffee and placing it down on its coaster.

"Sasha has been"—she gestured with her open hand—"trying me lately."

Ella looked down at her hands, resting in her lap. "Yes, well, I know Sasha's a good friend of yours, but I haven't always seen the version of her that you see."

"She has her good sides, but it's felt different since I stopped drinking."

Ella opened her hands to the ceiling, "Of course. That has always been my issue."

Courtney nodded. She took a sip of the coffee, a hazelnut flavor that Ella favored.

"I think I was still drinking when you and Sasha came into your powers, but not for long after. I kept with it for so long, years, before I had to make my first admission to myself, that beer wasn't good for me. But of course, I still wanted to drink. So, I switched to wine and martinis. And I was okay for a while with them. A couple more years to drink." Ella paused, the seconds stretching out, spooling out slowly, almost gently. She stared out the window, thinking about how a cabernet sauvignon tasted. Not even her drink. But it had been her last drink.

Courtney let her stare, until something brought her slowly back to the moment.

"Sometimes I'm even jealous of Sasha. I knew that I was in trouble, the way I was losing control of myself. I know that it is trouble. But I still wish I could just go and get completely plastered. Just one more time. You fool yourself for so long that there's this point you can be at just before you tip over into unconsciousness, when you're having so much fun and laughing so much, and that you'll know to stop yourself when you're there. That you'll be able to stop yourself when you're there. And that *that's* all you need to be at—that bliss point." Ella's eyes glistened. "God, I wish I were able to have one and stop there. If I could stop at one, I could stop after a couple, get to that bliss point. See! I'm already bargaining. If I really could go back, I would've started drinking beer again at the end."

"I wouldn't have figured you for a big beer drinker," Courtney said. The two didn't talk often about Ella's sobriety.

Ella laughed. "I get that a lot. Goes to show you can't help who you love." She looked out the windows again. "I don't know if Sasha is even at the point of trying to bargain. The 'I'll just have two drinks tonight' period. Occasionally you will only have two and so you think, 'See, I can limit myself. I'm not an addict.' But most of the time, two becomes four so easily and with such delight."

"I don't know," Courtney said. "We don't really talk about it."

"What happened? This time—that has you so off-kilter?"

Courtney told her about the dinner and the destroyed mug. Ella nodded as she listened, and when the story was finished, she said, "I'm sorry."

Courtney looked at her hands, remembering how she cried when they'd all left, told herself to have a good cry to let the emotions out, and then she'd fix the mug. And when she couldn't fix the mug, she covered her face and sobbed. "She hasn't even apologized yet."

"I feel for you in that regard. But what also concerns me is the irresponsible use of magic. What if she hurt him with the spell?"

"It would've been awful," Courtney said. She had not considered this possibility and did not want to follow that path too far. "She's an irresponsible person. She took Marni to a bar to drink, bad enough, but she ended up missing school the next day because of it. She ripped up a ticket from the Witches' Guard and then Howie March harassed me about it in the grocery store. I saw her accidentally break a piece of stone in her backyard patio last year and didn't smooth down the broken piece—which would have been easy enough with or without magic—and then cut herself when she was walking barefoot the next week. And then she still didn't smooth it for another month! I don't understand why the board picked her."

Ella raised her eyebrow and opened her mouth to speak.

"Well, I do," Courtney cut in. "But I don't know that I can get over this disappointment."

Ella nodded. She leaned back on the couch and allowed the statement to take its space in the room. "It's important to me that you're here, helping me build a future."

"Suffer now for a better future?" Courtney said with a sigh, and Ella steepled her hands beneath her chin. "They always make it sound so brave in historical accounts, but what if I don't ever get to see the better future? Shouldn't I get to live and know joy in my own life?"

"Where would you go?"

The question deflated Courtney. "Sometimes I dream of going down to North Carolina, where my family lives."

"It's a banned state," Ella said sharply.

And now it was Courtney's turn to nod and create a silence for the two to sit in. She thought about leaving, but where would she go? So she had to stay.

"What do you want to do. What's a better future here?" Courtney asked, and she could hear a petulant, childlike tone creeping into her voice.

Ella leaned forward. "It's not just for here, but it could start here. Think of the power we have, our magic. And yet we're so limited. What am I doing with my life? Planning parties? Making ice sculptures that can move? Tropical flora that lasts the afternoon no matter the weather? It's nice to see my clients happy, sure, but what if I could do more? If you could do more? If we didn't have to be confined to these little uses. These trivial, pretty things."

As she talked, her eyes shone brighter and brighter, and her words latched onto Courtney.

Chapter Thirty-Six

When Sasha returned home on Sunday, she ate lunch and poured a drink. After she finished, she leaned back in her chair, staring at the kitchen wall. She hadn't heard from Courtney all weekend, but Sasha hadn't texted her either. She started a load of laundry, emptying her travel bag and picking up discarded clothes from her bedroom floor. She had another drink and walked around the backyard, tossing fallen branches into the woods behind the house. She switched her laundry to the dryer. She decided to rearrange the furniture in the living room, floating the couch and the chairs and tables in the air and shifting them around with a wag of her finger.

She hated the new arrangement and moved it all back.

The light was beginning to leave the room, and she thought, Well I better go now. She changed coats twice, worried they were not giving the right message of contrition, and walked to Courtney's house.

When Courtney opened her front door, they stood and stared at each other for six seconds. Then Courtney stood to the side and said, "Okay, come in."

They walked into the living room and sat down opposite each

other. "You'll have to excuse me if I don't offer you any tea or coffee," Courtney said.

"All right, I deserved that," Sasha said. She looked down at her hands. "I feel like shit. I'm sorry. I know those are your favorite mugs and I can't believe I destroyed one. I messed up." She breathed in deeply through her nose, trying to hold back the tears, and continued looking down, unable to meet her friend's gaze.

"I'm pretty upset," Courtney said quietly.

"I get that. You're totally right—"

"I'm not done. You get so drunk that you forget about me, about the things that matter to me, or even my presence if I'm not in front of you. I had to chase you down at the Halloween party. And that hurts too, being forgotten."

They sat in silence. Once Sasha felt she could speak without starting to cry, she said, "I didn't know that."

"I'm not surprised."

Silence again, the soft ticking of a clock in another room crept in. "I'll do better. I won't drink as much, and so it won't be like you said because I don't want to forget about you."

"Sure," Courtney said with little enthusiasm. "It's worth trying."

Sasha shifted in her seat. "Do you want me to get you a new mug?"

Courtney shook her head. "No, don't bother."

"You're still upset with me."

Courtney sighed. "What if you weren't leader anymore?"

"I never wanted to be leader, and I don't care about being leader now. If we could do something to get the decision changed, I'd be glad."

"Okay, I'll talk to Ella. See if anything can be done."

Sasha nodded. "You were mad at me about that."

"I wasn't. I was just mad, in general, mostly at the board. I guess some of it got funneled towards you even if I knew it wasn't your fault."

Sasha stood up and started pacing around the room. "I get that. And I don't want that or anything else to stand between us."

Courtney agreed. Sasha wanted to stay, sit, and tell her about the trip to Vermont, but she sensed the conversation was done. They would need some space to let things settle before they could laugh and have a normal conversation. They said goodbye, and Sasha walked home.

Chapter Thirty-Seven

Courtney was brightness incarnate their next meeting. Ella said she was going to talk with the rest of the board. "You know it would make me so pleased to see you as coven leader," she had said over the phone Sunday.

Courtney woke up every day that week with a smile on her face and put on her brightest colors. It made Sasha smile to see her like that, pulling out stacks of books again, flipping for relevant spells and stories.

But Courtney didn't want Sasha to be happy about things between them yet. She was getting used to seeing only three of the orange mugs when she opened her cabinet, but she kept thinking, *Careless, careless of me and what's important to me.*

Since they returned from Vermont, Dillon was quieter, texting less and taking longer to respond to her texts. She managed to find out —feeling like she was wringing information out of him—that he was going to come up to Westchester on Saturday to see some friends.

Who? She typed.

He responded, *I don't think you know them.*

It was such a definite statement that he'd put a period at the end of it, not something he usually ended texts with.

Sasha pushed forward. *Can I meet you there?*

He told her he'd text her the address of the bar when they decided on one.

She stood up and shook her hands out and paced around her living room. She walked one way and picked up the rock that was linked to Marni's locker. She hadn't looked at it in several weeks, and the hall was empty of students. She walked the other way and picked her phone back up, checking if he'd texted again, even though she hadn't heard the message ding. She repeated this pattern back and forth for the rest of the day, adding trips to the kitchen for a drink. On her fourth trip to the kitchen, she thought of what she'd promised Courtney. But she wasn't out, and Courtney wasn't there, so there was no danger that she'd feel forgotten—not that Sasha really understood what she meant by that.

Sasha wanted to ask Dillon when she first woke up on Saturday about where they were going, but she waited until the afternoon. She called him, and as the ringtone pulsed, she thought, Will he pick up? He won't pick up. Please let him pick up. She held a drink next to her for courage.

He picked up. She tried to scan his tone, but he sounded same as ever. "You've had a busy week," she said.

"Yeah, work's been putting me through the wringer," he said.

"I'm glad we're seeing each other tonight."

"Yeah, me too."

The friend was someone he worked with who lived in Yonkers, and he would text her the address of the bar when they got off the phone.

Several minutes after hanging up, her phone dinged. He'd just texted her the bar name. "He can't even look up the address," she mumbled.

She began pacing again. When she looked at the rock, the hall was dark. She stood staring into the gray high school wall papered with posters, a deluge of exclamation marks in various fonts fighting for attention.

She tried on every dress in her closet, discarding them on the floor. As she went through more and more options, she began yanking them off her body with force. When they all lay in a pile at her feet, she sorted through them, and finally decided on a black strapless mini dress, which she put on with black tights and low black heels. She called a cab and pulled on her wool coat.

She couldn't find Dillon at the bar, which was crowded even though it was early. The crowd was dressed casually, and some people turned to look at Sasha. She went to call him, but stopped when she opened her recent calls list. Below his name was Margaret's.

It was an outgoing call from last Saturday night.

"Hey." She looked up, dazed, and it was Dillon, holding a full pitcher of beer and a stack of plastic cups. He held out an arm to hug her and she walked into it, still gripping her phone. "You found the place, great. I'll show you where we're all sitting."

She followed him, glancing again at the screen, wondering if maybe she'd misread, and it would turn up a different name this time. But it was still Margaret Darley.

It was a large group, about ten people including Dillon. "I guess grab a chair?" he said.

She took a chair from another table and scraped it across the floor. The woman sitting to Dillon's right moved her chair over for Sasha as Dillon introduced her to the people directly around them, and also mentioned the names of the rest of the group. Sasha didn't take in any of them. The woman didn't move the chair over enough for Sasha to get close to the table. Dillon took a plastic cup from the stack and poured her a beer. "You know what, I'm going to go get a screwdriver," she said.

When she returned with her drink, Dillon was in the middle of a conversation, looking away from her. Sasha sat. When he paused, she said, "Did I call anyone Saturday night?"

His friends laughed and shouted to each other around them. "What?" he said, leaning his head closer to her.

"When we were up in Vermont, did I call someone?"

He thought. "Yeah, actually you did. A family friend, I think? You said you thought of her because she lived in Boston."

"Did I talk to her?"

"I thought you got her voicemail because you didn't say anything, just were sitting on the couch with your phone to your ear and then hung up. Did she reach out?"

"No. Never mind," she said and took a drink. "Can we go somewhere else?"

"We'll probably go to another bar after this. Chris said there's a new place that's doing karaoke tonight."

"I meant can you and I go someplace else." She finished her drink.

He put a hand on her thigh. "Chris invited me to hang out tonight. We've been meaning to for a while, so I don't want to leave right away."

She opened her mouth to respond, but he turned back to the other conversation, and she pushed out of her chair and went to order another drink. She drank that one sitting at the bar, hunched low. She ordered another drink and returned to the table.

She set her drink down and wrapped both her arms around Dillon. He laughed a bit at the sudden hold, patted her arm. But she kept her arms there, willed them to be stone, to make the two of them into a sculpture. He tried to ease her off him.

"So much affection," he said with a laugh. And then in a lower tone, "What's going on? Why are you acting like this?"

"Like what? A caring girlfriend?" At the last word, she noticed him furrow his brow. She brought her arms down. Hadn't he said they were a couple?

He cleared his throat, and she picked up her drink. "Why are you drinking so much?"

"Since when is two drinks so much?"

"Two drinks in less than ten minutes?"

"Wow, I didn't realize you noticed me enough to keep track of my drinking."

"I…" He trailed off. "Never mind."

She glared at him. "Why don't you say what you were going to say?"

"I just sometimes think it's been a long time since we've known each other."

"What the hell does that mean?"

He shrugged. "I don't want to push this right now. I don't totally know what I mean, and you're drunk."

"So are you!"

Neither of them said anything for several seconds.

She stared into her glass. Was it a coincidence? His bringing it up right after Courtney had the other day? Maybe they'd planned it. "You're working together." She shook her head, "Why? Why are you doing this to me?"

"Doing what?" Dillon asked.

But Sasha stood up and walked to the door. She kept on expecting him to grab her arm.

He did text her when she was in the cab. *Uh, do you want to talk about this?* It read.

She typed out a response, calling him a liar, a witch fetishist, and a liar again. She erased it. She wrote, *Uhhhhhhhh, no.*

She put her phone down in her lap, took a deep breath, and unscrewed her flask.

Her phone dinged. She grabbed the phone, sloshing vodka onto her lap and the seat. It was a text from Dillon. *Wow. Okay.*

She threw her phone across the back seat, it smacked against the door. The driver glanced at the back, "Hey."

"I know," she snapped, "I know, I'm sorry." She took a pull from her flask. She didn't care if the driver saw. She remembered trying to hide the flask from Margaret on the highway with the cop. Had Margaret told Courtney about what happened in Boston? Did Margaret know Dillon's mother through Catherine? Were they all planning these confrontations together?

Stuck in her thoughts, plummeting downwards, she left the cab without paying. The driver yelled after her, and Sasha snapped to consciousness briefly to give her two twenties. It was too much to continue being in interaction with another person, and Sasha ran inside, not even caring to get the change.

She locked, bolted, and chained her front door and threw herself onto the couch. She held up a hand and summoned a glass to her. She lay on her couch, held the glass balanced on her chest. Her thoughts swirled darkly in her mind. Who did Margaret think she was burrowing into Sasha's business?

Sasha took her phone from her pocket. Margaret picked up on the third ring. "Sasha, I'm so glad to hear from you," Margaret said.

"I bet," Sasha said.

"Excuse me?"

"Who do you think you are, Margaret? I don't need your, like...your condescending preaching. And I don't need you spreading your assumptions about me to my friends. Things are going to be better with the coven now. We're making changes. Courtney's going to be leader like she should've been."

"Okay, but I'm really not sure what you're talking about. I haven't been in contact with your friends."

Sasha wavered.

"Are you okay, Sasha? I've been worried. And then you left a voicemail on my phone this weekend, but it was fifty-two seconds of silence. I wasn't sure what to make of that."

Sasha hung up the phone. Margaret called back, and Sasha ignored it. When Margaret called again, Sasha shoved her phone under a pillow.

Chapter Thirty-Eight

Lying in bed in the morning, Sasha remembered their fight from the night before. She tried to fall back to sleep, return to unconsciousness, but her mind pulsed too strongly with thoughts. In the bathroom, she stared at her reflection in the mirror. She stared until her features disconnected from representing someone named Sasha Hoffman.

"You idiot," she said to her reflection, the shapes of skin she had become. "You complete moron. No one wants to be with you. Why would he?" She had let herself hope, and she had let herself believe that there was something between them, a growing togetherness. She lay her hand, splayed out, over her reflection, and cracked the glass. The initial crack was loud, and then it splintered gently, reaching out beyond her fingers to the edge of the mirror, refracting her shapes further beyond recognition.

The wind howled that night, and her house lost power. She giggled, mid-sip. Her neighborhood lost power a couple times each winter. She usually brought out her lantern and lit large candles, but she sat on her couch in the dark, finished her drink, then poured another one.

Dillon didn't text again.

The next day, when Sasha felt an itching for human interaction, she grabbed the rock from the shelf. It seemed like years ago Courtney bewitched it. It even seemed another life when she'd stared at the dark hallway Saturday afternoon.

She set the rock on the coffee table so she could watch it while lying on the couch. She tried to read into Marni's face when she had her locker open. Marni was often alone, and she kept her eyes down. In the afternoon, a small girl with a large backpack chattered away while Marni nodded, taking out binders and notebooks. They were discussing an essay for English class and which books they were going to choose for the topic. Sasha didn't recognize any of the books they listed. This was more Courtney's area of knowledge. Sasha wondered if Marni talk about her schoolwork with Courtney. Courtney knew books. Courtney knew potions. Courtney even knew more about Sasha's family history than she did. Sasha didn't even have a particular skill in magic, the way Courtney did with potions, Pooja with written spells, Faye with transformation spells.

When Marni wasn't at her locker, she listened to the mishmash of conversations, footsteps, and other lockers being opened and shut. There were long strands of silence during class periods. Sasha loved those times especially, piping in silence from somewhere else calmed her. Silence its own sound.

Sasha drank straight vodka and ate Saltines. The sugar in orange juice made her jittery.

Margaret called again. She left a message. "I'm trying..." There was a long pause. Margaret's silence layered over the school's silence over the silence of Sasha's home. "I don't want you to feel like I'm judging you because I'm not. I'm just worried about you. What's going on, Sasha? Please call me back."

Courtney called also on Wednesday, and Sasha texted her, *Hey, I've been sick. Must be the flu.*

Later that day there was a knock on the door. Sasha glanced that way, then closed her eyes and turned into the couch. When her phone dinged, it was Courtney, saying, *I left a couple containers of chicken soup outside for you, my dad's old recipe. Feel better.*

Sasha drifted in and out of sleep. The first real human interaction she had in days was when she visited the liquor store. "What day is it?" she asked the cashier. Her voice felt weird in her mouth.

"It's Friday," he said.

In her kitchen, she took one bottle and put it in the freezer and tucked the rest into her pantry. She hadn't had a drink yet that morning, but she didn't pour one. Margaret and Courtney and even Dillon apparently would have expected her to. She wished they could see this, that she didn't have to have a drink. But why should she have to make notes of drinks had or not had?

The silence from the high school hallway tunneled into her ears, wrapping itself around her insides. She ran into the kitchen, downed three shots' worth from the bottle. She decided to make some toast, and maybe heat up some of the chicken soup after if she felt like it. She preferred to think of it as "the chicken soup" and not "Courtney's chicken soup." She took the meal back to the couch, where she saw Marni was at her locker.

A boy approached Marni. She turned to him. "Yes?"

He pulled self-consciously on his backpack straps. "Howie March wants to talk to you."

"What?" Marni said. Sasha grabbed the rock.

"You have to go see him," the boy rushed out.

"I wasn't not going to."

Sasha lurched up, suddenly in a rage, forcing a pair of shoes on, grabbing a coat. She dashed out the door.

Where would Howie be meeting Marni? And what stupid farce was this? Sasha called a cab to take her to the school. She skulked around the entrance and the parking lot, looking for Marni or Howie. She ran to the side entrance and looked in through the gym doors, but there was only a teacher setting up for class, rolling a metal cart full of basketballs to the middle of the gymnasium. When Sasha got back to the front doors, the cab was gone.

A student walked past Sasha towards the parking lot. Sasha grabbed her shoulder and the girl gasped. "You need to drive me into town."

"Um."

"I'm a witch. I'm your witch."

"O-okay, I guess. I was going that way anyway."

Sasha followed her to her car. Catherine would have requested the ride more eloquently. Catherine would not have even had to request the ride or point out that she was the student's witch. Maybe Howie wouldn't have even demanded a meeting with a young witch without Catherine being there or knowing about it first. He probably would have, Sasha decided. Maybe he hated Catherine more than he hated her.

Sasha didn't say anything to the student the whole drive. It felt like the longest four minutes of her life. She didn't know what to say to the girl. And when she thought, I should ask her name, it seemed the moment for introductions had passed. She pursed her lips, both desiring to say something and to keep quiet.

When the student pulled over to the corner of Main Street, Sasha jumped out of the car. She called behind her, "If you ever need anything..."

Sasha ran to the guard headquarters and burst through the door. The young guard at the front desk stood up with wide eyes.

"Where is she?"

He didn't say anything but glanced at a door. Sasha pushed through the door, dashing down the hallway she'd walked years before. There were muffled voices coming from Howie's office. The guard ran after her. "Mr. March is in a meeting," he yelled.

Sasha opened the door. Howie sat at his desk, and Marni sat on the other side, scrunched up with her hands folded in her lap, making herself as small as possible. They both looked up at her with surprise. Howie's face changed to annoyance, Marni's to relief.

"You can't—" Howie started.

"No," Sasha said definitively, pointing her index finger at Howie's face.

The guard behind her gasped. She heard him grab something off his belt. A gun? A taser? "I am pointing at him as a normal human would to emphasize a point. Not to cast a spell."

No one spoke. The room was still, at a pause. Howie watched her. He cleared his throat. "It's okay, John."

Sasha stepped forward and laid a hand on Marni's back. Her touch seemed to work as a tonic or permission, and Marni unfolded and shot up, bag in hand, at Sasha's side and poised to go.

"You do not call meetings with Marni or anyone else in my coven without talking to me first and without me being there."

Howie smirked and stood up also. "Your coven, Sasha? I hear that's soon not to be the case anymore."

How did he know? She had talked about it with Courtney only the week before. Courtney had said she'd talk to Ella about it. Was it Ella? Another board member? She kicked over the chair that Marni had been sitting in moments before, the metal clanged against the wall. Marni flinched.

"Mind your own damn business," Sasha snapped. She grabbed Marni's arm and pushed past the young guard, back down the hall and towards the exit.

Howie yelled after her, "You are my business, Sasha."

Chapter Thirty-Nine

What was that about?" Sasha demanded once they were outside, and down the block, Marni pushing her bike.

Marni sighed. "I don't even know. He was all, 'I just want to get to know you. I want to be friends.'"

"Ugh, he's disgusting."

"Yeah, he's a creep. Umm..."

"What?"

"It's just...my dad thinks I should go along with Howie. Keep him 'on my side.'" Marni took one hand off the handlebars to make air quotes.

Anger gripped Sasha's chest. "Howie is not on your side, and he never will be. He gave me all those lines about being friends when I was your age. It's the excuse he can trot out while he makes my life hell. That it's all for my 'good,' that he wouldn't do anything to give me trouble because we're 'friends.'" Sasha stared at the sidewalk. "What your dad said sounds like something my father would say, honestly. They think it's like the business world, like it's office politics, and you need to have people in your corner. But the guard's entire purpose is to keep us in line, intimidate us, and punish us."

"I know," Marni said quietly.

Sasha took out her phone to call another cab.

"Lock up your bike in town. We better go to Courtney's."

Courtney was surprised to see them. She thought Sasha was still sick, and Marni was supposed to be in school. She let them inside without comment and crossed her arms, waiting for an explanation.

"Howie pulled Marni out of school to have a one-on-one chat with her about 'being friends.'"

Courtney looked wide-eyed to Marni for confirmation. She nodded. "When did he tell you he was going to do that? Why didn't you tell me?"

"He didn't tell me," Sasha said. "I saw a student telling her to go see him on the rock. Anyway, he knew that there was talk about my not being leader."

Courtney's jaw dropped. "How did Howie know that?"

"You tell me!"

"What's that supposed to mean?"

Sasha threw her hands in the air. "I don't know. Did you tell him? Did Ella?"

Courtney stepped back. "I definitely didn't nor would I ever. We need to have a united front here. Please don't get paranoid. And I have a hard time believing Ella would."

"Does the board have to tell him?" Marni asked.

"I don't think so," Courtney said. "Just when there's a new coven leader."

"And no one on the board would have a personal friendship with him, right?" Sasha asked. Never had the words friend and friendship made Sasha so nauseated.

"That would be very surprising. Did either of you tell anyone?"

Marni shook her head no.

"Margaret. I ended up calling her the other day and said something about it."

"But I thought you said she and Howie hated each other," Marni said.

"Maybe it's all a front," Sasha suggested.

"That seems a little paranoid," Courtney mumbled.

"Who else could it be?"

Courtney had no answer. Marni shrugged.

"Maybe he's planning something," Sasha continued.

"But why now?"

"Because we're finally a coven again?"

"Maybe." Courtney turned to Marni. "You don't have to meet with him, at least not alone. Call one of us next time."

"I already told her that," Sasha said.

Days passed. Things returned to a certain normalcy. Sasha still hadn't heard from Dillon, but Howie didn't demand or request any more meetings. Ella sent Courtney an email that their coven's case was "under review." Courtney and Sasha were talking regularly again.

They were having dinner at Courtney's house on Saturday night when Marni said, "Oh, I saw that woman in town today, Sasha."

"Which woman?" Sasha asked.

"What was her name? Catherine's sister?"

"Margaret?" Sasha leaned back in her chair.

"Is that weird?" Courtney asked, fork poised over the take-out container she'd opened. "You did say she still has some friends in the area."

"What was she doing? Was she with someone?" Sasha asked.

"She was just walking on Main Street," Marni said.

"In what direction?"

"I don't remember, sorry."

Chapter Forty

Sasha disguised herself in her only white shirt, an Oxford shirt from the back of her dresser drawer, and a pair of navy pants. She put on an old peacoat she rarely wore and finished the look with large black sunglasses.

She had two rocks from her backyard in her pocket. She called a cab.

She didn't know where Margaret was staying, and she realized she hadn't asked her where she was staying the last time she visited.

The cab dropped her off on Main Street. Sasha kept close to storefronts, hoping their awnings would provide some cover. It was during school hours and before lunch hours, so only a scattering of people walked in and out of stores. Sasha walked in the direction of the guard headquarters, her heart pounding loudly in her ears.

She recognized Margaret's car a block from the headquarters. Sasha looked around but Margaret was not in sight. She crouched next to the car's back door, placed her hand flat on the handle and whispered a spell. The door sprung open.

Sasha slipped inside the car. She held the smaller rock clutched in her fist. Margaret kept a clean car, so she couldn't hide the rock among papers or bags. She looked around again. There was a woman on the other side of the road. A younger woman walking a large yellow dog.

Sasha wedged the rock in between the seat and back cushions of the middle seat, which were luckily gray. She hovered her hand quickly around the edges of the rock and the cushion, trying to blend the rock in further, smoothing out its texture. She surveyed her work and decided it would have to do. She was out the door, slamming it shut.

The dog barked, suddenly lunging at her, teeth gleaming and strands of spit flying towards her with each deep bark. Sasha gasped, falling backwards against Margaret's car.

"No, Cooper, no!" the woman yelled, pulling the dog back with the leash. "I'm so sorry, Sasha. I don't know what came over him."

Up close, Sasha realized she knew this woman. Marni's neighbor Brooke.

Sasha cleared her throat and pushed off the car. "Yeah, strange." She took a step away from the dog. "Well, good to see you, but I've got to get going."

She turned and started walking in the opposite direction.

Brooke called after her, "I've been meaning to come visit you if that'd be okay?"

Townspeople never called on Sasha like they did with Courtney and how they used to with Catherine and Deborah.

But Sasha did somewhat know Brooke, and she'd always been friendly, so she called over her shoulder, "Sure, that's fine." She could decide whether she actually wanted to let Brooke in or not if she did show up. She picked up her pace, keeping under the awnings, gripping the second rock still in her pocket.

She decided to walk home. On her route, she passed by one of the small lakes in her neighborhood. The last sheets of ice clung on and might be gone in the next week. She passed by this lake often, families skated on it when the ice was thicker, and in the spring and summer people went out in row boats.

She walked off the road, past the few trees that surrounded the lake. The water lapped quietly at the hard dirt shore. The ice was further from the shore, several yard away, and Sasha had the sudden urge to reach it.

She took off her gloves and shoved them in her pockets. She placed the palms of her hand together and pulled energy into her hands from her surroundings. Her palms warmed. She stood like that, eyes lowered, and palms pressed together, collecting the energy, until her palms began to sweat, and it felt like they would burn each other. She pulled her hands apart and quickly plunged them into the water.

Crouching, she stepped into the water small step by small step. She submerged up to her shoulders. The water around her lightly steamed. She wasn't yet to the ice, but she didn't care anymore about the ice. She looked around the empty expanse of the lake, the open gray sky.

It was all she needed. Because she was in the mood to declare that she of all people only needed one set of circumstances, and she'd never want for more. A small circle to herself, of warmth. Just a circle of warmth? No Courtney? No endless supply of vodka? No silk and velvet? No Dillon?

Sasha lay her head back, drifted in her little circle of the lake. Her hair swayed, a comforting weight around her. She closed her eyes, let a smile play on her face. The air was crisp. It was probably unhealthy—the cool air, the warm water. Who cares! She thought giddily. She let out a deep sigh of contentment.

Afterwards, she used a drying spell before walking home, because she knew it was what Courtney would tell her to do.

Chapter Forty-One

Sasha watched from her couch as Margaret got into her car. It was a shock to see her again, even though she was only seeing the back of Margaret's head and occasionally her profile. She didn't expect her to look different. It'd only been a couple of weeks since Sasha had seen Margaret, but her perception of Margaret was so shifted that Sasha desired that shift to be reflected physically also.

Margaret hadn't driven far after she left town and seemed to be parked on a residential street. When she returned to her car, she was still alone.

Sasha knew what she was waiting for, although she wouldn't admit to Courtney or Marni if they asked (or if they found out about her setting up the rock) because apparently it would be "paranoid." She watched Margaret to see if she met with Howie. She was waiting to see Margaret pull into the guard headquarters lot or walk to her car with Howie or another guard.

It didn't happen that first day. Or the second day.

Courtney called, because Sasha hadn't left her house or even texted. Was everything okay?

"Yeah, yeah," Sasha said with her gaze still on the rock. "Well, I'm feeling a little sick, so I've been staying in bed to let it pass."

There was a pause. Courtney said, "Again? Didn't you have the flu last week?"

"No," Sasha said. "I mean, it's just a cold. I'll be fine."

Margaret kept returning to town. She'd park on Main Street, be away for an hour or two, and then return to her car. Sometimes she carried bags with her or a coffee cup. Sometimes nothing. On the fourth day, when Margaret arrived in town in the afternoon, Sasha pulled on her boots and jacket and called a cab. She felt bleary from a lack of sleep. She'd sat on the couch watching the rock, and when she fell asleep by accident, she'd jerk awake when her glass fell or at some slight shift in the silence emanating from Margaret's car. Her legs and back ached.

In town, Margaret's car was parked at a similar spot as before. Sasha saw her walking on the sidewalk, her blond hair pulled up haphazardly and her hands in her pockets. She was walking towards the guard headquarters. Sasha started running. One stride from Margaret she reached out and grabbed her shoulder, shouting, "What are you doing? What are you telling him?"

The shocked face that spun around wasn't Margaret. A woman of similar age and height, the blond hair. Sasha was moving forward with momentum. She tried to stop, but she stumbled, pulling the woman down with her. Sasha's knees slammed against the sidewalk. She screamed. White dots flashed in her vision, and she shook her head. The woman sat sprawled, holding her left wrist and wincing.

"I'm so sorry." Sasha held back tears. "Is it bad? Tell me it's not."

Sasha tried to touch the woman's shoulder in a soothing way. But soothing didn't come naturally to Sasha. Her hand gripped like a claw. The woman pulled away, eyes wide. "What did I do to you?" the woman asked, shielding her wrist.

"Please, I'm sorry. I'll take you to the hospital. I'll pay."

The woman pushed off the ground, and muttered as she walked away about sending her the bill.

"Sasha?"

Sasha whipped around. It was Margaret.

"You," Sasha growled, standing up. Sharp pain in her knees made her wince, but she was quickly flush with anger. "What are you doing here? You've been here for days."

Margaret took a step forward. "I came to see you. I've been worried about you, and you wouldn't answer my calls."

"You haven't called me."

"Not in this last week. I knew you wouldn't answer."

Sasha shook her head. "You're lying. What have you told him about me?"

"Who?"

"Howie."

"Howie March? Why would I be talking to him?"

"I don't know. I don't know why you'd do this to the coven."

"Do what? I have no idea what you're talking about. Why don't we go somewhere to talk?"

"I'm not going anywhere with you."

Sasha turned away from Margaret. She didn't have a plan of where she was going. The guard headquarters loomed. Such a normal building, in the same style as the rest of the block. It put Sasha into a dark mood whenever she saw it. Even the mundanity was an affront. She was sick of it. She was sick of Howie, so sick of him. And then there he was—as if thinking of him had summoned him—walking into the parking lot and reading a piece of paper.

She shot a dark look over her shoulder. Margaret followed her. "You've been meeting with him, haven't you?"

"I haven't. I swear, Sasha. Why would I do that? Where is this coming from?"

Howie looked up at the raised voices. For a second, Sasha saw his face at a neutral, a face that could have been any townsperson's, simply observing their town. He met Sasha's gaze.

He smirked.

Bile raised in Sasha's throat. Her entire body burned with fire. She strode into the headquarters parking lot. Howie crossed his arms and raised an eyebrow in a sort of challenge. Sasha couldn't hear Margaret calling her name. She didn't hear what Howie said as she got closer to him and raised her hands. She couldn't look away from his face. She brought her hands towards one another, claws again, and across the closing distance between them, Howie grasped at his neck. She felt surrounded by a calmness, the silence of her home, the silence of the high school halls, the silence of Margaret's empty car. And the fire inside of her trickled out. Howie's mouth was open, an attempted scream. He was on the ground, scratching at his neck.

Sasha was pulled backwards, her hands pushed to her side, breaking the spell. She heard crying and a repeated muffled sound, which she realized was someone speaking. The words became clearer, like radio coming out of static.

"Oh my god, oh my god, oh my god." It was Margaret, who was the one holding onto her. Guards were pouring out of the headquarters. Howie on the ground, propping himself up on his elbows, pointing at Sasha. The guards ran and grabbed her. But she felt so light, and she was smiling.

"Okay," she said. "Okay." Soon they had her in handcuffs and her neck in the collar with two long metal rods attached, to hold her from a distance, and bring her into the headquarters.

"Okay," she said. "Okay." She meant to the guards, I'm coming with you, and I won't do anything. And she meant to something else, the universe, herself, Catherine, her mother, Courtney, I accept this.

More guards watched as Sasha was coordinated into the building. So many guards. Just for the three of them.

Chapter Forty-Two

There were chains on the wall of the interrogation room. Sasha sat at a table across from Howie March. They had kept her sitting in a cell for hours. He scribbled on a form, his pen scratching quietly. Two officers stood on each side of him, rifles in hand. Howie put a hand to his neck, massaging it. Stop, Sasha thought. Stop it. He capped his pen, leaned back.

"Here you are again." They stared at each other. His self-satisfied smiles were gone. "You're lucky, Sasha. Most other witches would be on their way to the electric chair. But your mother took the fall for you back then. I'm suggesting that you be sent to Maine. I hope you appreciate that because I didn't have to."

This was not an energy she could open up to. She would not thank Howie March. Or apologize as much as an "I'm sorry" bubbled against her lips. She didn't want to hurt people, she thought frantically, not even Howie. That woman she'd knocked over. She hadn't meant to. And her friend, her closest friend. Why had she thought Courtney was against her? She was sorry. She was sorry. But she wouldn't say it to Howie.

Howie continued against her silence. "You have a phone call. I suggest you call your father because we aren't planning on informing him."

He stood up and opened the door. The two officers grabbed hold of Sasha's arms and escorted her into the hallway. There was a phone on the wall. Sasha hadn't used a phone like this since she'd been in middle school. The officers held onto her as she dialed, loosening their grip slightly. She listened to the dial tone, swallowing, thinking of what to say. The call went to voicemail.

"Courtney," she whispered. "I'm here. I'm at the place again." She started crying silently. "Um, they say they're sending me to Maine, so I guess this is it. Goodbye." She hung up.

There were chains in the cell to wrap a witch to the floor, but Howie instructed the guards—two of them, rotating every other hour, guns in hand—to keep her unchained. "Unless you give us reason to do otherwise."

She lay down on her stomach. She crossed her arms and laid her forehead against them.

She thought of Courtney and Marni, no longer a coven. And how long before a new witch would come into her powers? Maybe the two would miss her also, as a friend.

Maine, though. Her mother was there.

After the first guard change, Sasha turned to be on her side, back facing them. What else was there to do, but turn, turn, turn.

CHAPTER FORTY-THREE

Courtney stood outside the guard headquarters. She usually went out of her way to avoid the surrounding area of the Witches' Guard. She didn't want them even thinking about her.

But the alarm went off.

What had Sasha done?

The alarm had blared while Courtney sped to the headquarters. Now the silence reverberated around the building. Courtney walked up to the door, despite every instinct telling her not to, and opened it. The front room bland as a doctor's reception area. There was a man in uniform sitting at the desk behind the glass divider. He stood up when he saw Courtney and drew his gun. He pointed it at her.

Courtney stood still and held up her hands. "I'm just looking for my friend," she said.

"Don't come any closer."

"Is my friend here?" she asked.

"You can't see her."

"What did she do?" Courtney whispered.

"We're not releasing that information."

"Okay." She stepped backwards. "I'm leaving now." And she slipped out the door. She ran to her car.

She called Ella the second she stepped into her house, shaking, crying, closing the door to shut the town out.

She was sobbing when Ella picked up. "Slow down. Take deep breaths," Ella said. Courtney did as she was told. "Okay, now, what happened?"

Ella hadn't heard yet. Courtney sputtered out the basic facts that she knew, and Ella cursed. "I'm going to call the rest of the board."

An hour later, the sky going dark, Ella texted, *I'm still working on it. I'm not sure what can be done. I'll call you tomorrow. Do not act rashly.*

Later, she would miss Sasha's call, her phone on silent while she lay in bed, staring at her ceiling, unable to sleep.

Courtney pounded on the front door in the morning until Marni answered. "Let's go," Courtney said, grabbing Marni's arm.

"Go where?" Marni looked at Courtney, eyes blood shot, no make-up on, her shirt buttoned wrong.

Courtney looked at the young witch. She didn't know. Had she not heard the alarm?

"Sasha's locked up."

"By the guard?"

"Yes. Something happened. I don't know what." Courtney started to cry. "She was probably drunk. But she's always drunk. Why did she do it?" she screamed.

Marni stood with a hand over her mouth. Courtney pulled at her, "We have to go!"

The two got into Courtney's car. Marni gripped the passenger side handle while Courtney took turns with abandon. Down Main Street, and then Courtney stopped in front of the guard headquarters. She couldn't go back in. It was so quiet.

. . .

Sasha woke up.

She tried to lift her head, groaned. Headache.

Howie had woken her. Or the baton he rapped against the bars had woken her. "Your sentencing came back quickly," he said. "They approved my Maine suggestion."

Sasha rubbed her eyes. She didn't respond. New guards came and dragged her to her feet.

They led her to the garage. There were several rows of patrol cars. Sasha was pulled to the front row, to a car with an open door.

The guards shoved her into the back seat. One followed and sat next to her. The other got into the driver's seat.

The garage door lurched up. Sunlight streamed in, and Sasha lifted her hand to shield her face. The guard next to her smashed her hand down.

"I wasn't—"

He raised his hand, ready to hit her again. She stopped talking.

Courtney jumped out of her car when she saw the garage opening. She ran. She didn't see the two guards until they were shoving her back with batons. She pushed forward. They slammed her to the ground. Marni dragged her backwards. She barely noticed. A car drove out and Courtney clawed her way up to half standing.

Sasha sat, staring straight ahead, her chin up, her back straight.

She didn't see Courtney and Marni in the parking lot. She was leaving. Going towards her mother, the woman, the witch, who had disappeared like smoke, who hadn't written her in all these years. The possibility of her pulsed, a point in the distance.

Epilogue

Courtney wasn't sleeping well.

She fulfilled her orders, but left the potions out in her mailbox for customers instead of inviting them in to chat. She was sure people were talking, but she didn't care.

Marni had asked if she wanted to get together. The last time they'd met as a coven Sasha had been with them. But they weren't a coven anymore.

Marni sat at the kitchen table, drinking tea from one of the orange mugs. She went on about school, purposefully pointless topics. Courtney half listened. She'd dropped off an order in the mailbox earlier and brought in the stack of mail. Junk, as usual. She sorted through it, uh-huh-ing.

And there it was—a slightly battered plain white envelope, her address handwritten. There was no return address, but Courtney didn't need it. She recognized the handwriting, the scrawl from their errand day to-do lists. She dropped the catalogue in her other hand and tore open the plain envelope. Marni looked at her with raised eyebrows. Her hands shaking with an urgency as if someone would yank it away from her, Courtney pulled out the lined paper and opened Sasha's letter.

Notes

The works of art Sasha sees at the Museum of Fine Arts, Boston were all at the museum or based on work at the museum I saw in October 2018.

Pair of finials for a Torah scroll (about 1766-1776) is by silversmith Myer Myers. They were made for the Touro Synagogue in Newport, Rhode Island. The painting of the woman watching a stage is *In the Loge* (1878) by Mary Cassatt. The John Singer Sargent paintings referenced are *Helen Spears* (1895) and *The Daughters of Edward Darley Boit* (1882). The painting of the woman in the bright dress is *Le Domino Rose* (about 1895) by John Humphreys Johnston, and was in the period room *Fireplace surround from the Elizabeth E. Spooner house, Boston, Massachusetts* (about 1880). The fictional painting *Aurora the Witch* was inspired by *Isabella and the Pot of Basil* (1897) by John White Alexander.

Acknowledgments

I would like to start by thanking my friends. My friends I grew up with, went to school with, and beyond. I have received incredible support, strength, and love from my friends throughout the years. They have so often been my first audience.

Thank you to my friend Scott, who read at least four different versions of this story, and told me when it was a short story that it could be a novel. Thank you to the rest of our writing group, Tyler and Gabrielle, who also read and gave feedback on the story. I appreciate all of your thoughtfulness, thoroughness, and good advice and support.

Thank you to the many teachers and professors I had over the years who gave me valuable feedback and advice.

I owe a huge thank you to my editors Becky Wallace and Hannah VanVels Ausbury, who helped me to bring this novel to its final form. Thank you to Coverkitchen for the amazing cover.

Thank you to my grandparents, aunts, uncles, and cousins. For all the love and support.

Thank you to my sisters. We learned to love reading together. Thank you to my parents, who taught us to love reading. To my dad, who gave us his love of the fantasy genre. To my mom, who brought us to the library what felt like every day growing up, and read to us every night before bed. Thank you to both of my parents for encouraging my writing.

Thank you to Anthony. For believing in me and in this story. I love you.

ABOUT THE AUTHOR

Iris Vradenberg is a fiction writer from New York. She currently lives in Maryland with her husband and their two cats. *Sasha the Witch* is her debut novel. Visit her at irisvradenberg.com for more.